Dead People From the Attic

Bud Scott

Copyright © 2018 by Bud Scott

All rights reserved.

Second Edition

ISBN 978-1-62806-198-7

Library of Congress Control Number 2018963172

Published by Salt Water Media
29 Broad Street, Suite 104
Berlin, MD 21811
www.saltwatermedia.com

Cover image courtesy of the author

Dedication

To Katherine
who always supports me in all my crazy endeavors

Acknowledgements

Special thanks to Julie Phillips, Ginger Honatke, Mike Glide,
Brahm Corstanje, and Dan Baines for supporting
this effort in the early stages.

Table of Contents

The Black Wreath 8

Not Tinkerbell 14

June in Atlantic City 20

If the Spirit Moves You 24

Henrietta 28

Photography Can Be a Dangerous Hobby 34

A Mother's Vengeance 38

Timing Is Everything 42

The Man Who Wasn't There 46

The Last Laugh 50

Midnight At the Ranch 56

The Great Amazon Adventure 60

Not Flander's Field 66

To Save the World 72

Yippie Ki Yay 78

Unconditional Love 84

Keeper of the Sacred Flame 88

Like a Thief In the Night 94

Any Road Will Get You There 100

All Out Of Bullets 106

The Treasure Hunt 112

Jinxed 116

The Gravity of the Situation 122

What Dreams May Come 128

Near Miss 132

A Little Bit of Sunshine	138
Ho, Ho, Ho	142
This Year I Resolve	148
The Hunt	154
More To a Name	158
Still, It Was a Nice Farm	162
Not Man's Best Friend	168
The Arbitrageur	174
More Than Meets the Eye	180
Maybe Next Time	186
The Impossible Bet	192
Dowsing For Oil	198
Off With the Faeries	204
Father of Inventions	210
Mother Knows Best	216
Private Plotnick	220
Loch Ness of the West	226
Missing Houdini	232
Wanna Bet	238
Love Conquers All	244
Auras and Gris Gris	250
Two Wheels Move the Soul	256
Private Eye	262
The Secret Life of Mr. Pomeroy	268
You Should Be In the Movies	274
Love and War	278
Women Get the Vote!	284

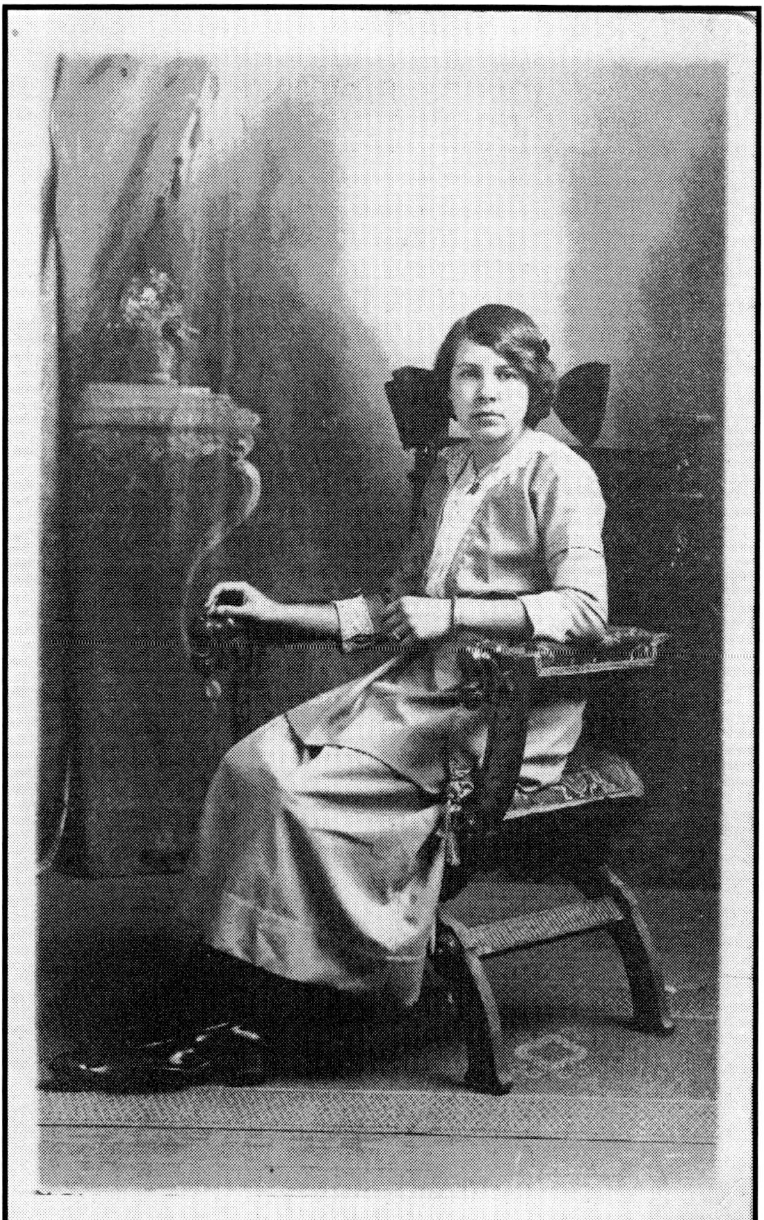

The Black Wreath

Alice Hobbs had been in love with her fiancé George since she was seven years old and he had carried her books to school for her. That had been back in 1905 when life was simpler. Her father was raising her with the help of the housekeeper since her mother had died of consumption. Her father owned a haberdasher's shop in Baltimore. Every day they thanked the Lord that the store had not gone up in flames in the fire of 1904. Had the flames traveled one more block her father's livelihood would have been nothing but smoke and ashes. Her fiancé's family didn't fare as well. Their dry goods store was near the center of the four blocks that burned to the ground. George's parents took what money they had saved and went to live with George's aunt in Pennsylvania. George, who was ten at the time, became an apprentice haberdasher in Alice's father's shop.

As the years went by Alice became more and more enamored with George. As she was blossoming into young womanhood, George too was smitten. He had been saving his money to buy Alice an engagement ring. It was a thin band of gold with five small diamonds set in it. After asking her father's permission, he proposed to her on July 4, 1917. She was not quite twenty and he was twenty-two. They made plans for a June wedding for the following year. It's said that man makes plans and God laughs.

Less than a month later George enlisted in the Army. He went to basic training at Camp Dix, the newly commissioned training facility in New Jersey. During his nine weeks of basic training he'd only been given leave once to come back and visit Alice. It was a tearful reunion because all that Alice could think of was George going off to war and never returning. It would never do to let George know this, so when he asked her why she was crying it was always, "I'm just so happy to have you home for a bit."

George regaled her with stories from camp and all the new friends he'd made. He told her how he'd be shipping out in mid-October, but that this whole mess should be cleared up by Christmas. At least that was the word going around the barracks. They were going to go over there and kick the Kaiser's butt and come back home in time for Christmas. This made Alice smile because she wanted to believe it; she was pretty sure he did.

Alice and her father took the train to Camp Dix to see George's platoon do their drill on the final day of basic. Afterwards they all went out for dinner as George was shipping out the next day. As they were having a cup of coffee after their meal, Alice said, "I've got something for you George." She slid an envelope across the table to him and watched eagerly as he opened it. A broad smile spread across his face as he looked at the picture. It was a studio portrait and she looked beautiful.

"It's so you won't forget me."

"That would never happen; I'll carry this with me always and I'll write to you everyday."

"Do you promise?"

"Yes, my darling Alice, I promise."

George shipped out the next day and Alice went back home and waited for the postman. The first letter arrived two days later, but Alice saw that it was postmarked New Jersey. Even so, her heart leapt at the sight of his handwriting. He didn't have much to say since they had just seen each other, but he told her of his undying love and thanked her again for the photograph. Now the waiting began and she was beside herself with worry when the next letter arrived a month later. Much of what he said had been censored, but he was alive and well at least as of November 16, 1917 and that was all she could have hoped for. She now had an address to reply to.

She wrote replies to every letter that came; there were usually three to five a week, even though they had been written on consecutive days.

Thanksgiving came with little to be thankful for. Nevertheless she put up a good front for her father. After Thanksgiving the steady flow of letters had slowed down to a trickle and soon Christmas was upon them. In his letters George stopped mentioning that the war would be over by Christmas, in fact he hardly mentioned the war at all. The few letters she had gotten recently had all been about them and their life together after he got home, like he was on an extended holiday. As 1918 rolled around, the letters came to a halt.

Alice didn't know what to do so she began to pray, not that she hadn't been praying before, but now she prayed with a deeper earnestness. Her prayers were not answered until late in February when she received a field service postcard that basically said George was in the hospital, he'd been wounded and hoped to be discharged soon. Also that a letter should be forthcoming. At first she was elated that he was alive, but then dread overtook her as she ran all of the worst case scenarios through her head. During all of this her father had been steadfast and held her hand and tried to soothe her fraying nerves.

When his letter finally arrived, he didn't go into much detail. He only said he'd broken his leg in two places and had a bit of memory loss. He'd need a cane to walk from now on and because of his injury they were shipping him back in about six weeks.

Alice was overjoyed, soon she would be reunited with George and they could finally get married. It was just a waiting game now.

When George arrived at the pier in Baltimore he was surprised that Alice wasn't waiting for him. He figured his cablegram got lost somewhere along the line. He took a streetcar to Alice's house, or at least most of the way. He had to limp the last block.

The house was closed and had a black wreath on the front door. His first thought was it must have been Alice's father. He knocked on the neighbor's door and asked about Mr. Hobbs. Mrs. McGuire told him that Mr. Hobbs had been taken ill and then died suddenly about three weeks ago. Then he asked if she knew where Alice was. He explained that he was her fiancé and he'd expected her at the ship. Mrs. McGuire looked down at her hands. When she raised her face to look at him there were tears streaming down her face.

"Alice died three days ago from the influenza. They buried her yesterday in Baltimore Cemetery."

George thanked her, left in a daze and took the next streetcar to the cemetery. He found Alice's grave and ran his fingers over the cold marble engraving of her name. He'd been through Hell and all that had kept him going was the thought of coming home to his beloved Alice. Now she was gone too. He had nothing left to live for. As he was kneeling at the grave, weeping and praying, he pulled Alice's picture out of his pocket and kissed her goodbye. Propping her photo against the gravestone he turned away and pulled out his service revolver.

14

Not Tinkerbell

We'd rented an old stone lodge in the mountains and stopped at a general store on the way. We needed some provisions and a block of ice for the icebox. The proprietor was friendly even when the entire family traipsed in to do the shopping, including my wife Edith, her sister Evelyn, and our two daughters Isabel and Kate, who were nine and ten respectively, and myself. We did leave Rocky, a Jack Russell terrier, in the car. He was barking up a storm because he hated to be left out.

The proprietor introduced himself as Jim, rang up our purchases and then asked us where we were staying. Once he found out, he went on and on about how the lodge was one of the nicest rentals in these parts.

"All stone, and plenty of bedrooms and indoor plumbing with hot and cold running water."

"Well Jim, is there anything interesting to do around here?"

"There's the caverns, they're about eight miles back the way you came; I expect you saw a sign for them. You might like the fishing down at the river, but I don't know if your girls would. There's a waterfall about three miles up the road past the lodge, and then there's the fairies, but that's about it."

As if on cue both of my daughters chimed in, "FAIRIES! FAIRIES! Daddy are there really fairies?"

Well I looked at Jim as if to say, you started this and you'd better finish it.

Jim said, "I've never seen them myself, but a lot of people who've come through here claim they have."

I gave him a dubious look, but played along. "So where are these fairies supposed to be, exactly?"

"There's a glade to the south of that waterfall I told you

about. That's where they've been seen most often. If you go up there and try to see the fairies, I'd advise leaving your dog at home or at the very least keep him tied up."

Jim looked deadly serious when he made this last pronouncement. Up until then I thought he was pulling my leg. In fact the look on his face scared me.

"Well, how about getting us that ice and we'll be on our way, we've taken up enough of your time."

All the rest of the way there the girls could talk about nothing but fairies. Speculating about their size, if they could do magic, if they lived in houses covered with moss. Edith and Evelyn got caught up in it too, and soon there was a lively discussion. My wife was an O'Halloran and she wasn't too far removed from the old country. Because of this she'd heard tales at the grandmother's knee about the fairy folk, and told the girls some of the fairies were mischievous in the stories that she'd heard.

Evelyn chimed in, "I remember some of those stories that Grand told were pretty scary."

We had just pulled up to the house and the girls were on me all at once.

"Can we go and see the fairies?"

"Can we go right now?"

"Can we Daddy?"

"Please."

I squatted down and looked them square in the eyes.

"Girls, there may not be any fairies at all, in fact I think Jim was playing a joke on us and is having a good laugh right now."

But they were having none of that. As I looked at them I saw one lower lip begin to quiver and then another; the waterworks came next. They both knew I couldn't stand up to that.

"We can't go today because it's too late and it'll be dark soon, but we can go see the waterfall tomorrow and check the glade for your fairies."

The tears stopped as if someone had turned the tap off, followed by squeals of glee.

That evening the girls were too excited to sleep, but finally wound down and fell asleep just before eleven. This was all to the good because after the long drive to the lodge I was beat and wanted nothing better than to sleep late the next day. The adults got to bed not long after the children, but the morning came too early.

By seven in the morning the girls were up, and I heard my wife shushing them and telling them that Daddy needed his sleep, but by then I was awake and smelling the coffee brewing.

I stumbled out of the bedroom and said, "Is everyone ready to go see a waterfall?"

The reply was, "Yes, and fairies too!"

Edith said, "We're not going anywhere until everyone has a good breakfast and I have time to pack a picnic basket for lunch."

So we all sat down to bacon and eggs, pancakes, fresh squeezed orange juice and coffee. I even slipped Rocky a piece of bacon.

Edith said, "Don't be feeding the dog at the table, he'll just start begging."

I gave her a sheepish look and went to shave while the girls cleared away and washed the morning dishes and helped their mother get the hamper ready for lunch.

After breakfast and a shave I was feeling much better and we all got loaded up in the car, including Rocky.

"Should we leave Rocky here?" I asked.

"No, why should we?" Evelyn asked. She had taken a liking to him and vice versa.

"I just thought maybe there was something to what Jim had said."

"Well we're not leaving him."

"OK, I've got a length of rope in the back; we can fasten it to his collar and tie him up if we have to."

This got me an ugly look from Evelyn, but she acquiesced.

The waterfall was magnificent, cascading over the rock face and falling about fifty feet into a large pool that fed the stream. Despite its grandeur we made our way in short order to the glade. We found a nice grassy spot to put out our blanket and set the hamper nearby for lunch. There were quite a few birds, frogs and other various critters, but no fairies.

Having been there for a while, we decided to unpack the lunch hamper. It was just then that Rocky, who'd been dozing in a patch of sun, perked up, but it wasn't because of the rustle of the hamper. He got up on all fours and cocked his head and stared at thin air. Then his head moved from side to side like he was tracking something. Suddenly his hackles came up and he began a low growl. Suddenly he was off like a shot chasing something. Luckily I'd had the foresight to tie the rope to his collar and the other end to a small bush. He got to the end of his tether, but instead of stopping short he kept going; the rope just ripped through the leaves of the bush. Rocky went off into a thicket, growling, barking, jumping and snapping at something. Moments later we heard a yelp and then a few more, then everything went quiet.

"Rocky! Rocky! You OK boy, where are you?"

Then we heard whimpering and I made my way into the thicket and saw Rocky laying on the ground with his back to me. When I got to him I couldn't believe what I saw. His ear was bleeding; it had small chunks missing from it like the bite of some animal. Then I saw the rope all around his legs and thought he'd gotten tangled up. Rocky had been hog tied — all four legs with a nice neat knot. At that moment I felt something buzz by my ear and I turned to see what it was. For the briefest instant I saw a hideous grinning face with a mouth full of pointy teeth; it was attached to a nearly skeletal body, hovering about three feet off of the ground on rapidly beating wings. No sooner had I registered all of this, it was gone.

I gathered up Rocky, Edith, Evelyn and the girls, got in the car and drove as fast as I could back to the lodge. The girls were in tears partly because of Rocky and partly because they hadn't seen any fairies. We doctored Rocky up but he wouldn't come out from under the bed the rest of the time we were there. No amount of tears would persuade me to take the girls back to that glade though.

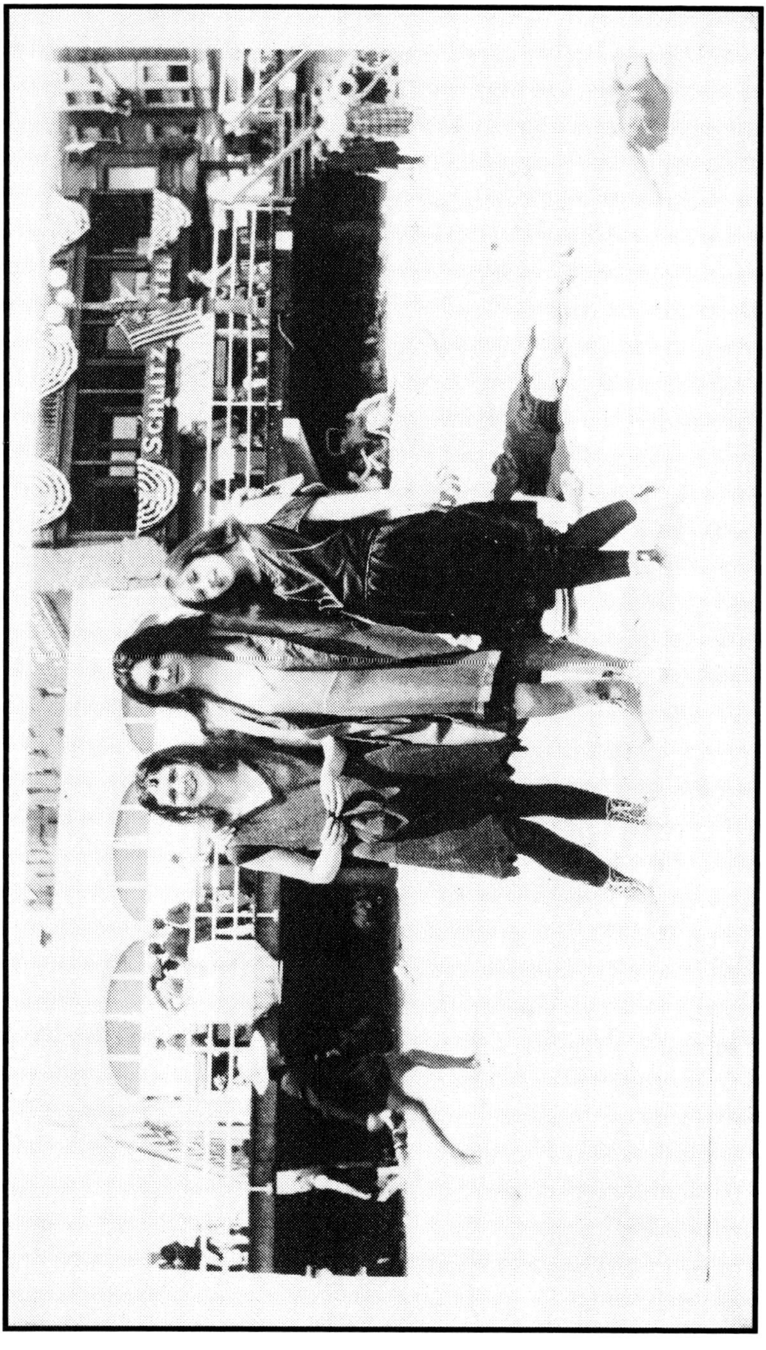
SCHLITZ

June in Atlantic City

God, we were so young then. That's me in the middle — June, with April on my right and May on my left. It was that summer of 1927; Lindbergh had just crossed the Atlantic and anything seemed possible. Having taken the train in from New York we were there for the day without a care in the world. We had already visited the Steel Pier and were just lounging on the beach when this photo was snapped. That evening we went dancing in one of the hotel ballrooms, I don't remember which. I do remember our dance cards were full.

That was the last summer we were all together. I went off to Vassar but only stayed through the fall of 1929 when the crash happened. April might have been the lucky one of us three when the stock market crashed. Her father lost everything — the house, the car, every dollar in the bank account. He killed himself, but first he killed his wife and April. She would have turned twenty that next month. At least she didn't have to live through the depression.

May moved out to California and got married. Her husband had something to do with the movies. She sent me a couple of postcards and then we lost touch. Those movie people didn't seem much affected by the depression. Seemed like the worse it got, the more movies they came up with.

We weren't hit as hard as some folks, but times were still tight all the way around. I worked for a while as a stenographer, the one skill I'd picked up at Vassar. The other thing I picked up at the time was cigarettes. They made you look elegant and sophisticated — little did we know.

After about a year of being a stenographer, I met the love of my life, Howard. He came from a good family, had just passed the bar, and was starting out in his father's practice. We got married in the spring of 1933 and proceeded to have children in rapid succession, two boys and one girl. The first boy only lived for about an hour; he was premature and back then most didn't make it. So the family consisted of Helen and Robert and Howard and myself.

I love those children with all my heart. Howard died in 1963 of a massive heart attack, but he provided for us well. I loved him too even though I was certain he was having an affair, but back then you turned a blind eye.

I don't know if it was the stress of Howard's death or just the luck of the draw, but I was diagnosed with breast cancer and had a double mastectomy. I was depressed and borderline suicidal. I was taking pills to help me sleep and pills to keep me going during the day. I was seeing a psychiatrist and lucky for me she got me into a support group for cancer survivors. So, after a few years I got off the pills and got my life straightened out, only to be diagnosed with lung cancer. I was sixty, the kids were grown, and I'd started enjoying visits from my grandchildren. I wasn't ready to give up yet.

They took out about a third of my right lung and told me I had to quit smoking. I had thought breast cancer was hard, and losing my husband, but giving up the cigarettes was the hardest thing I've ever done. I had headaches, my hands shook, I craved them like a drowning man craves something to cling to. I stopped cold turkey and kept telling myself if I wanted to see my grandkids grow up I had to do this thing.

I haven't had a cigarette now for ten years. The grandkids are all in high school and although I'd been cancer-free for the past decade, the X-ray showed a large shadow on my lung and they wanted to do a biopsy.

It came back positive and apparently it was a very aggressive cancer and without surgery the doctors gave me about six months to a year. With surgery, depending on what they found and if they could get all of the cancer and leave me with enough lungs to breathe, maybe five more years.

I was seventy now and tired of doctors, tired of life in general, but not quite ready to give up. It was spring and I told my daughter that as soon as the weather warmed up enough I wanted to go to Atlantic City one last time. I wanted to see the Steel Pier and go down the boardwalk.

By the time June rolled around I was on oxygen and too feeble to walk even with my walker. Helen and Robert showed up at my door with a van they'd rented. They rolled me up in my wheelchair and fastened it down and we were off to Atlantic City. I dozed most of the way there, but perked up a bit once we got there. Robert and Helen took turns pushing me down the boardwalk. By this time I was in a lot of pain, and the pills weren't doing a lot, but I put on a brave face for the kids.

When we got to the entrance to the Steel Pier I told them I was tired and just wanted to go home now. I took a couple of pain pills and woke up as they wheeled me back into the house. I had a full time nurse by then and she admonished them for keeping me out so long and I was too tired to argue in their defense.

It was a good day despite the pain and I'd wanted to go out on a good day. That was why I'd been suffering through the pain — you see I'd been squirrelling away a pile of the pain pills for a couple of months now. I think the last count was forty-two.

The nurse got me into bed and gave me my pill, which I took, saving as much water in the glass as possible.

I said, "Thank you Edna, for everything you do for me. I won't need anything else; if I do I'll ring."

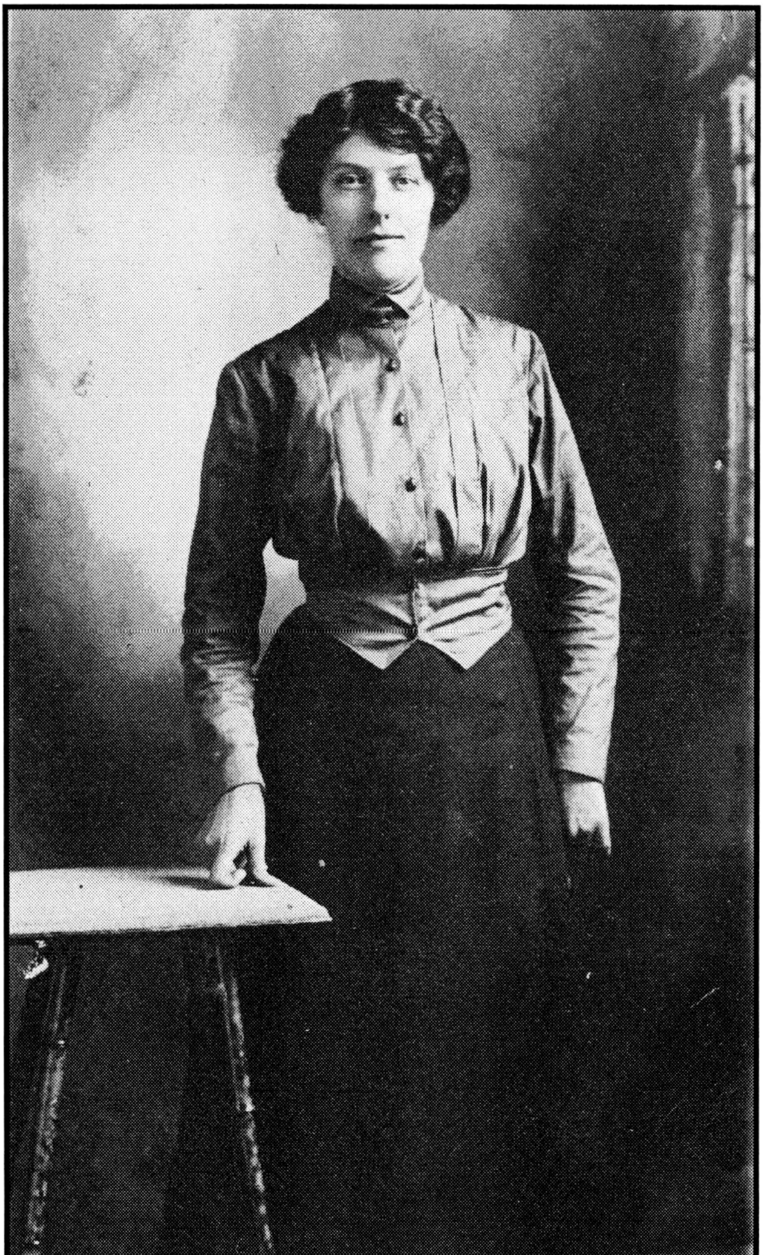

If The Spirit Moves You...

Although distantly related to Mina Crandon, Belle always tried to distance herself from her. Mina was known in Boston as Margery the Medium and used less than ethical means to contact the spirits. Belle on the other hand, even as a small girl, had the gift. In fact, she couldn't recall ever not having some kind of connection to the other world. Her parents tried to keep it quiet, but as she grew into young womanhood her connection grew stronger. She became a member of the Spiritualism movement and began holding séances shortly after the First World War began. Her séances were like no others — no darkened rooms, no Ouija boards, in fact none of the trappings of the current mediums. All Belle had in her sitting room was a small bamboo table that would move, levitate, and tap out answers to the sitter's questions. She would tell people that she had no idea how it worked but that she would feel a surge of energy through her body just prior to the manifestations beginning. She did this in broad daylight and never charged any money for her service. That was unheard of. She would tell her sitters that this thing was not of her but from somewhere else and as such she was only a conduit and could not charge for the service. (She had money in her own right from a trust fund so could afford to be beneficent.)

It was the broad daylight that had the disbelievers baffled. Most mediums performed their miracles under the cover of darkness. She would have no more than three sitters and herself all positioned around the table. The table would be bare, with no cloth to conceal any mechanism of any kind. Yet she would get results nine out of ten times. The majority of her clients were women who had lost a son, husband, or sweetheart in the war and wanted desperately to communicate with them. This was another reason that Belle wouldn't charge anything; she felt it was taking advantage of their grief and desperation.

Most sessions would begin with some prayers and a hymn or two before they would gather around the table. Sometimes they would sit and other times stand, but they always had their fingertips on the table top. Belle would ask if one of the client's deceased spirits was present. The table would tip and tap out once for yes and twice for no. Once the affirmative had been tapped, the questions would begin. This part of the séance could last up to three hours depending on the questions. Afterwards Belle was completely spent and would excuse herself while the ladies helped themselves to tea and cakes before leaving.

Belle would conduct séances two or three times a week and had a waiting list of people wanting her services. The séances took so much out of her that it usually took her a day or two to recuperate, but she felt that this was her calling so she persevered.

One day her group consisted of a young woman, an older lady, and a middle-aged man. Belle had no problems with a man in the group, but she sensed something strange about this one. Nothing she could pinpoint, but he made her feel uneasy just the same. Belle had long ago learned to listen to that little inner voice, so she was keeping a close eye on him.

The séance progressed as usual. The ladies asked their questions in turn and when Belle got to the gentleman she was prepared for anything. The gentleman told of his only son Phillip who had died at Verdun and felt that his spirit wasn't at rest. Belle asked if the spirit of Phillip was near, and got a single affirmative tap. She asked if he had died in Verdun — another single tap. She went through a series of questions that the gentleman posed. Just as she was beginning to think she'd misread him, he declared he had no son and proceeded to debunk Belle as a fraud.

Belle felt as if she had taken a blow to the solar plexus. She had committed her life to this cause of Spiritualism and this man comes in her house and lies to her and then has the audacity to call her a fraud.

The two other women had stepped away from the table and left Belle across the table from her accuser. Belle began to inform the gentleman that she was no charlatan, and although she couldn't explain it she assumed they had contacted the spirit of some young man named Phillip who had died in Verdun. She also let him know in no uncertain terms that he could leave and was not welcome back.

Unperturbed by this the gentleman began feeling all around the table for wires and mechanisms that didn't exist. At this point Belle was so outraged that she was beyond words. Her fingertips still rested on the table top, and suddenly she felt a powerful surge of energy flood through her body and down her arm. Before she knew what was happening, the table began to quiver. Then it began to dance back and forth from two legs to the other two legs like a small child who needs to use the bathroom.

The gentleman in the meantime had halted his investigations and was staring dumb struck at the table.

"That's impossible," he said.

The table, seemingly of its own volition, lifted off of the floor. It moved with a swiftness that was hard to describe and hit the gentleman square in the forehead. There was a sound like somebody thumping a ripe watermelon. With a groan the man collapsed to the floor. The table resettled into its usual position as if nothing had happened.

Belle fearing grave damage had been done, made an extensive examination. Much to her relief, she found the table to be undamaged.

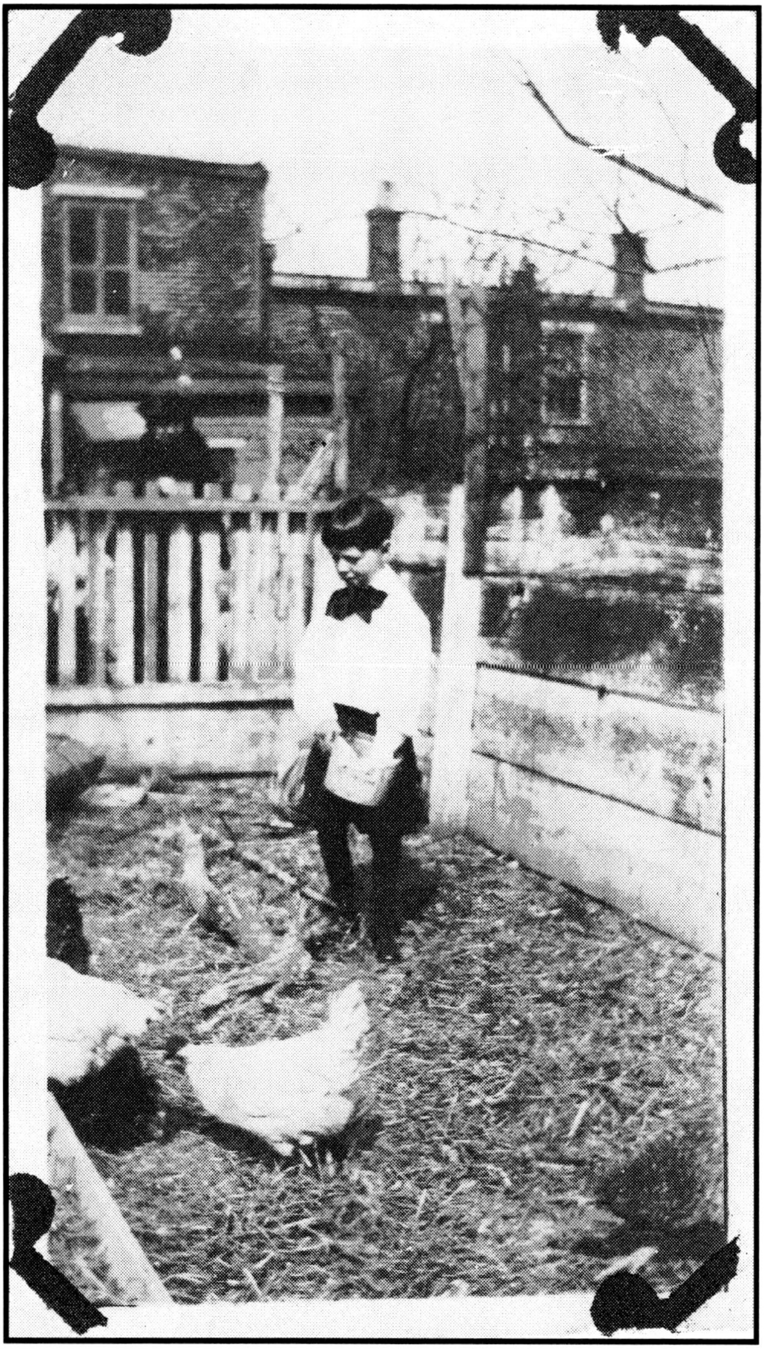

Henrietta

"Child, you get them chickens fed or you'll be late for school."

"Yes Mama. Mama, do you think Henrietta is feeling alright?"

"Lord child, how many times have I told you not to name the chickens. They're here to lay eggs, not to be pets."

"I know, but she always looked like a Henrietta to me."

"Don't you "but" me young lady. Now get them fed and gather up those eggs and get on off to school."

"Yes Ma'am, but..."

At this point Mama would just give me that stare, you know the one, the one that would send a shiver down your back. I got everything done and made it to school on time, but I couldn't stop thinking about Henrietta. Just something about the way she was pecking at her food like she didn't really care and she hadn't laid an egg for close to a week. Mama knew I didn't name all the chickens, just the special ones, the ones that have a personality. Most of the chickens are just stupid.

Henrietta had five toes on each foot instead of the normal four and she was big. Until recently she would lay a couple of eggs a day. I think she might have poor eyesight because sometimes she'd see a bug and cock her head sideways to get a better look at it. Then she'd pounce on it and most of the time missed so she'd start chasing that bug all over the place. Sometimes she'd run right into the wall and nearly knock herself out. She would fall over, then get up and stagger a bit and shake her head. Then she'd go on like nothing happened. I laughed so hard the first time I saw her do it, I thought I was going to pee my pants.

That night when Mama was tucking me in to bed she said,

"You know why I don't want you naming the livestock don't you?"

"I guess it's so I don't get attached to them, but they ain't like pets. It's just Henrietta is funny sometimes."

"Aren't like pets," she corrected. "You know from time to time we have to sell off a pig; that's where our bacon and ham and sausage come from. We sell some of our eggs too, and when the laying hens get too old..."

"I know, they end up in the stew pot. Henrietta isn't that old is she?"

"Well she hasn't been giving us any eggs for about a week now. We can't keep feeding her if she isn't producing eggs."

"But she'll starve if we don't feed her. Oh, you mean it's time for the stew pot."

"I'm afraid so. See this is why I don't want you naming chickens."

"Mama, do chickens have souls?"

"I don't think so dear."

"Can I ask God to bless Henrietta anyway?"

"She is one of God's creatures; I don't see any harm in it."

I said my prayers and included Henrietta.

The next day was Saturday and I had my share of chores to do. These kept me busy until late afternoon. It was then I saw Papa talking to Mr. Wright our neighbor from about a mile up the road. I go to school with his daughter. They looked over at me a couple of times and I saw Mr. Wright nodding his head. Then they disappeared around the back of the chicken coop.

Sunday morning I was up early to feed the chickens and gather the eggs, when I noticed that Henrietta wasn't there anymore. So today was the day for the stew pot. Poor Henrietta. When I got inside to get ready for church, Mama wanted to know if I'd been crying. I couldn't tell her I'd cried because Henrietta was gone, so I told her I got some dust in my eyes while feeding the chickens.

At church all I could think about was whether chickens have souls. I finally decided they don't, because who would want a bunch of chickens running around in Heaven.

Sunday dinner was always a special meal and this Sunday was no exception. Mama was rolling out dumplings, cutting up green beans, making biscuits. She had something simmering in the pot that smelled so good, 'til I found out it was a chicken, or should I say Henrietta.

"Mama, I don't feel so good. Can I go to my room and lie down?"

Mama wiped her hands on a tea towel and then put the back of her hand to my forehead. "You don't have a fever. You go lie down and I'll come get you when it's supper time."

I shuffled off to my bedroom and buried my face in the pillow and began to cry. I must have cried myself to sleep because the next thing I knew Mama was waking me up telling me it was time for dinner.

"I'm not hungry."

Well Mama knew something was wrong if I said I wasn't hungry.

"Should I get Doc Simmons to come over? Where do you feel bad?"

"I can't explain." Then the words caught in my throat and I began to sob. "I can't eat Henrietta, I just can't. I know it's her day for the stew pot, but I just can't do it."

"I knew you'd become too attached to that chicken and I was afraid something like this would happen. What if it wasn't Henrietta? What if it was just some anonymous chicken that you didn't even know? Could you eat it then?"

"But it's not, it Henrietta!"

"No, it's not Henrietta. Remember when Mr. Wright was here yesterday?"

"Yes."

"Well he and your father had a long talk about little girls and their chickens. It seems Mr. Wright's little girl has a similar situation except that chicken is still a good layer and not ready for the stew pot. Your father traded Henrietta for one of Mr. Wright's chickens. I think we got the short end of the stick because Mr. Wright got the bigger bird out of the deal."

"Mama, all of a sudden I'm feeling better and I'm starving. Let's eat."

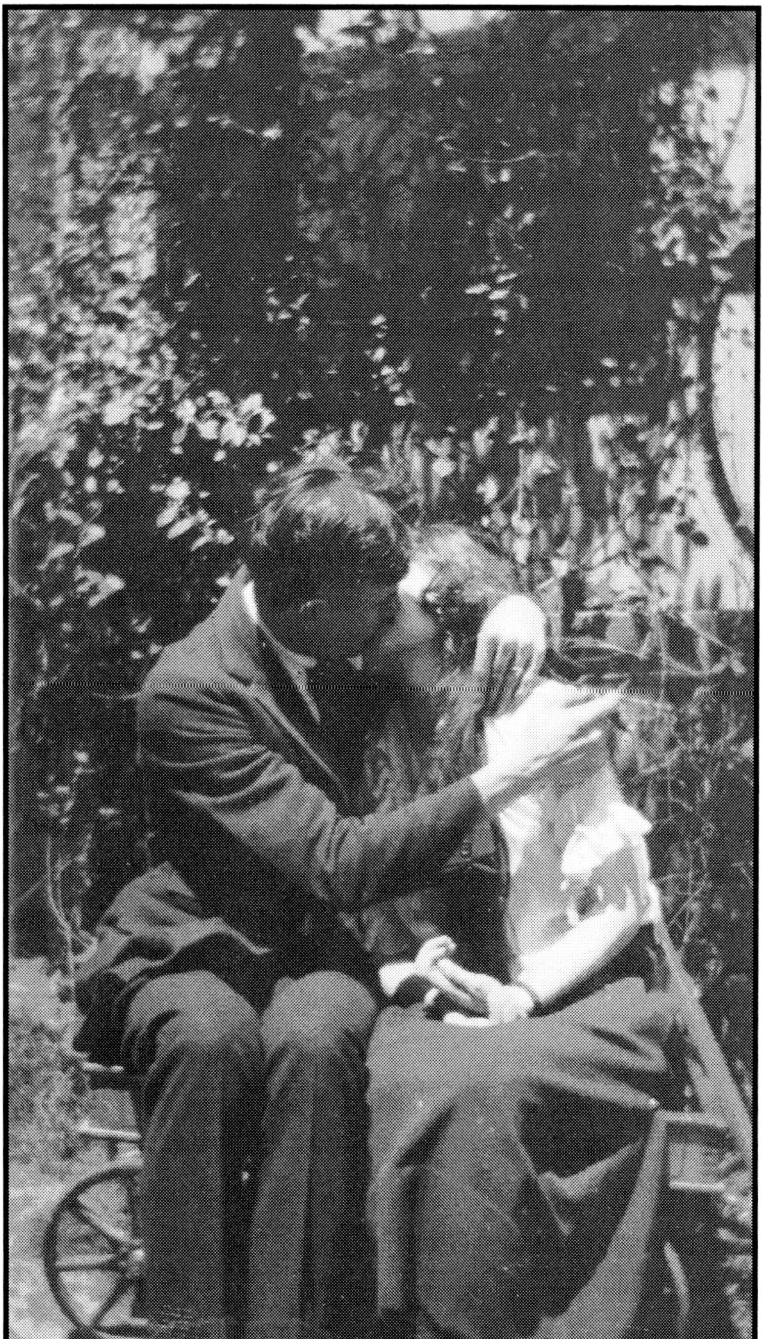

Photography Can Be a Dangerous Hobby

I never knew how dangerous a Brownie box camera could be. I snapped this picture at a weekend-long house party. One of Dickey's nouveau riche friends was throwing this shindig and Dickey insisted I tag along. I felt a bit out of place just being a working stiff, but Dickey told me not to worry about it. After I got there I realized that the guest list ran the gamut from the Hoi-polloi to Bohemians and everything in between. I didn't stick out as badly as I thought. I was a bit of a novelty to some with my camera, but soon nobody even noticed I had it. I didn't even know who they were at the time. I just thought it would make a great snapshot.

I found out later that his name was Claude Pierce, some distant relative of Franklin Pierce, 14th President of the United States. The lady in question was Edith Long of the South Hampton Longs. As I say, I knew none of this at the time; it wasn't until I had developed the film and showed the prints to Dickey that he pointed them out to me.

Dickey said, "You've got a gold mine there, son. You see the ring on his finger? Well that ain't Mrs. Pierce he's kissing there."

I had no idea what he was talking about when he said, "gold mine." He went on to explain.

"I'm pretty sure he doesn't know you took that picture since your camera is still in one piece. I'm also certain that he wouldn't want Mrs. Pierce to know about his dalliance. Even though he comes from a well-heeled family, it's her side of the family that has the real wealth and if she cut him off, he'd be as poor as you are. No offense."

I wasn't offended, but still a bit in the dark about the photo.

I guess Dickey saw the bewilderment on my face.

"Damn son, don't you see? That is the perfect blackmail photo. No telling what he'd pay to not have that sent to his wife, or worse yet published in the society column. I bet you could get a couple of thousand easily."

My mouth must have been hanging open at this point because Dickey reached over and closed it for me.

"You'll have to be careful in your approach though; he's been known to run with a pretty rough crowd. I've heard he lets some bootleggers use the family boat house from time to time."

I explained to Dickey that I had no intentions of blackmailing anybody, no matter how badly I needed the money.

"Oh yes, those gambling debts. Well this could pay them off and give you some walking around money to boot. This is a sure thing, son."

That got me thinking. I guess Dickey saw the gleam in my eye and the slight nod of my head as I thought over the possibilities.

" OK, here's what you need to do ..."

Dickey laid out a plan so slick and so intricate I couldn't believe he'd come up with it on the spot, but that was just the kind of mind that Dickey had.

I only made one mistake when I sent that first letter. Just by sheer force of habit I'd put my return address on the envelope. That one mistake was my undoing. They came in the middle of the night, broke down my door and threatened me at gun point unless I told them where the photo and the negative were. So I told them, not being the heroic type. I thought they would leave then but they ransacked my apartment and busted up all of my photography equipment. Then the one with the gun pistol whipped me and they kicked the shit out of me. Then they left.

I told all of this to Dickey from my hospital bed.

Dickey said, "Oh son, what did I get you into. I had no idea. I mean I never thought you'd get hurt. Well you are well out of it."

I said, "No Dickey, remember you told me I should have another copy of the negative in a safe place. Well I did listen to that. So now the price just went up because now it's personal."

Dickey's mouth fell open at this last remark. I reached over and closed it for him.

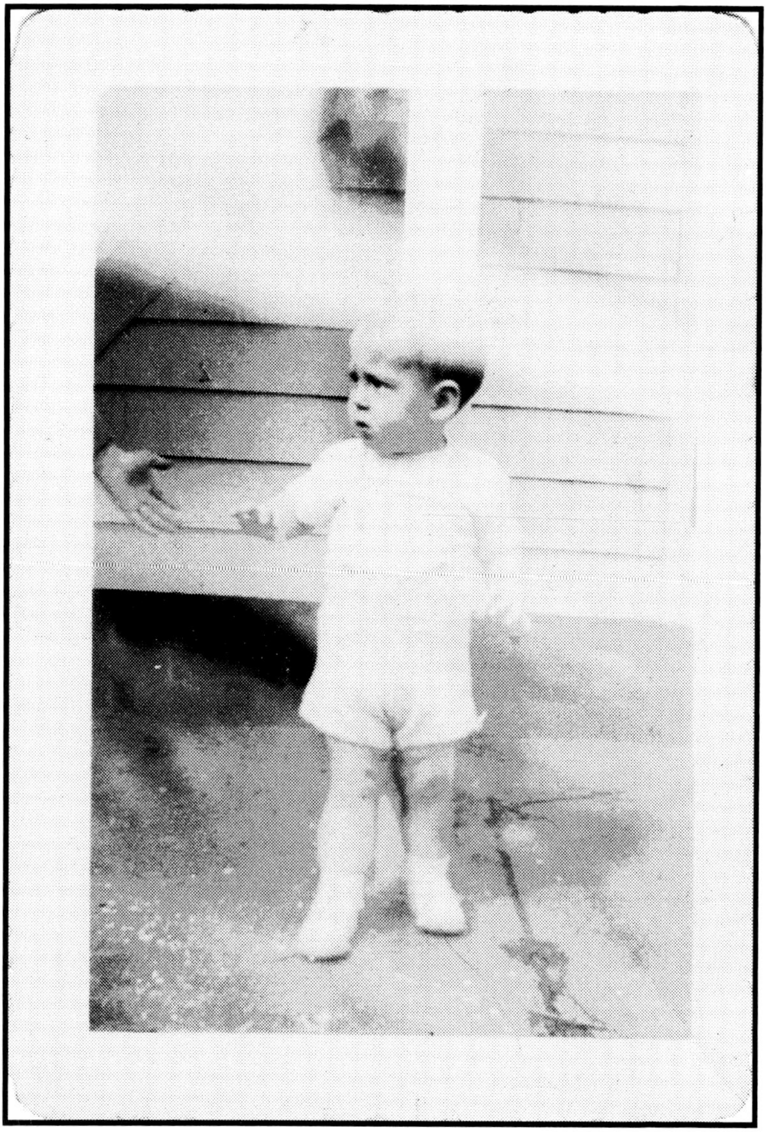

A Mother's Vengeance

The day they came for me they told me that Billy will be well taken care of.

"But he's only nineteen months old; he needs his mother," I cried.

They kept promising me as they tugged me away from him. It broke my heart the way he looked at me, like he'd never see me again.

"You be a good boy Billy. Mommy will be back soon."

"I knew he didn't understand what was going on and I willed myself to not cry. The matron from the orphanage was standing by to scoop him up as soon as I was out of sight.

It was really all Harold's fault. Harold, that's his father, had been a good bread winner until about a month ago. That's when he got fired from his job. Then last week he suddenly died. I was beside myself with grief and worry. What was I going to do? Funerals are so expensive, and I was barely scraping by taking in laundry. Luckily it was just me and Billy now. I'd had a miscarriage a few months before, never thinking I'd be grateful for it. I knew with a newborn and Billy that things would be much worse."

The man sitting across the table from Mildred was furiously taking notes.

Mildred continued, "Harold had swept me off my feet just a couple of years ago. He'd had money then, like all the rest of those high-flyers speculating on the stock market. Then the crash came and he was very nearly wiped out. He'd stashed a couple of hundred away against hard times, and boy were these hard times. Being used to a champagne life-style didn't set well with his beer budget and he went through that money pretty quickly.

Then Billy came along and he knuckled under and got a good job as a civil engineer. He'd gone to college and had some old school ties. They were able to get him a job at least; that was better than most had. He wasn't happy though; he hated being tied to a desk. He hated having to punch the clock; he hated his life and all it had become. He began to stop off at the bar on the way home. At first he'd come home a bit tipsy. As the months progressed his drinking got worse. He started missing work and that's when they fired him."

The man at the table looked up from his notebook and and started to ask a question, but before he'd gotten his mouth open Mildred was off again.

"He started picking up odd jobs here and there, but he never brought home any money. He never seemed to make it past the liquor store on the way home.

The arguments started soon after the drinking started. He seemed to blame me for all his woes. Some nights he'd come home smelling like a distillery and take out his frustrations on me. After that I couldn't show my face in public for a few days. The night he found out that I was pregnant again was like a dam had broken inside him. First he blamed me for being pregnant, like I could do that all by myself. Then the punches started flying, not at my face this time but at my stomach. After three days in bed I lost the baby and the last shred of respect I had for him."

She paused for a breath and plunged on.

"I thought he might hurt Billy, but so far he'd never laid a finger on him. The night before he died he must have run out of money. He'd come home early, and although not stone cold sober, he was as close as he'd been in a long while. I thought now was a good time to try to reason with him, but it was like talking to the wall.

Harold interrupted me mid-sentence and said, "Tomorrow I'm taking Billy to the orphanage and we can go to California and start over."

I said, as calmly as you please, "Here's a couple of dollars pin money I've been saving. Go get us a bottle so we can celebrate our new life together.

He snatched the money and was out the door in a flash. When he returned the only bottle he had was sloshing around in his gut. He stumbled into the back door and was greeted with a frying pan to the skull. It took three more whacks before he didn't get up any more."

There was a wan smile at the corners of her mouth that didn't quite reach her eyes as she looked at the police officer taking notes.

"So that's why I did it, and I'd do it again."

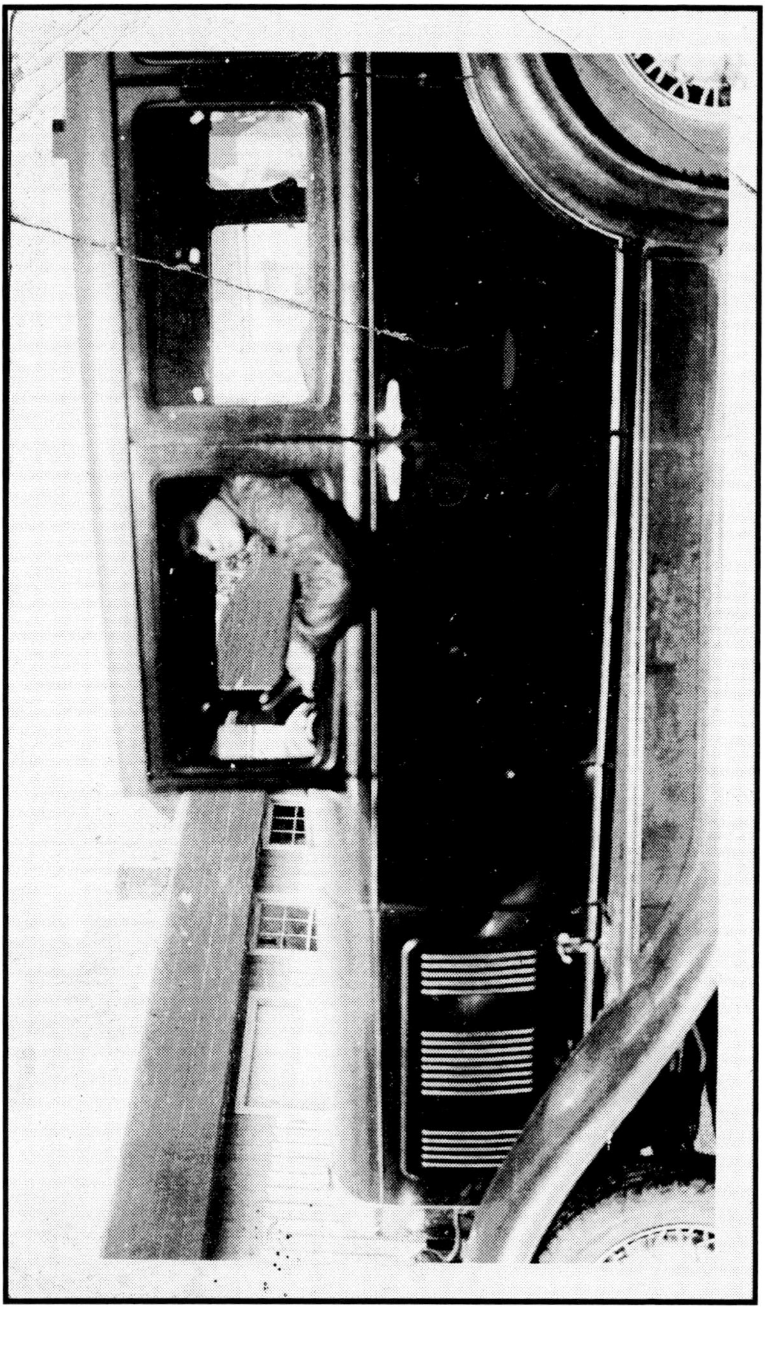

Timing Is Everything

"Gus, why do I always have to stay with the car?" Charlie asked.

"Charlie, you are the best driver I know and a darn good mechanic to boot, but you can't guarantee me this jalopy will start up when we come back out, now can you?"

Gus' spirits rose for a moment, getting praise from Charlie, and then were dashed just a quickly.

"No, I guess I can't, but I know what's wrong. There's a bad float in the carburetor. I just need to get it to a garage that's got the parts and I can rebuild it."

Gus didn't have time for this; he was in a hurry. He and Arty, his business associate, needed to go talk to the the bank manager about withdrawing some funds and he didn't want to be late.

Charlie began to whine, "I get bored just sitting here waiting for you guys; it would be different if I had something to do."

"You should have brought some of your comic books with you; you know how you love them."

"But I've read all of them."

Looking up, Charlie spotted a drug store.

"I can go over to the drugstore while you guys are taking care of your business."

"You can't leave the car running; somebody might steal it."

"I didn't think of that."

Damn Charlie, if he wasn't nearly Gus' brother-in-law, Gus would have ditched him long ago. He was a great driver and a good mechanic, but other than that he wasn't the sharpest tool in the shed.

Gus pulled out his pocket watch and flipped it open. He had to be at the bank in three minutes.

"Charlie, you wait right here while I go get you a couple of comic books."

Gus was half way across the street when Charlie thought of something.

"Gus, Gus, get me some Juicy Fruit gum too."

Gus just threw up his hands in exasperation as he continued to run across the street.

Moments later Gus ran up to the car and shoved a bag into Charlie.

"Here, a couple of comics and some Juicy Fruit."

"Gee, thanks Gus."

But Gus was already off at a trot headed to where Arty was standing on the corner. Arty had his pocket watch out and was tapping his toe with impatience.

"What's going on Gus? I see you talking to Charlie and then dash over to the drug store and back. Ain't we got a job to do? The Brinks truck started unloading a minute ago. We should have already been there."

Gus gave him a cold hard look and asked, "So are you calling the shots around here now?"

Arty looked down, scuffing his toe like a school boy. "No, you're the boss Gus."

"OK, then let's go."

Just as they were pulling their guns out they heard the squeal of tires and saw one of their rival gangs screech to a halt beside the Brinks truck. One of the Brinks guards dropped his money bag and ducked behind the truck. There were three guards in all — one in the bank, one in the truck, and the last one taking cover behind the truck. The one in the truck slid a small panel open

44

and began to spray the rival's car with bullets. Glass shattered, headlights burst, the radiator started gushing steam. Then out of nowhere three police cars arrived with their guns blazing. Gus and Arty quietly holstered their guns and began to walk around the block away from the foray. They circled the block and came up behind the car that Charlie was tending.

"Wow, Gus, you and Arty were lucky you didn't get caught in the middle of that. You guys might have gotten killed. I guess you missed your appointment."

Gus said, "Yeah, I guess we did. I'm not so sure I want to do business with a bank that was almost held up."

Gus thought, if I had been on time, that would be me lying there in a pool of blood. If I hadn't gone for those comics and gum, that would be me.

"Hey Charlie, that drug store has a soda fountain. How about I buy you an ice cream sundae. Shut the car off and let's go get one."

Charlie's face lit up like the night sky on the forth of July.

"Can I get a cherry on it?"

"You can get whatever you want."

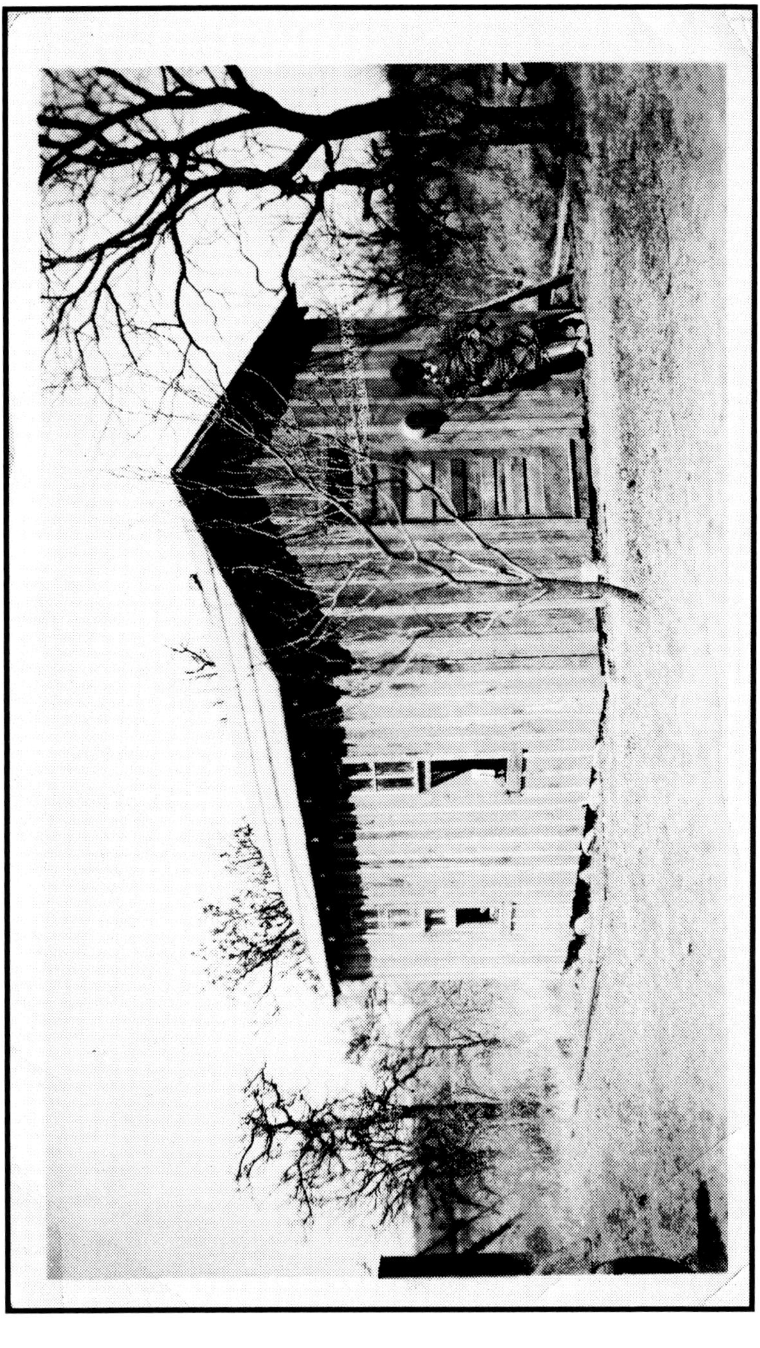

The Man Who Wasn't There

Abner Tyler lived in this two-room house all of his life. His father had built it about the time he was born. He was part Cherokee or Chippewa, nobody could remember. They just remember his Grandfather's wife was part Indian. That never set too well with the folks in these parts but they kept themselves to themselves.

Folks would see Abner walk into town about once a month with his mule in tow, to get provisions. He always paid cash according to the proprietor; nobody knew where he came by his money. Some speculated he'd robbed banks on his way back from serving in the Spanish-American war. Some say he saved Teddy Roosevelt's life and was paid a handsome sum for that. Some say he was a shaman and alchemist and turned iron ore into gold. There were nearly as many theories as there were people in town.

Abner never married but he did have a dog for many years. It would trot into town with him behind the mule and then sit and wait patiently while he did his shopping. It was a non-descript brindled mutt with a chunk of an ear missing, probably from a coyote. The dog had no name that the townsfolk ever knew, they just called it Abner's dog, if they spoke of it at all. It was a strange sight to see though, Abner leading the mule and the dog bringing up the rear. When they got to the general store Abner would tether the mule. Then Abner would wave his hand over the dog's head, almost like he was petting him and then he's say, "Stay." The dog would plop down on his haunches and probably would have stayed there 'til the judgment day. Once Abner was through with his shopping he would snap his fingers in front of the dog's face and say, "Come." The dog would stand up and shake himself from head to toe like he'd been doused with water;

then he'd fall in line and the small parade would leave town.

Once, while Abner was in the store, the mule got it in his head that he'd had enough for the day and sat down. When Abner came out he just looked at the mule and gave a tug on his lead, but the mule persisted. Abner didn't say a word. He put his parcels on the boardwalk in front of the store, undid the top button of his shirt and pulled out a small leather bag that was hanging on rawhide around his neck. Opening the bag, he fished around and came out with a pinch of something between his fingers and waved this under the nose of the mule. The mule's nostrils flared, but it did not move. Then Abner leaned over and whispered something into the animal's ear. Immediately the mule stood up, Abner strapped his parcels on to the mule and headed out of town.

By all accounts Abner was an odd duck, but he kept to himself and didn't stir up any trouble. He had a small garden that grew the meager produce that kept him going. On occasion someone would see Abner pack up the mule and head out into the desert. He'd be gone for several days or maybe a week. Some speculated he was hiding a gold mine out there somewhere. Others thought he had an Indian squaw that he visited. Some suggested he went out there to commune with the Devil himself. There was much speculation on this topic.

Abner usually came into town around the middle of the month, but the middle of the month came and went and so did the end of the month. The townsfolk had become a bit concerned because Abner was getting up there in years. The preacher was approached to go and check on him but he respectfully declined as Abner wasn't one of his congregation. So the Sheriff road out to check on Abner. The dog had died quite a few years before so the only thing to fear out there was Abner himself.

Everything looked normal to the Sheriff, until he saw the mule's carcass in the corral. It had been there a while because it was pretty well picked clean. The skull poked out of the scrub grass and seemed to be grinning. At this point the Sheriff had a bad feeling. As he knocked on the door and called out Abner's name, the door swung open. The sheriff stepped in — the front room was a sitting room and kitchen, the floors were swept, the dishes cleaned and put away. Nothing seemed out of place. He kept calling out Abner's name, getting no reply. He pushed open the door to the little bedroom in the back and that was when the odor hit him and he gagged. There was Abner stretched out on the bed wearing the same black outfit he always wore, with his hands folded on his chest holding a Bible. On the wooden crate beside the bed were two twenty-dollar gold pieces and a note with three words on it, "for my funeral."

Some people thought he'd killed himself, others just figured he somehow knew it was his time. Either way, after the funeral, which was attended only by the preacher and the grave diggers, Abner was pretty much forgotten.

A couple of years later, oil was found near Abner's property, and Mr. J.D. Jones real estate agent, always looking to make a fast buck, thought now was the perfect time to unload the Tyler property. He'd picked it up for a song, but needed the cash flow right now. When opportunity knocks you don't slam the door in it's face. The oil company wanted some photos of the property so Mr. Jones took his trusty Brownie box camera out and took some shots of the existing building, etc.

It was after the film was developed that people started talking about Abner again. You see the shot he took of the house had Abner standing out front.

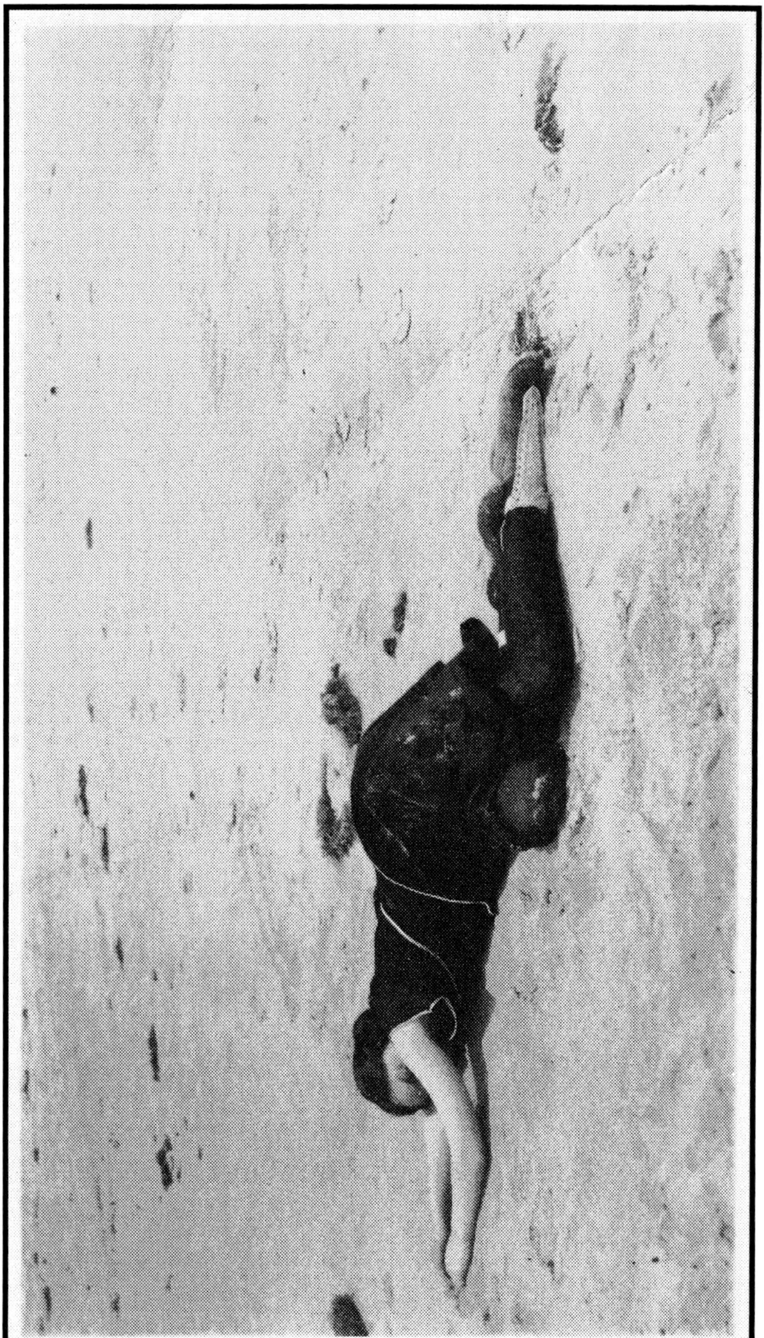

The Last Laugh

The four of us, Maggie, June, Harry, and myself, had rented two beach cottages for the week — one for the guys and one for the gals. We'd waited until September when the crowds were gone and the rental was not quite so dear. There was a long deserted stretch of road leading to the beach and of course, nature called. I pulled over to the shoulder and scampered off into the bushes and scraggly pines. After I'd finished, I thought I'd have some fun with them. I came out from behind one bush only to be obscured by another. At this point my head and shoulders were just visible. I began to shout.

"Help! Help! I've stepped into a bog or quick sand or something like it." As I said this I began to flex my knees and slowly sink down behind the bush. It was hard the keep from laughing as I did it.

My gal Maggie was beside herself. She was yelling at Harry, "Do something!"

"Oh he'll be alright," Harry said.

By this time, I was completely behind the bush and did all I could to stifle a laugh.

Meanwhile Maggie and June were getting a bit frantic and trying to push Harry out of the car to go and help me.

Harry shouted out, "OK enough Paul, you've had your fun, come on out."

"For the love of God, I can't hold on much longer," I said as I violently shook the bush.

Now Maggie and June were halfway out of the car and Harry was thinking I'd taken the joke too far.

Harry said, "Girls, get back in the car, now!"

As they got back in, grumbling and complaining the entire time, Harry put the car in gear and calmly drove off.

I realized they were going to just leave me, and it was at least ten more miles to the beach. I jumped out from behind the bush waving my arms frantically. "Stop! Stop! It was a joke."

For some reason it didn't seem as funny as it had a moment ago. Nobody spoke to me for the rest of the trip, although I apologized profusely.

When we arrived at the cottages I was feeling pretty low and wished I hadn't pulled that prank. The girls looked at each other and nodded, then Maggie said, "Have you learned your lesson?"

"Oh yes!"

She even managed to get me to promise no more practical jokes for the rest of the week. That promise lasted until the next day. We were down on the beach having a picnic lunch and enjoying the day when I saw a ghost crab scuttle by. I casually reached over and grabbed it before it got too far and dropped it into the picnic basket.

Moments later Maggie reached into the basket, but nothing happened. She pulled out a sandwich and there dangling from the waxed paper was the ghost crab. She screamed and the sandwich went one way and the crab the other as she flung both of them. I was able to catch the sandwich before I fell back on the blanket in peals of laughter. It was funny to everyone except Maggie. I was given the cold shoulder for the rest of the afternoon.

When she was finally talking to me again I told her I just couldn't help myself, but that I'd try to behave. She was appeased for the time being.

"Paul, that was your last chance. One more and I'll not speak to you for the rest of the week and you needn't bother calling on me when we get back."

Well that put a crimp in my style; I was beginning to fall for her but didn't think it could work out if she had no sense of humor.

The rest of the week was pretty dull and uneventful. We'd beachcomb, swim, or picnic during the day. At night we'd play cards, dominoes or read.

As I said, uneventful right up until the day before we left. We were all tired that day because we'd stayed up into the wee hours playing Gin Rummy. It was early afternoon and we'd just finished lunch. I guess it was the full bellies, the warm day, and the lack of sleep the night before that caused us to choose naps as our next activity.

We'd been asleep for maybe a couple of hours when there was a pounding at the cottage door. It was June in a very agitated state. We came out rubbing our eyes.

"What's up?" I asked.

"It's Maggie, she's disappeared. She said she wasn't sleepy and was going for a swim. I told her not to go alone, but she said she'd be OK, that she was a good swimmer. I didn't think anything more of it until I just woke up and she wasn't back. I checked her room. I looked over the dunes at the beach but didn't see anyone. I thought maybe she'd be over here."

"We just woke up when you came pounding. Let me get my shoes and we'll go looking for her."

Harry said, "We should check the beach first, if that was the last place you knew she'd be."

On the other side of the dune was nothing but a long stretch of deserted beach as far as the eye could see in both directions. There was the occasional chunk of driftwood and piles of seaweed but not a living soul to be seen. We split up; June and I went south and Harry went north. We were several hundred yards apart when I heard Harry yelling and waving his arms frantically.

"Over here! Over here!"

Harry was standing next to what looked like a large piece of driftwood from a distance.

We came at a run and that's when I saw Maggie, sprawled out on the sand. She didn't seem to be breathing.

"Oh my God, Maggie!" said June.

I started to go toward Maggie, but Harry grabbed me by the shoulders and said, "It's better if you don't."

I sank down to my knees and put my head in my hands and began to weep.

June and Harry turned away from me but I could see through my tears that their shoulders were heaving with tears of their own.

It was then that Maggie burst out laughing and June and Harry joined in.

"How do you like a taste of your own medicine, Paul? We'd been planning this one all week."

It was at that moment I knew I was in love.

56

Midnight At The Ranch

It was nearly noon, a cloudless day, but there was a definite chill in the air. It may have been the altitude or the time of year or a combination of both. Puffs of steam rose from the nostrils of the large black stallion on the other side of the corral. He seemed to fit his name, "Widow Maker."

It was Dot who was supposed to ride him around the corral while Natalie and I watched. Dot was the new-comer to our little group. She was going to stay behind at college over the Thanksgiving break because her parents were traveling out of the country. I decided to invite her and my best friend Natalie home to the ranch for the break. Natalie had been there the year before and knew what to expect, but Dot, the big city girl, was like a fish out of water.

Natalie and I hatched up this plot and spun out a story for Dot. We told her how "Widow Maker" hadn't actually killed anyone but he had injured three riders and four grooms, one of them seriously enough that he was in the hospital for three weeks. Natalie chimed in, "I had to ride him last year and he was as gentle as a lamb. I think he just doesn't like men." Dot gave her a dubious look.

Last year I had given the same story to Natalie and she was so scared that I thought she was going to be ill. The night before her ride she was sitting on her bed with her arms around her legs and her knees up to her chin. She was rocking back and forth muttering, "I can't do this, I can't do this." All the while tears were streaming down her face. I broke down and had to tell her that the horse was named "Midnight" and he wouldn't hurt a fly.

"Really?", Natalie asked.

"Really, cross my heart and hope to die."

Now she was crying in earnest, but with relief.

Natalie said through sniffles, "I should be mad at you but I'm so relieved I can't be. Just don't do anything like that again."

I promised never again, but here we were and it seems to be different now that Natalie is in on it.

That evening we tried to wind Dot up, but she wasn't having any of it. She acted as if she rode man-killing stallions every day and tomorrow would just be more of the same.

I guess somehow we knew if Dot passed this test it would solidify our friendship. She'd only been in our circle for a couple of months because she was a freshman and we were sophomores. Dot was way smart though; that was the reason she'd been accelerated and was taking sophomore level classes. That was how we'd run into her. We knew she came from New York and that her family had money, probably old money. She didn't like to talk about her family; we sensed some problems there but didn't want to pry. So she was still a bit of a wildcard to us, but this would show Natalie and me what she was made of.

The time had come and Dot strode towards the great horse. She had her riding britches on under her coat. As she approached the stallion he snorted and pawed the ground with his hoof. Dot reached into her pocket and produced an apple and held it out to the great beast. He bent down and sniffed it, then plucked it from her hand. It was gone in less than a minute.

Dot looked him over. He was nothing but rippling muscle from hoof to head. His powerful flanks twitched slightly as Dot stroked them. He was a jumper if ever she had seen one. Dot took him by the bridle and spoke to him quietly. She scratched him behind the ear and then swung up into the saddle. She started him off at a trot on her first lap around the corral, then up to a canter. She brought him up short right in front of us and leaned over and whispered into his ear. Patting him on the neck she turned him toward the center of the corral and took off. She had him at a full canter as he came to the fence. Dot leaned into him and they were airborne and landed as easy as you please on the other side. She rode him maybe a hundred yards into the field and came back, jumped the fence once more into the corral.

Natalie and I were sitting there dumbfounded. We'd never seen anything like it. Dot trotted up to where we were and gave us a look as if to say, "So do I get into the club?" After that look had passed between them and been acknowledged, Dot said, "I guess I forgot to mention that daddy has a stable full of champion steeple chase horses."

Dot dismounted and the great horse nuzzled her neck. She reached into her pocket and pulled out another apple and handed it to him. As she patted his neck, she said, "You did good out there Midnight."

I looked at her in astonishment. "How did you know his name?"

Dot looked at me and said, "Yesterday I asked one of the grooms."

It was then Natalie and I knew we'd been had.

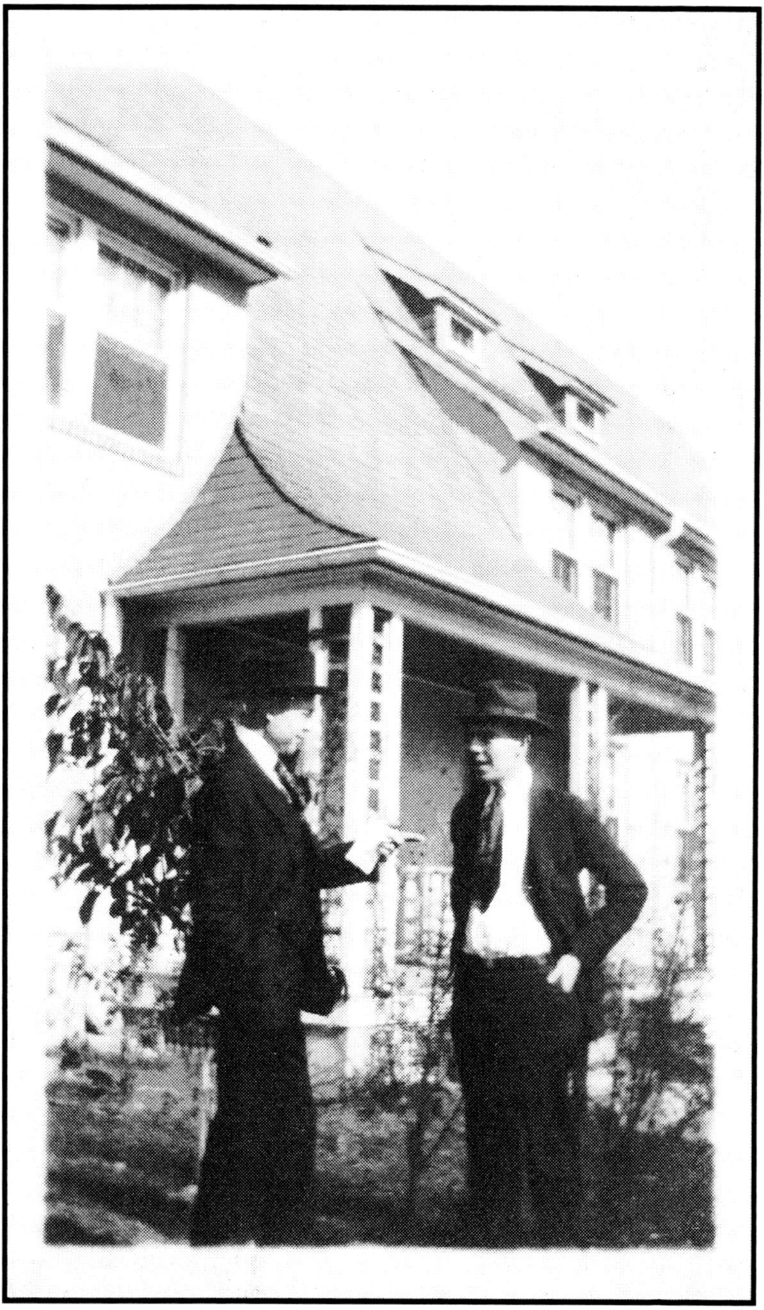

The Great Amazon Adventure

My buddy Charlie had just told me the most remarkable thing. He said he was going to the Amazon to look for Col. Percy Fawcett and possibly discover the lost city of Z while he was at it.

"What makes you think you'll be able to find him Charlie? After all, he disappeared over ten years ago."

"It's not just me, there is a whole expedition that's going."

"How in the world did you even hear of it? I mean we don't live in the big city and none of our friends are what you'd call explorers."

"I answered an ad in the newspaper. They were looking for 'Young, physically fit, not married, and preferably no family ties whatsoever.'"

"You do fit the bill, all except for Margaret. I thought you two were getting serious and were going to get married."

"We were, but all of a sudden she said she wasn't ready to settle down. I have no idea what I've done to cause her to change her mind. In that envelope I've given you is a letter to Margaret explaining where I've gone and why I'm leaving, along with the engagement ring I was going to give her. You must promise not to give it to her until I'm on the ship headed for Brazil."

"You have my promise, but aren't you even going to say goodbye to her?"

"It's all in the letter. It's better this way. My will is in there too and I've left everything I have to her."

"But Charlie, she's the one who broke it off. Why would you leave her anything?"

"You dumb galoot, I still love her, but if I can't have her I might as well shake off the dust of this one horse town and see the world."

"But haven't you read the reports in *The National Geographic* magazine about the savages and the insects and the diseases? They say there are some flies that lay their eggs under your skin and then they hatch out and you've got maggots living under your skin. They've showed pictures of twenty-foot-long snakes and spiders the size of your hand."

"It can't be all that bad. If it was why would people keep going back? Col. Fawcett had been lots of times."

"The last time he was there he disappeared without a trace and hasn't been heard from for over ten years — his son and another companion too."

"Well this expedition is about ten times that big with all of the modern equipment. They have a wireless set that transmits and receives. They have an airplane that can land on the water — it'll be used to scout ahead of the expedition and to drop supplies and possibly to get somebody out in a hurry, all of the latest snake bite anti-venoms, and a complete stock of medical supplies."

"That's great Charlie, I'm glad I'll be staying right here where the worst I have to worry about is the common cold."

Charlie looked at him and shook his head, "Don't you long for adventure? Don't you want to go someplace that's never been explored?"

"Well Charlie, I've just asked Maude to marry me and she has accepted. I think that should be enough of an adventure for me. I was getting ready to tell you when you broke your news. When do you leave?"

"The ship to Brazil leaves in a week. I need to be at the docks bright and early that day."

"I guess I couldn't talk you into staying for a couple of months; I wanted you to be my best man."

Charlie's resolve wavered for a moment and then he said, "There'd be no way of catching up with them if I waited that long."

On the docks a week later we all showed up to see the intrepid explorer off — Maude, Margaret, and me. Charlie was surprised to see Margaret there, but put on a brave face. We all went on board to check out Charlie's quarters. They were small but tidy with all of the necessities — a bed, nightstand, clothes cupboard and a bathroom down the hall. His quarters were a bit cramped with four people in it so they made their way to the rail near the gang plank. Dr. Rice, the leader of the expedition came on board. Since Charlie had met him once for an interview he made the introductions.

A loud steam horn blew just then and then came the announcement, "All ashore that's going ashore."

Up until this point Margaret had been subdued, but now burst out in tears. She pulled out the envelope that Charlie had given to me and began waving it around.

Margaret pulled off her gloves and Charlie saw the engagement ring on her finger. She said, "I will marry you Charlie and I'll wait for you to get back."

At this point, my old pal Charlie was in a bit of a predicament. He'd only signed up for this lunacy because Margaret called everything off, but he was a man of his word and would now have to go through with this fool-hardy expedition.

I got Dr. Rice off to one side and whispered into his ear. Moments later he was throwing Charlie off the ship and having his luggage dropped off at the end of the gangway.

Charlie was astounded and relieved. He asked me what I'd said to Dr. Rice.

I smiled and said, "I told him that this little show was for his benefit and that you'd been secretly married earlier in the week."

Charlie said, "And you gave that envelope to Margaret even though I explicitly told you to wait until I was out to sea."

"Yep," I said.

I couldn't read Charlie's expression and was preparing myself for a punch in the nose, when suddenly he burst out laughing.

"I'm so glad I've got you as my best friend."

"So, can I put you down as best man at my wedding?" I asked.

"Only if you'll return the favor."

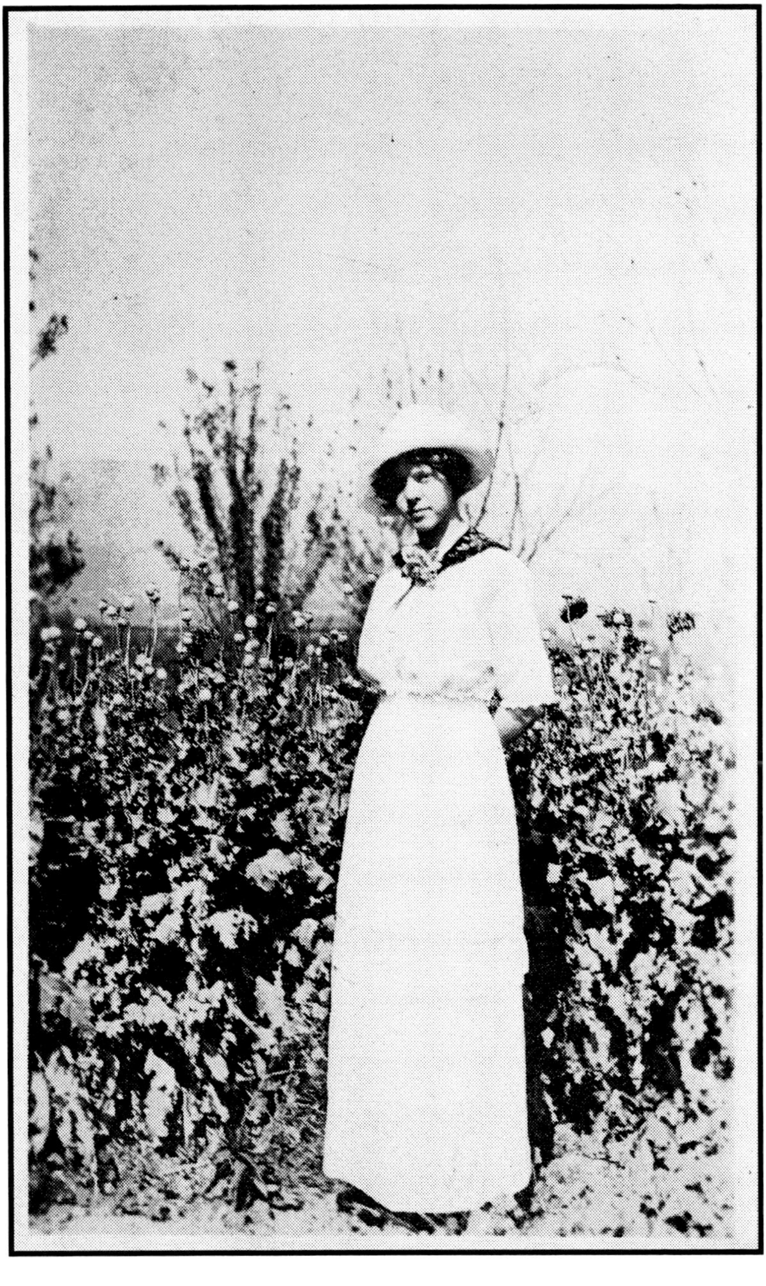

Not Flander's Field

Myrtle should have been a boy, but that was not to be. Her mother died shortly after she gave birth. At first her father considered putting the child up for adoption because his lifestyle wouldn't allow him to raise her. He dabbled in many things, some that weren't quite legal. That environment was no place to raise a daughter. Money wasn't a problem so he shipped her back east to her maiden aunt to raise. Myrtle had the finest nannies, the best schools, and when she turned twenty she wanted to go back to California and find her father. He'd been mostly absent during her life, but had sent birthday and Christmas presents regularly.

When she arrived at the address her aunt gave her, there were no grand reunions. Her father was not even there. The servants said, "He is away on business."

She quizzed them on what kind of business he was in and got vague answers. The closest to the truth was import-export. Prohibition was in full swing and he was running booze down from Canada. Myrtle knew none of this, but wasn't content to wait around until he showed back up.

Her father had graciously given her the run of the place and access to the car with its driver. She took the car to San Francisco, the Chinatown district. She loved Chinatown back in New York and escaped there as much as possible, unbeknownst to her Aunt. Her Aunt may have suspected, but Myrtle never got caught. She'd picked up a bit of Cantonese along the way and intended to use it today. She went from the grocer, to the fish monger, to the herbalist always asking the same question, and always receiving the same answer. Always getting the shake of a head. Her last stop was a seedy looking restaurant, a hole in the wall. Old men were hunched over their bowls of noodles when she approached the proprietor. He smelled of fish and smoke and grease. She asked her question and he looked her up and down then grabbed her wrist with a boney hand and began to drag her toward the back. As quickly as he had grabbed her he had a knife blade at his throat. The old men briefly lifted their heads from their noodles, saw it was none of their concern and continued to eat. The proprietor having been bested, spat out a long list of profanities as well as the answer she'd been looking for. She thanked him and left.

Deeper into Chinatown, towards the more disreputable sections she strode. She was glad that she had a revolver as well as her knife. She strode with purpose and no one challenged her. After a few wrong turns, she made it to the address she was given. At the end of an alley was a heavy wooden door that had been painted green at one time, but was now just a ghost of its former color. She rapped on the door with the handle of her parasol. A small window in the door slid open and an old man stared out at her.

"Go away," was all he said before sliding the window shut.

Bang, bang, bang went the parasol and once again the window slid open. This time before he slid it shut she rattled something off in Cantonese. This gave the old man pause. She then pulled an item from her bag and showed him. He cocked his head as she twirled it between her fingers. Slowly the bolts were drawn from the door and it swung in. The room was dimly lit and a haze of smoke lingered in the air. The old man motioned her to a room in the back. The air was clearer her and the lighting better.

The old man scrutinized her then asked, "Do you have more of those?"

Myrtle nodded.

"How many?"

"Hundreds, maybe thousands."

"Why do you come to me?"

"I was told you might be interested."

"May I see it?"

She handed over the item and he pulled out a knife to cut into it then he looked up and asked, "May I?"

"Do what you want; that one is yours to keep."

After slicing it open and giving it a thorough examination, he said. "These aren't ready yet but will be in another week."

"I will still have them in a week. Are you interested?"

The old man made some noises, and stroked his wispy beard. Reaching over for a pencil and paper he began writing out some Chinese characters, scratched through a few and started over. When he was done he wrote a number down that Myrtle could read and slid it over to her. The offer was respectable, but she knew she would lose face if she didn't haggle. She reached for another pencil and scratched through his number, wrote down another and slid it back. A smile broke over his face as he took the paper and then a frown as he shook his head. The paper went back and forth several more times before Myrtle, feeling that she had not lost face, capitulated.

A week later the old Chinaman and a couple of helpers showed up at the ranch that Myrtle was now calling home. Her father was off again, but this transaction didn't concern him.

Remembering her days at school, she never thought that her botany lessons would come in handy. Not until she had stumbled upon the huge field of poppies growing wild on the outskirts of her father's ranch and remembered that opium comes from the poppy. She really had no idea how, but had nothing to lose by running a bluff in Chinatown. As it happened she'd struck gold. It made her giggle to think that her father had never even noticed them, being too busy as a bootlegger, a fact she had recently found out.

The old Chinaman and his helpers were done and had their truck loaded to overflowing. Myrtle had kept back a small batch to plant the seed for next year. She waved as they left and put the fifteen hundred dollars in her bag. She was thinking it might be nice to stay in California for a while.

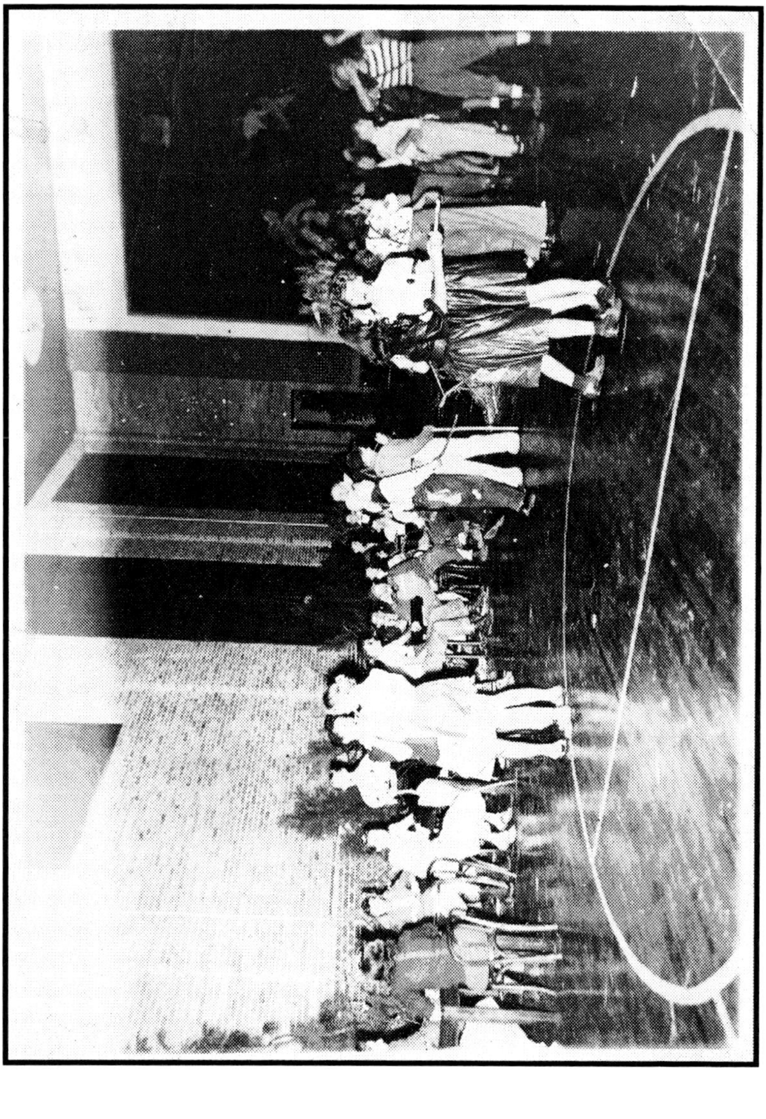

To Save The World

I didn't want to be here at a stupid kid's party, but they made me come. I really didn't see how I could accomplish anything here. I was supposed to be looking for a certain boy; his name isn't important. After all, you wouldn't know him. I had no description or photo to go by, just a name. I began to casually ask around, all the while getting strange looks.

"What are you supposed to be?" asked one girl.

I looked around, thought for a moment and said, "I am a person from the future."

She looked me up and down and said, "That's a pretty weird costume."

I must have read the year wrong because I was wearing stuff that was from the mid-1960's –plaid bell bottoms, wildly colored paisley print shirt, a fringed vest and a string of love beads. At least I had my long hair pulled back in a ponytail so face on, it didn't appear that long.

I asked her if she knew the person I was looking for.

"Oh yeah, he's here somewhere. I think he's dressed like a pirate."

At least now I had a name and "dressed like a pirate."

This was a huge Halloween party and there must have been thirty pirates in the crowd.

I began to mingle as best I could. The stupid outfit I had on was not helping me to be inconspicuous, but that couldn't be helped now.

I'd talked to about ten of the pirates, all giving basically the same answer, "Not me, I think he's over there somewhere."

I drifted over to the punch bowl, took a cup and sat down.

A moment later a very pretty girl with fairy wings sat down beside me and began to chat.

"You're not from around here are you?"

"No," I said, wanting to keep this conversation to a bare minimum.

"Me either. I'm visiting some relatives here in town. They made me come. I didn't really want to. What are you supposed to be anyway?"

"I'm from the future."

"Wow, they sure do dress funny in the future. Do you want to dance?"

"No, I'm looking for somebody."

She abruptly got up and stalked off, but that was just as well.

I'd finished my punch and was about to search again when this scrawny kid in a pirate outfit came strolling up and looked me over.

"I hear you are looking for me. Well here I am. What do you want?"

I was a couple of years older than him. He was maybe fifteen or sixteen. The kid was showing some bravado I'm sure he didn't have yet, but give him a few years.

I stuck out my hand and said, "Hi my name is Paul and I've got a business proposition for you."

He looked at me suspiciously, but also with a hint of excitement.

He shook my hand and told me his name.

I said, "Let's go outside, I've got something in my car I'd like to show you."

We got to the car and I opened the back door and pointed at a cardboard box on the seat. "It's in there."

He leaned into the car and began to open the box. At that moment I pulled out what looked like a Taser and sent fifty-thousand volts through his body. He collapsed on the back seat.

I pushed him the rest of the way in and then drove off.

When he came to we were in an abandoned warehouse and he was securely taped to a chair. He wanted to know what was going on, where we were and why.

"I will tell you everything, because you deserve to know."

I pulled out a fifth of whiskey and made him take a drink.

"You'll be needing more of this soon, but I want you to be clear headed while I tell you what is going on. I have been sent here from the future and my job is to find you and kill you."

"You're crazy! Why do you want to kill me?"

"I don't want to kill you, but it's for the good of mankind. It's a sacrifice for me too; I can't return because the technology for time travel doesn't exist yet. The future I come from is bleak. There are only about a hundred thousand of us left and most of them are sterile from the radiation."

"What has that got to do with me?"

"I'm getting to that. There is a time in the future where you have become rich and famous. Your wealth and fame are only superseded by your egotism. Somehow against all odds you become President of the United States. The records are sketchy since the internet went out. It seems in your first year in office things were not going as well as you had anticipated. There was talk of impeachment, among other things. Like I said, the records are sketchy, but from what we've been able to piece together you decided to start a war thinking it would divert attention from you. You launched nuclear missiles — think one hundred times as much as Hiroshima or Nagasaki. There was no provocation. They landed in mainland China killing almost half a million people."

The captive gave a visible gasp. I gave him another swig of the whiskey.

"After that there were retaliatory strikes, and the population of the world was cut in half within a week. Firestorms raged all over the world. Then nuclear winter set in as all of the poisonous dust accumulated in the atmosphere and blocked out the sun."

There were tears running down his face now.

"I would never do something like that, never in a million years."

"Oh, but you did do it. The survivors banded together and used all of the limited resources they had left to build a time machine and send me back. I only have to kill you and with my knowledge of the future I can live like a king. Here, drink some more of this."

He took about four more gulps of the whiskey and now his speech was slurring.

"I won't, I won't, I won't."

The whole time he was crying and I noticed he'd wet his pants.

"I'm sorry."

I pressed the device that looked like a Taser to his neck but it was set for five-hundred-thousand volts. This time he didn't wake up.

I left him on a bench outside of the gym with the bottle in his hand.

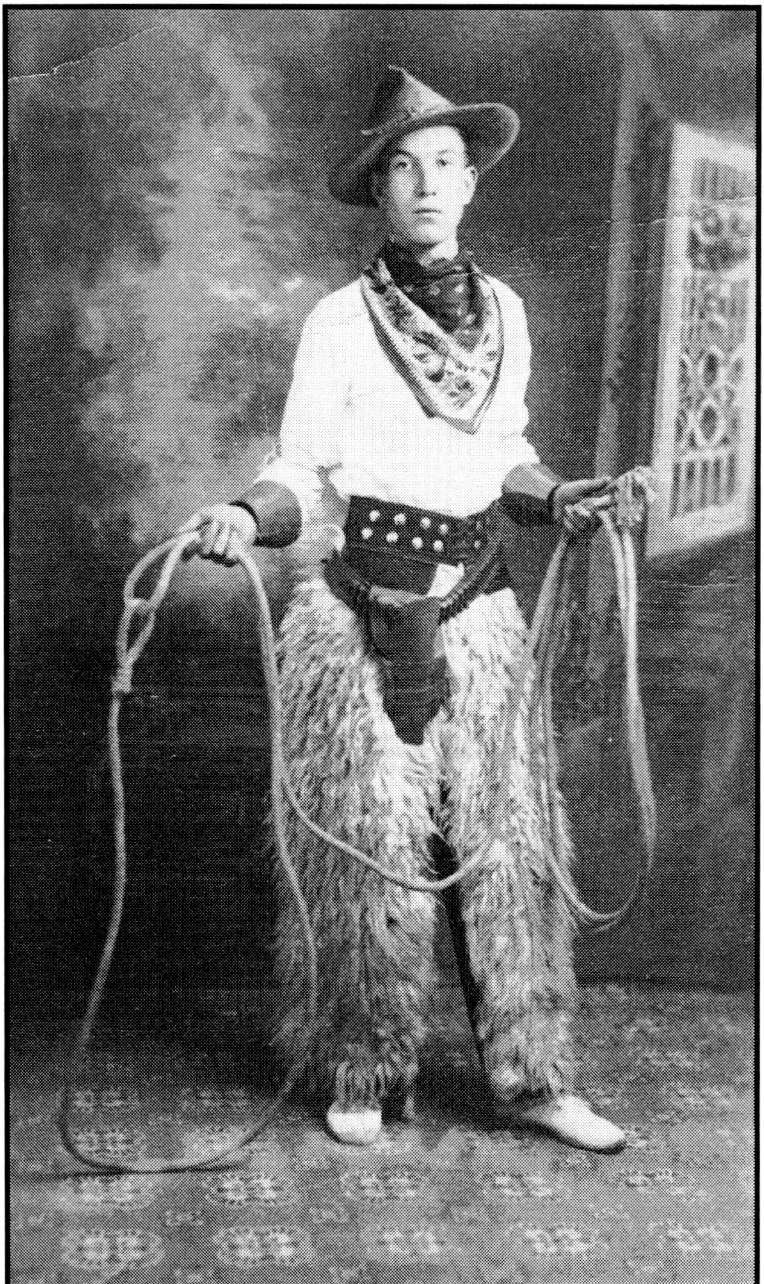

Yippie Ki Yay

Elmer Woodcock III came from a well to-do family. His father and grandfather were bankers in Boston and it was just assumed young Elmer would follow in their footsteps. Elmer had other ideas.

Ever since he was a young boy, Elmer loved reading all the westerns he could get his hands on. He mostly had to do this in secret because if he was ever caught with "that trash", it would be thrown out immediately. Some of what he read did get by the censors because it was history. Although he was fixated on all things "cowboy" he unintentionally developed a deep understanding of history, albeit a thin slice.

His grandfather passed away when Elmer was eighteen and off at college. The old man had understood Elmer better than anyone else in the family. His grandfather had once told him, "Elmer, banking isn't for everyone. Sometimes I wish I'd never gotten into it myself."

This statement had run through Elmer's head for years. After the funeral Elmer said, "Father, I don't know if I want to be a banker."

His father looked at him with a mixture of disappointment and disdain, but only said, "Now is not the time to discuss this, we'll talk about it after you graduate."

Elmer went back to college and graduated Suma Cum Laude with a degree in History. That was one battle he'd won with his father, getting him to concede to a history degree instead of something related to economics. So at twenty years of age with a degree in history he went to work at the bank. He began as a teller and would work his way up the ranks. He never brought up the matter about not wanting to be a banker to his father. He had an entirely different plan.

After a year working in the bank Elmer didn't report to work one morning. His father called the house and was told that Elmer left the same time as usual. His father sent someone out to look for him but to no avail. It was as if Elmer had vanished.

It was Elmer's twenty-first birthday, that apparently nobody had remembered except his mother who gave him a peck on the cheek and said, "Happy Birthday." The other thing that everyone had forgotten except Elmer was that he came into a hefty trust fund on his twenty-first birthday. Elmer was going to celebrate that fact.

His first stop was the photographer's studio. Here he had a full length portrait made of himself outfitted in full cowboy regalia. He paid extra and had a rush put on the order and was told he could have the prints by the end of the day. The next stop was to buy some off the rack clothes and a suitcase. Finally, he went to the train station, bought a one-way ticket to Wyoming, and checked his bag. He had a few hours before the train left so he got something to eat and then picked up the photographs.

He mailed one to his father, writing on the back: "I've always wanted to be a cowboy but you wouldn't listen. I have taken a job on a ranch in Wyoming. Tell Mother not to worry."

He guessed at this point he'd burned his bridges, but he didn't care. He was on his way to fulfill his dream.

It took the better part of a week to get to Wyoming. When he arrived, there was a beat up farm truck waiting for him. It was full of supplies for the ranch. The driver's name was Jed and he stuck out a callused hand and shook Elmer's. He looked Elmer up and down, then he asked, "You know what you're getting yourself into son?"

Elmer replied in the affirmative and Jed just shook his head. "Those hands haven't seen a single day of hard work. I've seen greenhorns before, but you're about as green as they come."

Elmer's face turned red with anger and embarrassment. All he said was, "I'll be fine."

After the first year Elmer was no longer the greenhorn he'd been when he showed up. He could ride, rope, and shoot nearly as well as anyone on the ranch. The work had been hard and the calluses on his hands were catching up with Jed's. Elmer couldn't be happier. He looked back at the photograph in the cowboy duds and had to laugh; nobody dressed like that. He showed it to Jed once. Jed tried to stifle a laugh but it burst out of him like water breaking through a dam and it was contagious. By the time they had finished they had tears running down their faces.

Elmer sent letters back east, but never got anything in return; eventually he stopped sending anything at all.

During his fifth year on the ranch he was checking a horse's hoof for a stone because it had begun to limp. Some of the other ranch hands found him slumped in a heap against the paddock wall. Elmer had been fiercely kicked and had taken the brunt of it on his left leg. His leg was broken in two places and Elmer was in and out of consciousness as they bundled him into the back of the farm truck and drove him into town. There was no hospital, only the town doctor. The doctor set Elmer's leg the best he could and gave him something for the pain. It was nearly two months before Elmer could walk without help. Well not exactly without help, because now he needed a cane. The doctor didn't set the bone exactly straight and now Elmer walked with a limp. Elmer's days as a cowboy were at an end.

Elmer headed back east. Bankers didn't need two good legs, but neither did history teachers. Elmer thought the latter would be more rewarding and took a position as a high school history teacher. He'd regale the students with stories from the ranch when it would help make a point with his lesson. The students seemed to hang on every word. At the end of the school year as his students were about to graduate he pulled out the much alluded to photograph of himself in cowboy duds. This he passed around expecting giggles and stifled laughs, but none came. What he did get was looks of awe and wonder.

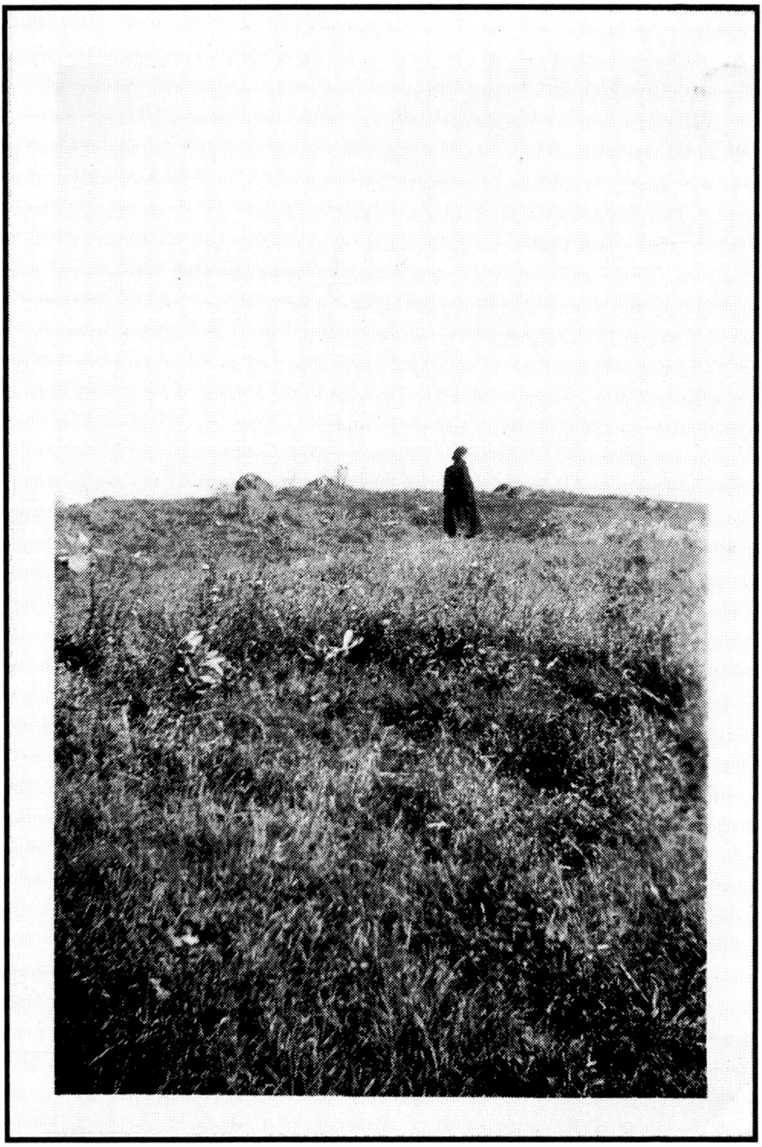

Unconditional Love

The funeral was over and Rachel needed some time alone, so she headed aimlessly up the hill. Today she had buried the love of her life. They'd been together for more than thirteen years. It had only been in the last year that she had seen his health decline. First it was small things like staying in bed longer than usual. He'd always been an early riser and was invariably up and ready for the day before she had even gotten a cup of coffee. Then she noticed he wasn't finishing his dinner, but she didn't say anything even though she'd noticed he was losing weight.

One morning a couple of days prior, she had checked on him because it was nearly noon and he'd never stayed in bed this long before. His breathing was labored and she told him she'd be right back as she rushed out of the house to get Doc Jones. By the time they had gotten back, he was gone. Now she was walking up the hill carrying her grief like a sack of bricks. She ended up at the precipice and gazed over at the steep drop down to the water and jagged rocks. "Nobody could survive that drop," she mused. Then a shiver wracked her frame from head to toe as she realized what she was thinking.

Why had she come all the way up here? Was it that she just needed to be alone or did her sub-conscious have some sinister ulterior motive? She sat down on an outcropping of rock and let her legs dangle as she dropped stones over the edge. She watched them plummet down and make tiny splashes in the water or ricochet off the rocks jutting from the bottom. The more stones she dropped the more she began to think that it might just be possible to survive the fall, but not for long, and it would be painful if you weren't killed instantly.

She sat there and looked out over the water and began to

cry. She had held it all in until now but now the flood gates were open and they wouldn't stop until she was all cried out. She was hugging her knees to her chest when the crying fit abated. Rachel felt a tug at her dress sleeve but didn't see anyone. She looked around like someone waking up from a dream and tried to figure out how long she'd been there. The sun was much lower in the sky than it had been when she arrived so it must have been a couple of hours at least.

As she stood up to head back she heard a sound like a gunshot that was very close by. She jumped off of the rock she'd been sitting on and back on to the path. No sooner than she'd done that there was another loud report and the entire chunk of the outcropping that she had just been on fell away into the ocean.

Rachel stood there dumbstruck. That could have been her. She could be laying in a heap at the bottom of the cliff. She stood there for a moment and shivered. She needed to head back; there were people waiting for her. She needed to pull herself together and get back home. It wouldn't be easy after a loss like this, but life goes on.

She started back down the hill, counting her blessings. She had a good home and two loving little girls. She knew that they were devastated too. She had no right to go off and leave them when they needed her. She began to trot down the hillside and when she saw her two little girls she went down on her knees and embraced them. Just then she heard her husband say, "I know it's hard to talk about now, but maybe soon we could get a puppy for the girls. I know it will never replace Rover. Just think about it."

Rachel looked over to him with tears brimming in her eyes and said, "That might be a good idea; just give me a bit of time to get over it. It's not every day you have to bury your best friend."

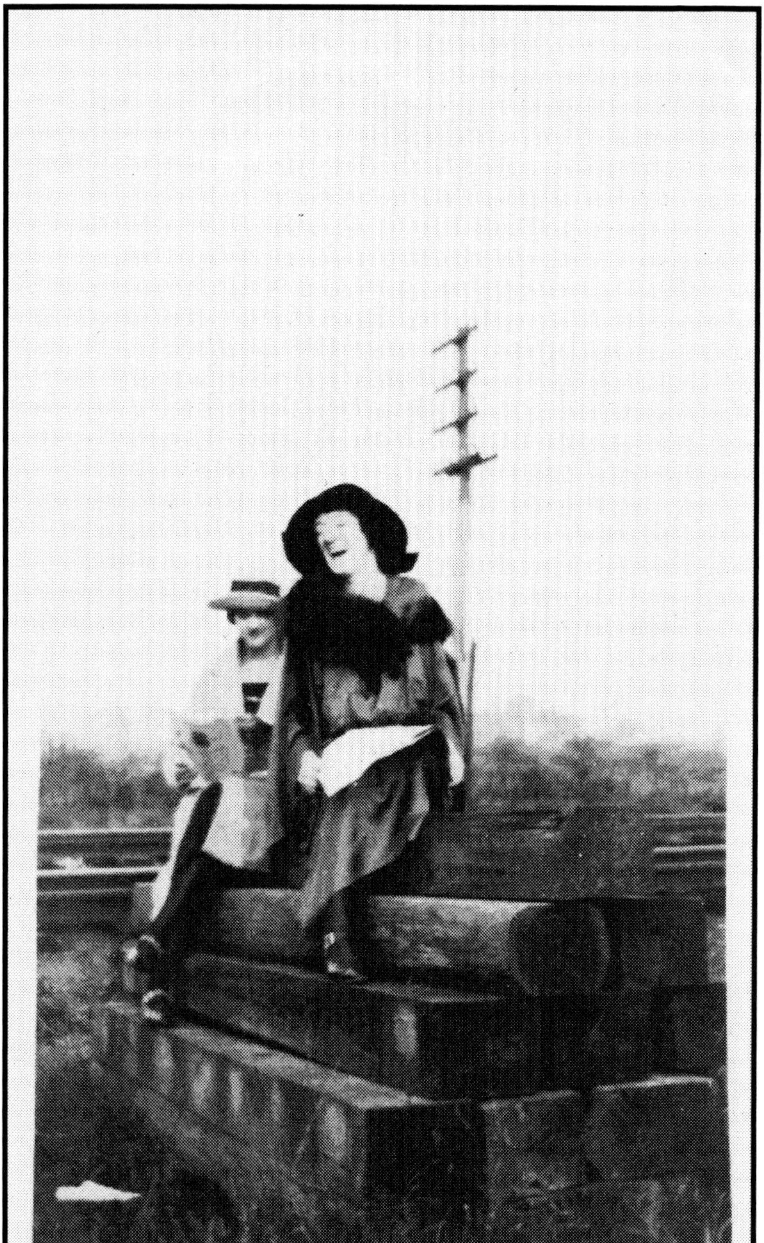

Keeper of the Sacred Flame

Anyone who didn't know her thought that Aunt Minnie was a bit odd. Those who knew her understood that they didn't know her at all. I was her ward, as Minnie never had any children and she had adopted me when I was about three years old. I probably knew her better than anyone. I knew her real name was Minerva and she was older than she looked. I was to find out later she was much older than she looked, but I'm getting ahead of myself.

As I was growing up she taught me all of my lessons. I think at one time she may have been a teacher, among other things. My lessons consisted of the normal reading, and writing and arithmetic, but as I found out later there were also some things that "normal" children didn't learn. For instance, along with my alphabet I learned to read hieroglyphs and alchemical symbols. She also taught me Latin and Greek. We would take walks in the woods and she would quiz me on different plants and their uses. If they were poisonous I would have to also know the antidote. I just thought this was the type of education that every young lady received. We also went over manners, and mine were passible as were hers, but she would often warn me that sometimes you had to throw manners out the window for the greater good. I never really understood that but nodded and went along with it.

It was not long after this photograph was taken that Aunt Minnie became ill. I was twenty-three by then and it seemed like it was time to pay her back for all of her kindness toward me. She would not let me get a doctor, saying, "They can't do anything for me."

I would bring her broth, help her to the bathroom, and give

her a sponge bath, but I really wasn't doing anything to make her better. After about a week she seemed to rally. She was sitting up in bed when I came in and she patted the bed beside her. I sat down and she began to talk.

"Jane, it's time I tell you a few things. I was hoping I would have more time, but my time is drawing short."

I began to protest but she just gave me a look that meant "Be quiet and listen."

"I am old Jane, much older than you think I am. I am close to three-hundred years old and even We don't live forever. I am a member of a secret order known as The Keepers of the Sacred Flame. There are nineteen of us around the world and all women. There are certain rites and rituals we perform year after year that keep the universe in harmony."

I had begun to look at her like she'd lost her mind or was delirious.

"I am neither crazy nor delirious, and yes I can read your mind sometimes. Think about it for a moment, Jane. Look at the grand house we live in. We have servants, we never lack for anything, and I have no source of income. How could that be? I guess I could be living on a vast inheritance and I guess in a way I am. As I said there are nineteen of us worldwide and some are younger and some are older. I am one of the oldest. We have each along the way acquired large fortunes due to the longevity of our order. We have been around a long time; we saw the first Pharaohs of Egypt ascend to the throne. We have no need of money. Even if each of us lived to be one thousand we would not be able to spend it all, but we don't live ostentatiously. We live comfortably and try not to attract too much attention to ourselves."

I nodded as if for her to go on.

"Jane, I didn't pick you to be my niece, the universe did. I was told when the time was right I would know who was to be my successor. When your parents died in a fire and you were going to be taken to the orphanage, I heard a little whisper, "She is the one." I have learned well to heed those whispers; they don't come often but woe betide the person who ignores them. I didn't listen to one early on and it was nearly the death of me, but there isn't time for that story. I have taught you arcane and esoteric knowledge. Although you don't understand all of what I've taught you it will stand you in good stead even if you are to refuse the offer that I am going to present to you. Yes, it is an offer and you can refuse if that is what you want to do. We always have free will; without that we are nothing. It's not always easy, though the past twenty years have been relatively uneventful. Twenty years is just a drop in the bucket when you are talking about millennia."

I had begun to fidget on the bedside because this was just too much to take in all at once.

"Let me get to the point. I will die very soon; it's only with the help of the other eighteen that I have the strength to tell you all of this. If you accept, you will be given great power, wealth and responsibility as well as an extraordinarily long life. You will give up a family and close friends; you will become a nomad of sorts. If you live somewhere too long, people begin to talk about the woman who doesn't get any older, who keeps to herself and seems a bit odd. That's how the witch trials began, but I digress. I need an answer from you and although this was not how I planned it, I need it now."

I chewed at a finger nail as I let all of what she'd just told me sink in. I nodded my head in ascent. Then Aunt Minnie leaned over cupping my face in her hand and whispered a single word into my ear. When she did it seemed like the universe exploded behind my eyes. I collapsed on the bed beside Aunt Minnie. When I came to, my beloved aunt had passed on. For just a few moments I felt the presence of the other eighteen in the room with me. I was being bathed in love and consolation. Then they were gone, but I knew I could contact them if the need was urgent. For now it was just me, Jane, Keeper of the Sacred Flame.

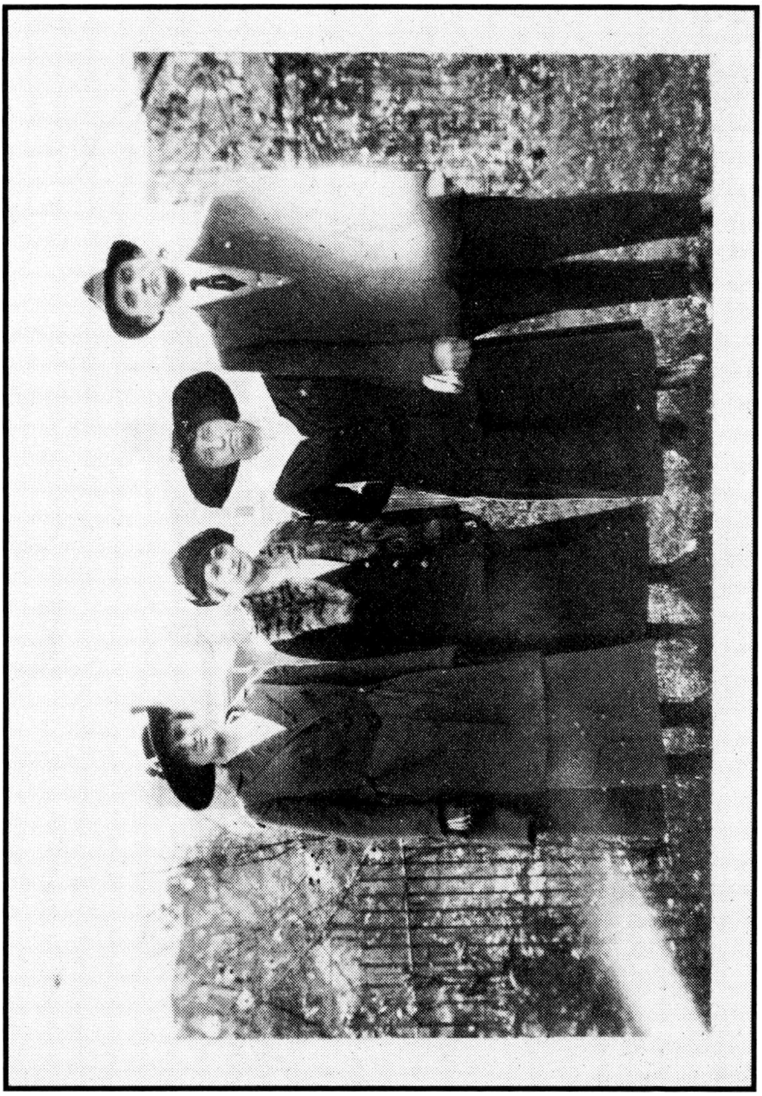

Like a Thief in the Night

Joe ran a successful import-export business while his wife stayed home and raised the two girls. By the norm of the day the girls should have been married and out of the house long ago. The problem was, every time a young gentleman came to call he never returned after meeting their father. It wasn't that he menaced them, but that he just laid it out in no uncertain terms that if they weren't interested in marriage to one of his daughters that they needn't come back.

The girls, Natalie and Dorothy were well on their way to becoming spinsters at twenty and twenty-two respectfully. Rose would plead with her husband to not give the girls' suitors such an ultimatum.

She'd say, "Joe, just let nature take its course. No young man is going to commit to marriage before he knows either of the girls. How would you have felt if my father had talked to you like that?"

But Joe was adamant; he knew what young men wanted and he was having none of that. Perhaps if one seemed suitable he could come to dinner and they could get to know him, but so far there were none.

Joe was also a bit of a snob since they had moved to a ritzier neighborhood in 1921. This was about a year after he left his job as a receiving clerk on the docks and opened his own business. The girls had been ten and twelve then. They hadn't been poor but now they were much wealthier than they'd ever been. No matter how Joe tried to downplay it, the signs were everywhere. He rode around in a new Roamer; they had a cook, maid and butler.

All of this had also come to the attention of the authorities who suspected that Joe's import-export business was just a front for bootlegging. The problem was, they had no proof. They had raided his warehouse and inspected all of the crates and bills of lading. Everything tallied except for the lifestyle that Joe and his family were living.

One fine day a gentleman came calling on Natalie, and since her father was at work, her mother let them sit in the parlor and chat until Joe arrived back home. Joe arrived and gave the young man "the talk." The young man stood his ground, saying he did intend to marry her after a suitable engagement period so they could get to know each other. The young man was named William Gordon and he received an invitation to dinner the following evening,

William Gordon turned out to be a very likeable young man. Joe actually started to warm to him by the time dinner was through. William suggested a six-month engagement and Joe told him he'd think it over. After dinner Rose, Dorothy, Natalie and William played cards while Joe read his newspaper; all the while Joe kept an eye on William.

Joe, being nobody's fool, began to check out William and his family. He was afraid that he might have a gold-digger as a future son-in-law. Everything that William had told them checked out. He came from a fairly wealthy family and was currently working as an accountant at a bank with hopes of becoming president of the bank one day.

William returned for dinner the next week and Joe announced that the engagement was on. After consulting the calendar, they decided to be married on the first Sunday in May. Natalie couldn't have been happier unless Dot was engaged too.

The weeks passed and William was invited over for dinner several times a week and Natalie went to meet his parents as well. Joe liked this young man who had high hopes of being bank president. As the weeks progressed, Joe began to drop subtle hints around William. For instance, would he want to have alcohol at the reception? After pondering this for a moment, William said, "Joe, I know that booze isn't legal, but I think it's a stupid law. If there was some way to have some booze at the reception, that would be great. I want the genuine article though, not that stuff that'll make you blind."

Joe just smiled and nodded his head, thinking, "This boy has possibilities."

Joe said, "What would you say if I offered you a job that pays a lot more than you make at the bank?"

"What kind of job?"

"Working for me in the family business."

"No offense Joe, but I did some checking up on you through the bank and with the cash flow that you have I don't see how you can pay me a lot more than the bank."

Joe smiled, "Well I guess we've both been checking up on each other, but that isn't the business I was speaking of. I also run a more lucrative business since Prohibition started. I do it right under the noses of the government. I'm one of the largest wholesalers of perfume in the United States. If you tally it all up I probably sell about ten-thousand gallons of perfume a year."

William looked skeptical. "Women don't buy that much perfume; there must be booze in those bottles."

Joe smiled, "I knew you were a sharp one. I sell it wholesale for three dollars a quart. That way I don't have to bother with rebottling and labeling."

"That's a hundred and twenty grand a year. Your accounts don't show that. What do you do with the money? Sorry, that's not my business, it's just the accountant in me."

"Not a problem. I bought this house with cash, the car out

front was paid for in cash, and I get a new one every year. I own quite a bit of real estate and I have a substantial reserve tucked away. I'm going to need it too for this wedding."

"So how do you keep track of it all? Who's your accountant?"

"That's where you come in. I'm prepared to pay you twenty thousand dollars a year to keep my accounts straight. I've got everything in a ledger now but it's beginning to be too much for me to keep up with."

"I'd need to see the books before I commit. I could meet you at your office one evening and we could go over them."

"No need for that, I have them here."

Moving a panel on the bookcase, some "books" swung out exposing a safe. Joe deftly spun the dial and opened the safe. William got a glimpse in there as Joe pulled out the ledger; it was full of stacks of currency.

William started looking through the ledger. There were accounts dating back ten years — well over a million dollars.

William said, "Wow this is amazing, but I will have to decline."

As he said that he pulled out a badge and a revolver and said, "Joseph Ascarni, you are under arrest for tax evasion."

Joe who was seated behind his desk grimaced, then clutched his chest. Then Joe stopped breathing and went limp.

This outcome had never occurred to William. It was just Joe and himself in the library. He put his revolver and badge away. He was waiting for the bribe, but none was coming now. He looked at the safe and it was still open. He emptied the safe of the cash, stuffing it in all of his pockets, his stockings, his hat and coat. He put the ledger back and locked the safe and closed the panel. He left by way of the side door and was never seen in those parts again.

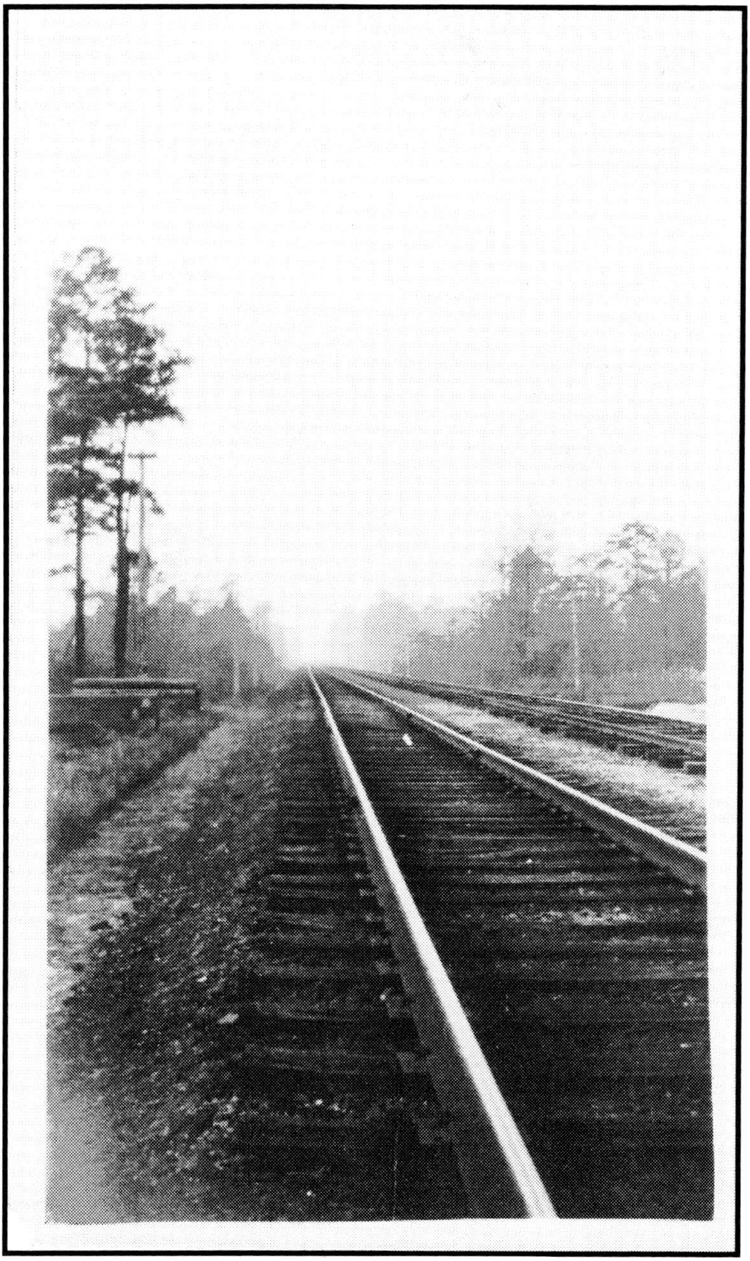

Any Road Will Get You There

James remembered someone once said, "Go west young man."

It sounded like good advice to him. If he followed the tracks he'd eventually end up in Chicago, but something interesting might turn up along the way. You just never knew.

All he had were the clothes on his back, a bed roll, and the couple of dollars he'd saved up. Leaving might be a hardship, but they'd never treated him well. He had his pocket knife for protection and his wits for what they were worth. He'd be OK, at least that's what he told himself.

He'd been walking all day and had seen a few trains come barreling through, but when he looked back down the tracks the view hadn't changed. As far as the eye could see the tracks spread out in front of him and receded behind him. If it hadn't been for the rest of the scenery, he might as well have been standing still. It was also beginning to get dark and he was going to need a place to sleep.

He saw several small fires down the embankment from the train tracks and went to investigate. He'd stumbled into a hobo jungle. An old man greeted him and told him to sit by the fire and warm himself. The temperature was going down rapidly as the sun sank.

The old man stuck out a hand that hadn't seen soap and water for a long time and said, "My name is Bob. You just passing through?"

James said, "I'm headed to Chicago. You know, 'Go west young man.'"

Bob nodded his head sagely. "You got anything to eat in the bundle?" pointing at James' bed roll.

"Some cheese and bread. I did some odd jobs for a woman and got some food and this coat."

"Tell you what, you share your cheese and bread and I'll share my beans and coffee."

"Deal," said James.

"You got any money on you?"

"I've got—"

The old man cut him off, "Don't be telling me how much money you have nor anybody else. There's some jokers 'round here would bash you over your head for two bits. I suggest if you have any money you put it in your shoe. I heard tell that some woman a couple of towns back got her throat cut, and the guy got clean away."

"What kind of person would do that?" he asked as he fingered his own pocket knife.

"I don't know, must be crazy though."

Yeah thought James, must be.

He slept by Bob's fire that evening and was up at first light. Bob was nowhere around so James packed up his meager belongings and went into town looking for some odd jobs. He helped a farmer muck out some stalls and earned himself some breakfast and a bit of food to carry him through 'til tomorrow, but no money.

The walking that day was much like the day before. As evening fell he spotted another cluster of campfires and headed toward them. To his surprise there sat Bob with his beans on the boil and he welcomed him like an old friend. They sat and talked and Bob said he'd heard of another murder just like the last one.

James said he didn't want to talk about that; it might give him nightmares. He told Bob he's taken his advice and moved his money. Now all he had in his pocket was a handkerchief and his pocket knife. Once again he slept beside Bob's fire and like the day before he woke early, but Bob was already gone.

This morning's trip into town yielded him no work, so he had to dig some money out of his shoe and went into a diner. He had a hearty breakfast and stuck a couple of ham biscuits in his pocket for later. While he was eating his breakfast at the counter he overheard a couple of men talking about a murder that had happened the night before in the town. It sounded just like the last two to James.

As he walked out of town headed west, James began to think. How had Bob known about those other murders? How come he was gone so early in the morning? It wasn't likely he'd run into Bob again, or so he thought. The rest of the day was just mindless, one foot in front of the other.

As darkness fell he saw a bunch of campfires off to the side of the tracks, but he hesitated to go over. What if Bob was there? Could he not let on that he suspected him? He approached the nearest campfire and to his relief it wasn't Bob. Then he heard from the next fire over, "James, come on over here." It was Bob, and James couldn't ignore him.

They chatted about their day and this time James brought up the most recent murder. Bob was curious because he said he hadn't heard anything about it. This sort of put James' mind at ease, but not entirely.

James slept late the next day and the sun was already up. Bob was sitting on a log by the fire.

"I thought you'd never wake up."

James rubbed his eyes and sat up. "I thought you'd be long gone this morning."

"I thought I'd stick around for a change."

They both saw them at the same time; there was a sheriff and his deputy coming down the embankment and headed straight for them.

Bob didn't seem concerned at all, but James was a bit frightened.

When the officers got there the sheriff said, "Are you James Wolley?"

"Yes sir," he said.

"You need to come with me."

"But I didn't do anything. What about Bob? I think he killed three women," James said pointing at Bob.

"You escaped from Danvers State Mental Asylum and we're here to take you back."

"What about Bob? He's killed three women!" He said once more pointing at Bob.

Bob just sat there with a knowing smile on his face.

While the Sheriff had distracted him the deputy had snuck up behind James and knocked him unconscious with a blackjack.

The deputy looked at the sheriff and said, "Who's Bob?"

The sheriff just shrugged.

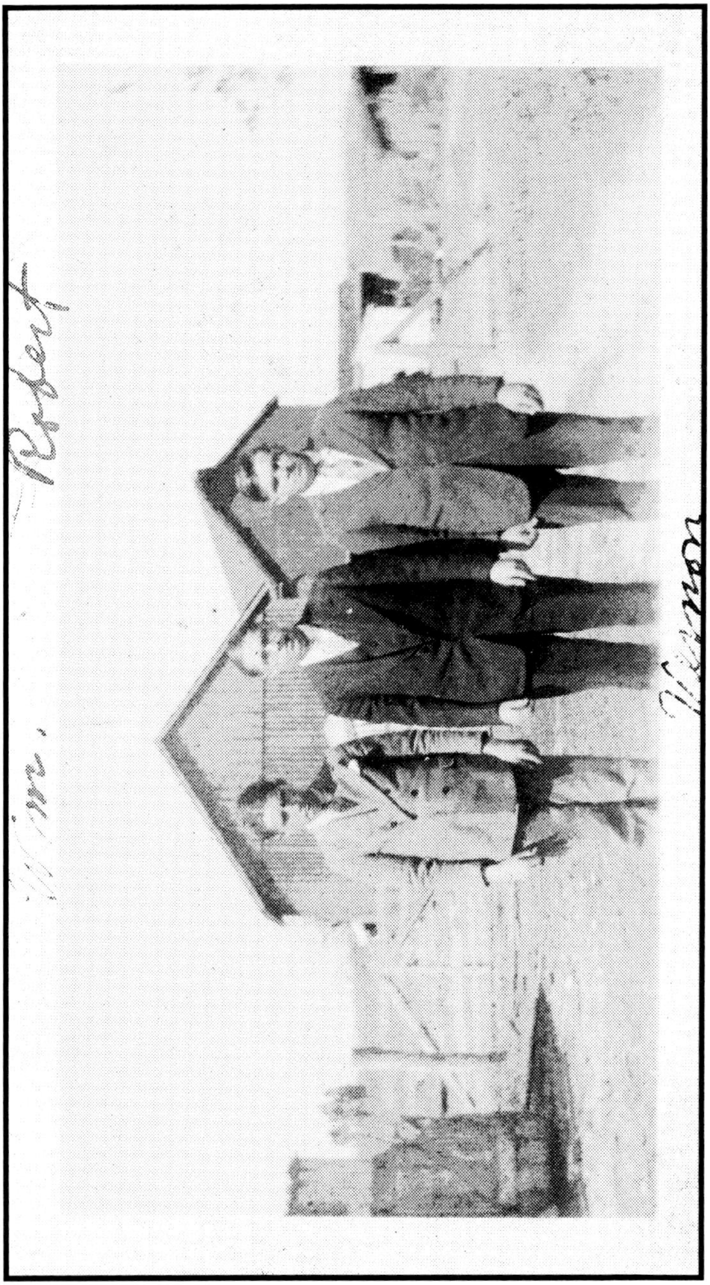
Wm.
Robert
Vernon

All Out of Bullets

Vernon tried to raise his two boys to be honest and upstanding community members. It had been difficult after their mother had run off like she did. William was two and Robert was four when she left. She just packed her bag and got on the train said she was going to visit her aunt in California. That was the last they saw of her. That was fifteen years ago.

The Depression was hard on everybody, but more so on cityfolk. Vernon and the boys had the farm, and as long as Vernon could make a go of it they'd at least have food on the table. After the boys' mother left, Vernon contacted his sister who lived in Kansas City and offered her the job of raising the boys while he kept up the farm. She readily accepted and soon she was a part of their family.

Vernon worked six days a week and on Sundays he'd take the family to church. The boys would fidget and squirm until they were old enough to sit still. By that time, they were working on the farm when they weren't in school. Neither of the boys liked school very much but thought it better than farm work.

William, the younger of the two, had always been picked on. He was thin, and always got Robert's hand-me-down clothes. They hung on him like somebody had dressed a scarecrow. William was the reader in the family and got better grades than Robert. He was partial to reading history and especially liked anything to do with the Wild West. Some days he fancied himself and his brother as Frank and Jessie James or Butch Cassidy and the Sundance Kid. He seemed to be drawn to all the outlaws.

There was a shotgun and a hunting rifle in the house, but the only gun that really interested him was a colt revolver that had belonged to his grandfather. The story was that General Grant had given it to him for some heroic deed in the Civil war. William wasn't clear on the details, but coveted the gun.

Once a month his father would take everyone and go into town for provisions. It was on one of these days that William, about fourteen at the time, asked to stay home. His father reluctantly gave in but told him not to get into any mischief. William told him he wouldn't.

The dust had barely settled on the long dirt lane leading to the farm when William had the Colt out and was shooting imaginary bad guys in his bedroom. He had a handful of bullets that he'd found in the drawer with the gun, but knew he would have to wait until the family was much closer to town before he could actually shoot it.

It seemed to William that every minute was taking an hour to pass. He'd given them an hour to get to town and knew it would be several hours before they returned. He took the revolver out to an unused pasture and set up a tin can on a rock. He backed up about thirty feet. Taking the loaded revolver, he held it down at his side and pretended to quick draw on the tin can. He had the pistol pointing roughly in the direction of the can when he pulled the trigger. Well, he attempted to pull the trigger. It was harder to pull than he had anticipated. They made it sound so easy in the dime novels he'd read. So still pointing it roughly in the direction of the can he used both hands to pull the trigger. This time the gun went off with a deafening roar. It also kicked back and hit him so hard in the chest it made him stagger backward. The can remained unharmed.

He tried again, this time knowing what to expect. He missed the can but saw a chip of stone fly off. His third attempt knocked the can off its perch and sent it flying. William thought he'd done enough for today. Even though they lived in the middle of nowhere, there was a neighbor about a mile away and sound carried pretty far over this flat land. William's arms where tired from holding the gun too. It was a lot heavier than he thought it would be, and his chest hurt from his first shot. He went back to the house and put the gun away, knowing he'd be back to it next month.

After about a year of this, he had become pretty proficient. He had also noticed that most of the ammunition was gone. How would he explain that? He needed more ammunition and that required money. That was something he had none of. Even if he had the money, how could he explain buying bullets for a gun he wasn't supposed to be using?

He tossed and turned and couldn't get to sleep. The full moon illuminating his bedroom didn't help at all. With a flash of sudden inspiration, he got up and snuck out of the house. It was half past eleven and everyone was asleep, including the townsfolk. He took the horse and rode him bare back to the edge of town where he tethered him to a shrub. Better to do this on foot.

He went to the back of the General Store without a plan other than to break in, steal some ammunition and leave. He didn't know what he'd do if the door was locked. Fortunately, it was not locked, in fact it was wide open. As he was about to enter he heard hurried footsteps and a stranger came busting out of the store with his arms loaded with all sorts of stuff. The stranger stopped and stared at William and in that moment's hesitation William picked up a piece of lumber that was propped up against the back wall. He swung it like a baseball bat and made contact. The stranger dropped all he had as he fell to the ground unconscious.

William ran and woke up the sheriff and all the commotion had awakened the storekeeper. The Sheriff hauled the stranger off to the jail. The store keeper was so grateful he gave William a five-dollar store credit as a reward.

If it struck anybody strange that William was there in the middle of the night, they never asked about it.

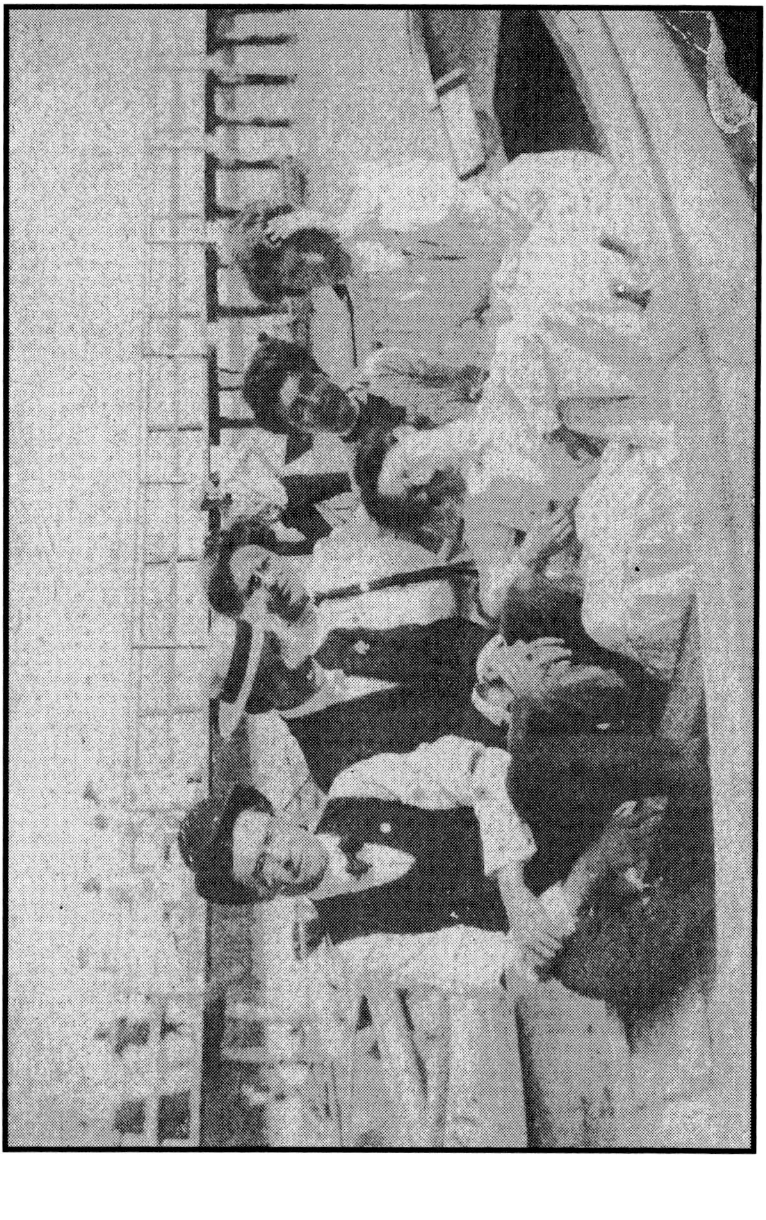

The Treasure Hunt

George and I (I'm the one in the bowler hat) were rowing the ladies out to the island for a picnic. We were only interested in two particular ladies. Ruth was my sweetie and Gwen was George's. For the sake of propriety Gwen and Ruth had each invited their sisters. Ruth's sister was Kate and Gwen's was Anne. So the six of us with a large picnic hamper rowed out to the island.

The island was about half a mile from the harbor and not very large. All totaled it might have been a square mile. It had a nice sandy beach though, that was perfect for our outing. The far side of the island was rocky and the middle rose up about thirty feet and had a few trees and shrubs. Some people said there were wild pigs on the island, but I'd never seen any.

The weather was gorgeous; the sky had the occasional cloud and there was a light breeze. George and I took turns rowing and we landed about an hour after we left. The ladies were excited because none of them had ever been to the island. George and I used to come here as boys and play pirates. We would draw maps and have one location where "X" marked the spot. We were always sure we would find buried treasure and be rich, but instead we grew up and became accountants. Not rich, but comfortable.

We pulled the boat up on the shore far enough that the tide wouldn't take it away and leave us stranded. The ladies wanted to explore and so we told them that you could walk the circumference of the island in about a half hour. Meanwhile, George and I collected a pile of driftwood and got a small fire going. We spread out the picnic blanket and got the hamper out of the boat. Then as if on cue, the ladies rounded the opposite shore and headed our way.

They said they'd been treasure hunting and showed us what they'd found. They had a collection of tiny shells and some bits of sea glass. Their greatest find though was carried in the fold of Anne's dress. There were close to two pounds of blackberries that were luscious and the biggest ones I'd ever seen. We saved them to have with the pound cake that was packed for dessert.

We were all starved, the ladies from their walk, and us from our rowing. We tucked into the food in the hamper like we were castaways seeing our first good meal. Of course Gwen and Ruth had outfitted the hamper with all we would need. There were ham sandwiches, deviled eggs, three bean salad, and pickles. A large jug of lemonade was there to quench our thirst and the pound cake for dessert. Just so we didn't appear to be heathens there were also plates, glasses, silverware, and napkins.

By the time we had finished our lunch and packed up everything I suggested we go on a real treasure hunt. I produced a tattered map from my coat pocket and began to lay out the story of how I had obtained it. Since it's provenance seemed credible everyone was excited. I got a couple of shovels out of the boat and a compass from my pocket and we began to look for the first landmark on the map. It seemed to be on the other side of the island and described a rock formation that looked like an eagle's head.

Ruth said, "We saw that when we walked the island. We all thought it looked like some kind of a bird. We can take you right to it."

"Lead on," I said.

As we rounded the far end of the island the ladies were getting excited and pointing at the rock. We followed the directions on the map and ended up near the center of the island. The final step was to find the tree with an "X" carved in it and dig thirteen paces due east of that tree.

We found a tree that may have had an "X" carved in it at one time, and could barely be made out through the bark. After pacing off the requisite number of steps, George and I began to dig. We had no idea how far to dig, but after about two feet we hit something hard and began to dig around the object. We had to widen our hole to be about three feet around before we exposed the object. It appeared to be a box wrapped in oil cloth. It took George and I a lot of prying with shovels and hefting and hauling to get it out of the hole.

Once it was out, it was indeed a box about eighteen inches square and a foot tall. The ladies were beside themselves with excitement. George and I unwrapped the oil cloth to expose an old box with bands of metal that were very rusted despite the oil cloth and of course a lock. We hacked at the lock with the shovels to no avail. Then George had the idea to pry the hasp off by getting a shovel behind it. This worked. Due to the rust it just fell apart.

Now was the moment of truth. We raised the lid on creaking hinges and peered inside. At first glance it appeared to be empty, but there was a folded sheet of paper in the bottom that looked a lot like the map I had.

I reached in and unfolded the paper and began to read it.

August 4, 1732

This chest has been buried knowing that in the future two men and four women will discover its contents. As you are reading this now, you know this to be true. The two men are destined for greatness, but if and only if two of the ladies present can answer one question each.

At this point George and I pulled ring boxes out of our pockets and each of us got down on one knee and asked Gwen and Ruth to marry us.

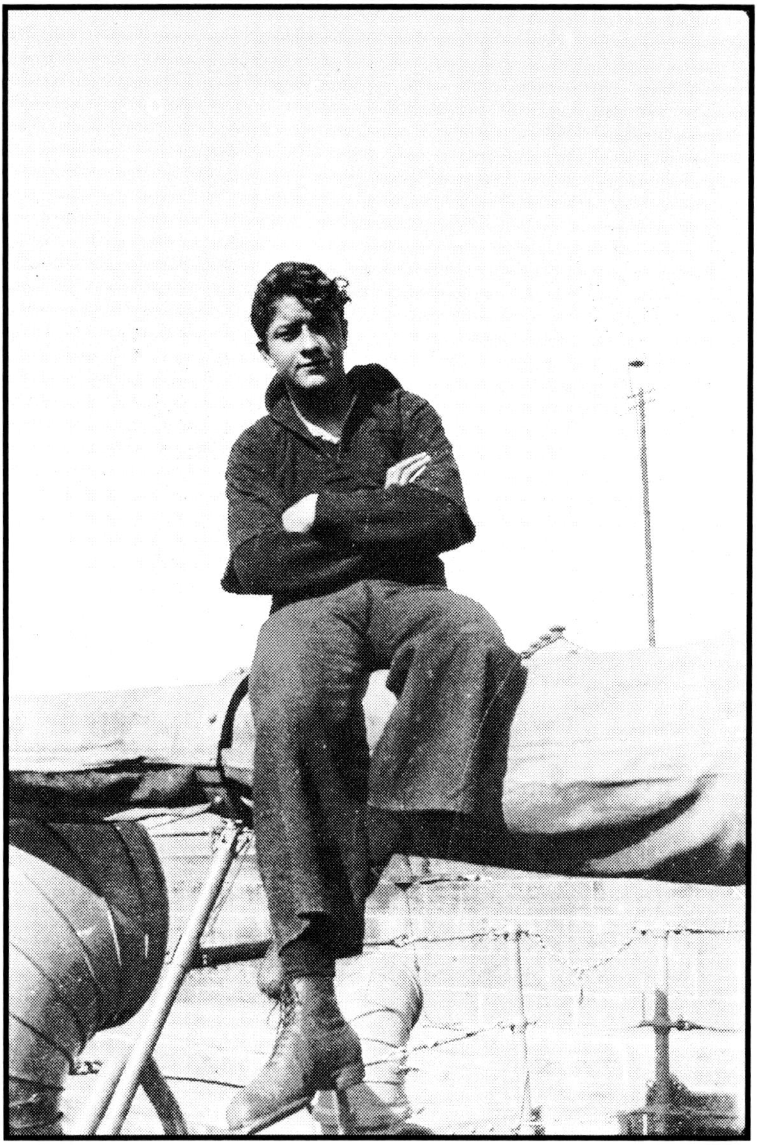

Jinxed

I'm not a superstitious man, no more than any other sailor, but I told the Captain that I'd wait for my pay right here above deck in the bright sunlight.

The Captain said, "You're acting like an old woman, McGreevy."

"Be that as it may, I'm not going below decks anymore and I'll not be crewing for this ship again."

The Captain just walked away shaking his head. I heard him mutter, "Nothing ever happened in broad daylight."

Maybe not, I thought, but I wasn't going to risk it after what I'd seen.

We'd made a run to Jamaica delivering agricultural supplies and bringing back rum. We weren't a day out when things began to happen. At first you could chalk them up to coincidence ... the only light bulb in a passage way burning out and leaving you in total darkness, one of the gauges on the boiler getting stuck — things like that. We were in the mess about a week out of port when somebody mentioned one of those little things. Then somebody else chimed in and before long everyone in the mess had a story. Individually they weren't much, but put together it seemed like the ship had a jinx on it. She was an old ship and I figured that she just needed some overdue maintenance. My opinion didn't prevail though. The rest of the crew were nearly certain that there was a jinx on the ship. It wasn't until the night before we docked in Jamaica that I became a believer.

I was taking a shift shoveling coal into the boilers. The engineer had shown us where the gauges needed to be and told us if they dropped below a certain point to give her more coal but not so much they went into the red zone. There were two of us shoveling and had been at it for nearly an hour when the engineer came around. He wanted to know how long we'd been at it and when we told him, he frowned.

"You've been shoveling steady for almost an hour, no breaks?"

"Yes sir," we both said in unison.

The engineer looked at the gauges and they were rock steady right where they had been since we got there.

"Have these gauges moved at all?"

"No sir," we replied.

He pulled a wrench out of his overall pocket and gave one of the gauges a tap. Suddenly the needle swung over into the red."

"Stop shoveling!" he commanded.

The engineer started turning a large valve, but it wouldn't budge.

"You two, get over here and help me."

With all three of us turning, it finally broke loose and the pressure gauge went down into the normal range.

With the crisis averted, the engineer went around to the rest of the gauges and gave them a tap. Each one gave a small fluctuation before settling down in the normal zone.

"That's the damnedest thing I've ever seen; all four gauges were stuck in the same position. I've seen one or two get stuck, but we have four, so at least one will give an accurate reading. A few more minutes of you boys feeding her coal and the boilers would have most likely exploded and nobody survives an explosion like that."

When we docked I had half a mind not to get back on her, but I signed up for the complete voyage and if I didn't go back I'd get no pay. So, I went to a bar and got a drink and then began to ask the bartender a few questions. He was reluctant to give me any information until I told him my tale and slipped him a silver dollar. He looked around and then wrote an address on a scrap of paper and then drew a sigil on the back and told me to show that to the woman I was going to see.

It wasn't far from the bar and from the outside seemed like any of the other shanties. I knocked on the door and a voice beckoned me to come in. The inside was dimly lit with all sorts of things hanging from the rafters — snakeskins, bundles of herbs, and dessicated small animals, to mention a few. At the end of the room, sitting in a plush chair behind a small table, was an old woman. She pointed at a chair on the other side of the table, so I sat.

She pulled some cards from a pocket of her skirt and said, "Would you like to know your future?"

I handed the piece of paper over to her that had her address and the sigil on it. She looked at it for a moment and then set fire to it in the candle flame.

"You seem to need some help."

That was an understatement, and I told her my tale. I told her I just wanted to get back safely and never set foot on that ship again. She told me she could make up an amulet that would protect whoever had it on that ship, but that it would be expensive. I handed her a twenty-dollar gold piece and asked if that would do. She eyed it and then bit down on it and examined the mark. She nodded and began to assemble the items and to mumble something over them. She told me I could hang it around my neck or keep it in my pocket and as long as I had it on my person I would be safe.

I made the return voyage without incident and that's why I'm waiting topside for my pay.

The Captain came over and handed me my pay envelope and after I'd looked through it and jumped to the dock I had a thought.

"Hey Captain, you could probably use this."

I threw him the pouch but it didn't quite get to him. He took a couple of steps and picked it up.

"What's this for?"

"It will keep you safe," I said.

"Bah," he said as a few hundred pounds of agricultural supplies that were being loaded fell to the deck just where he'd been standing moments before.

He looked at me, he looked at the pile a mere foot away, he looked at the amulet ... and stuck it in his pocket.

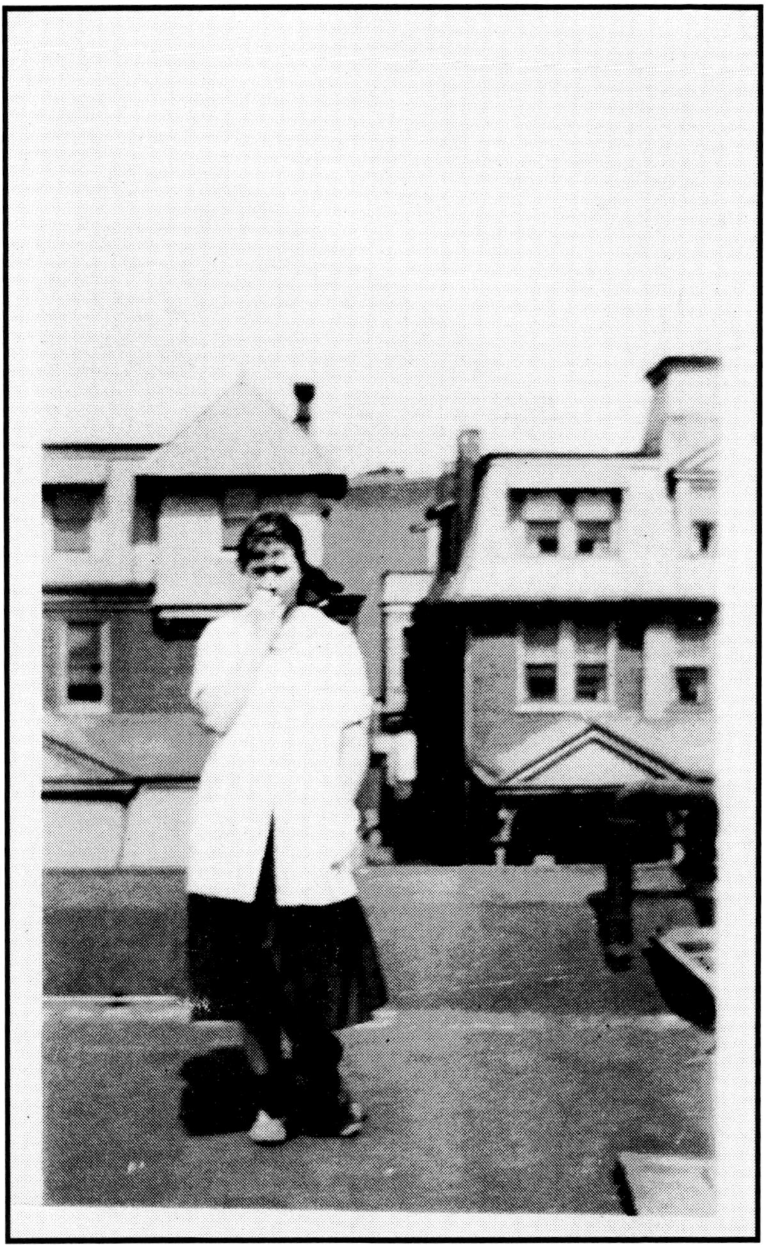

The Gravity of the Situation

I wasn't supposed to be up on the roof, at least not alone. The last time they caught me up here they locked me in my room for a week. They don't understand that when I'm up here and can look down on the rooftops I feel some serenity. The voices in my head are still there but they are at abeyance for a few brief moments. I don't know why; they used to be worse up here.

They think I'm crazy but I'm not. I can't say as much for some of the others here though. There are only six of us and mostly they keep us separated and none of them have ever wanted to come up on the roof with me. I've asked them numerous times.

There isn't anyone here my age, so I don't have a lot in common with them. We do eat meals together and in the evenings we listen to the radio shows in the parlor. Mrs. Crosley is the exception; she isn't allowed to listen to the radio with the rest of us because she just won't stop talking. She carries on a conversation with some person the rest of us can't see. Sometimes she will even get into heated arguments and start shouting.

They wheel old Charlie in and set the brakes on his wheelchair because even though he sits there with a vacant look on his face, he'll go racing down the hall in that wheel chair given half a chance.

Well I might as well tell you about the rest of them.

Mr. Gorsuch seems pretty normal except he does things over and over again. For example, he'll come in a room and close the door and open the door and then close the door and he'll do this four more times before he is satisfied the door is closed. He's the same way with light switches and a bunch of other stuff, but if you didn't know that you'd think he was normal.

Miss Helen Palmer looks normal too but she thinks it's 1880 and that the house we all share is hers. She also thinks we are all her servants. I'm the upstairs maid and she scolds me sometimes because her bed is made incorrectly.

Andrew is a marvel. He can draw anything and it looks like a photograph but he can't look you in the eye or carry on a conversation. I used to try to get him to talk and once or twice he'd begin and then start to stutter so badly that it was just pointless.

Then there is me. I have voices in my head, but doesn't everyone? Mine are just more insistent than some people's. They never make me do bad things — well nothing really bad. There was just one time and I didn't do anything wrong. It was because of that incident that I'm here.

I better explain.

Our family lived in the third floor apartment of a building with five floors. The roof was a public area where people would go to escape the summer heat or gaze at the stars. I went up there a lot and even had a chair with a sun umbrella over it. I'd take a book up there and read most of the day. I would have to watch my younger brother Oliver sometimes and mother wouldn't let me take him up on the roof. She always said it was too dangerous for a five-year-old to be up there even if I was with him.

Of course because he wasn't allowed to go up there, that was the first place he'd want to go when mother left us alone. For about six months I resisted his pleading, but one spring day when it was unseasonably warm I gave in to him and the voices in my head that kept telling me everything would be fine.

He loved it up there and everything was fine. He ran around on the roof flapping his arms like he was flying. When we got back down I had to swear him to secrecy. I told him if mother ever found out there would be no more trips to the roof. Everyone knows how hard it is for a five-year-old to keep a secret, but he was able to do it. He never told mother.

We'd been going up every chance we could get and each time we were up there and he was running around and jumping the voices became more and more insistent. I was always able to stifle the voices until that one day.

It was in the early fall and still fairly warm but there was a strong breeze kicking up. We were up there and I had on a light jacket and Oliver had on a wind breaker. As usual he was running around and jumping, but now he was jumping into the wind while he held his coat open. He was so small that the wind would catch his coat and he would hang suspended for a second before he'd land again. He thought this was the greatest thing.

"Look, I'm really flying."

It was then the voices came on hard and heavy and I couldn't stop them. They were telling me that he could really fly and that I should tell him. I knew it was wrong but they just kept saying it over and over. They told me he could fly if he only jumped off the building.

I said, "Oliver, you can fly if you jump off the building."

He cocked his head and looked at me like I was crazy and I may have been then.

"Really?"

"Yes, really," I said.

No little brother ever doubted what his big sister told him. He took off running into the wind and a few steps before he got to the edge, he tripped and went down on the gravel roof. He scraped his arms and chin. I scooped him up and ran back downstairs to our apartment with him. All the while the voices in my head are screaming at me to let him fly.

I cleaned up his scrapes and sent him to his room.

Mother found me in the living room with my knees pulled up to my chin, rocking back and forth.

I was just saying over and over, "No, little boys can't fly."

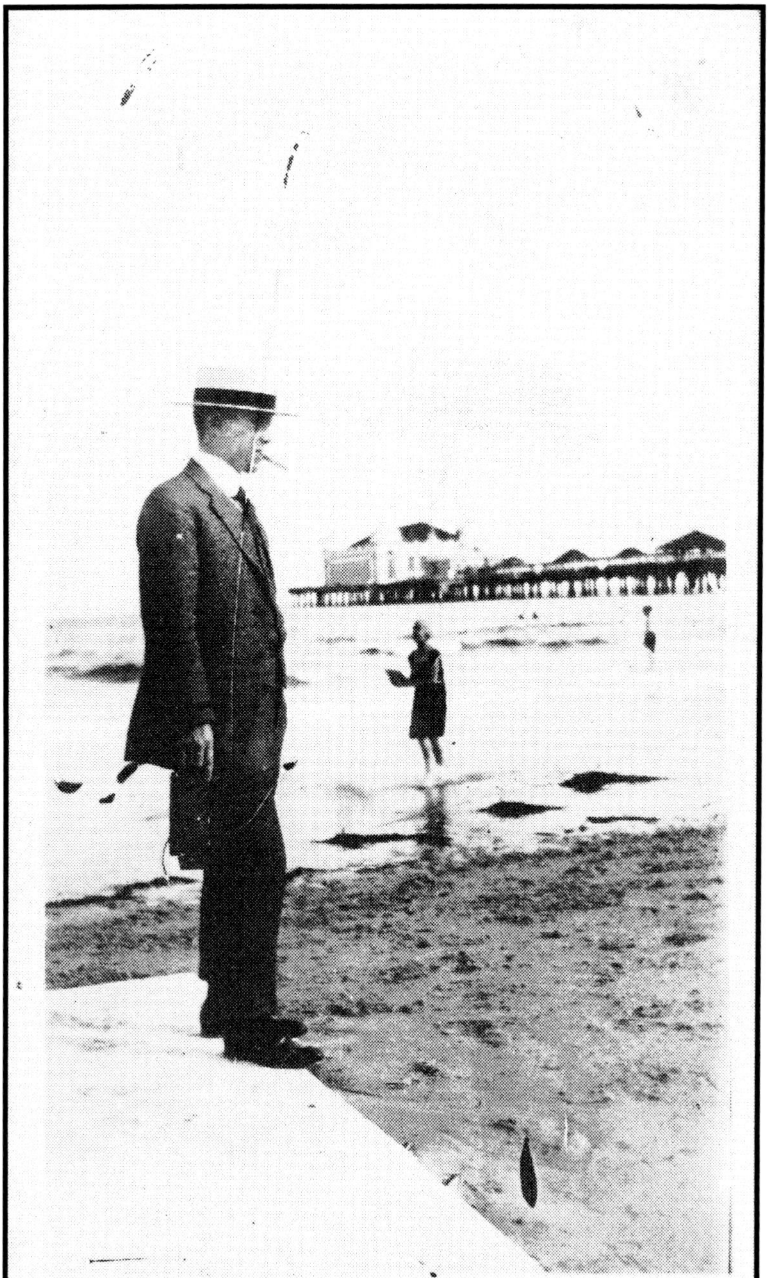

What Dreams May Come

I've been having this recurring dream. It's always a very vivid dream and everything seems to stand out in high relief. I'm a young girl beachcombing while a man with a camera stands some distance away smoking a cigar. It's a pleasant dream and I always find the most wondrous shells and bits of driftwood. The man never seems to pay any attention to me, but I feel he would come to my aid if need be.

I have long since been a young girl and have never needed a man to come to my assistance. I guess I'm what they would call a spinster in days gone by, but times have changed. This is the 1920's and a woman of independent means need not harness herself to a man for security. That being said, the gentleman in the dream troubles my mind. At times I wonder if deep down I want a protector and then at other times I just say, "Bah, it's only a dream."

One night I was having this dream and came across a very beautiful shell. I had never seen one like it. It was about four inches long and shaped like a spiral. Each spiral alternated pink and blue. I held it up and it was almost iridescent in the sunlight. I may have been mistaken but I thought the gentlemen looked over as I held it up. I knew that this would be perfect on the window sill of my apartment.

The morning after that dream when I awoke, I found I was gripping something tightly. When I opened my hand I gasped in amazement. The shell from my dreams was in my hand, but how could this be? Was I going insane? I decided there had to be a logical explanation to this, but what that was I had no idea.

Later that day I took the shell to a friend of mine to look at.

He was the curator of the American Museum of Natural History. He examined it and said it looked like a sea snail shell, but he had never seen one like it. Then he wanted to know where I got it. I told him that I'd rather not say at the moment, and he left it at that.

So at least I am not delusional; other people also see the shell. It is real, but how?

It was several more nights before I had "the dream" again, same stretch of beach, same man with a cigar. This time I found a chunk of sea glass that was perfectly shaped in the form of a seahorse. It was a gorgeous shade of teal, and this too I thought would look good suspended in front of the window with the seashell on the sill.

Once again I awoke to find the object clutched in my hand. I was seriously beginning to question my sanity. Although it seemed possible to cross time and space while in a dream state, that's all it was. There was nothing substantial about dreams, at least that was what I thought. I didn't know what to think anymore.

My dreams were normal for about a week and then I had "the dream." When I'm in "the dream" I don't realize I've been there many times before. It always seems like a new experience. This time as I was beachcombing I found two pieces of driftwood laying on each other to form an 'X." Well I thought "X" marks the spot, so I dug down a bit and came up with an old coin that was black with age and unreadable. I dug some more, but that was the only treasure to be found. The gentleman with the cigar seemed to be looking my way, but could have just been gazing out at the sea.

When I woke up, I was much relieved to find I had no coin in my hand. As I got out of bed I heard something hit the floor with a ring of metal. I looked down and there was the coin. I was going insane. I wondered if any other parts of my life were falling apart and I hadn't noticed. I took a mental inventory and found the only anomaly were these things appearing from my dreams. I remembered once at a séance that a ring had appeared from beyond the veil. Was this the same thing?

Once again I went to the curator of the museum. He cleaned up my coin and examined it. It had a date of 1780 and was a Spanish coin; other than that he couldn't tell me. This time when he asked me where it came from, I said I'd been beachcombing and found it under an "X" marks the spot piece of driftwood. He didn't ask any more questions.

I had a blissful month free from "the dream."

The night I had "the dream" again, I noticed something different. The gentleman with the camera and the cigar was no longer there. The stretch of beach I was on was utterly devoid of people. Clouds were gathering as if for an impending storm. I was beachcombing as usual but not really finding anything. I noticed some movement out of the corner of my eye and looked around. It was just a ghost crab, but a very large ghost crab. Then I saw another and another. Soon there were hundreds of them and they were getting closer. Several would run up and nip at me and then scuttle back off. One brave one ran up and grabbed my heel and I started screaming. I woke myself up screaming. My heart was thundering in my chest; I took a few deep breaths to calm myself. I told myself it was just a bad dream, but I'm not sure I was convincing. I threw back the covers and examined my heel. There was a red mark from the pinchers, but no crab. I then saw movement under the covers. I grabbed the poker from the fireplace and beat the covers until the movement stopped. When I peered underneath the covers, there was the mutilated remains of a crab. I'll never sleep again in that bed, or possibly any other.

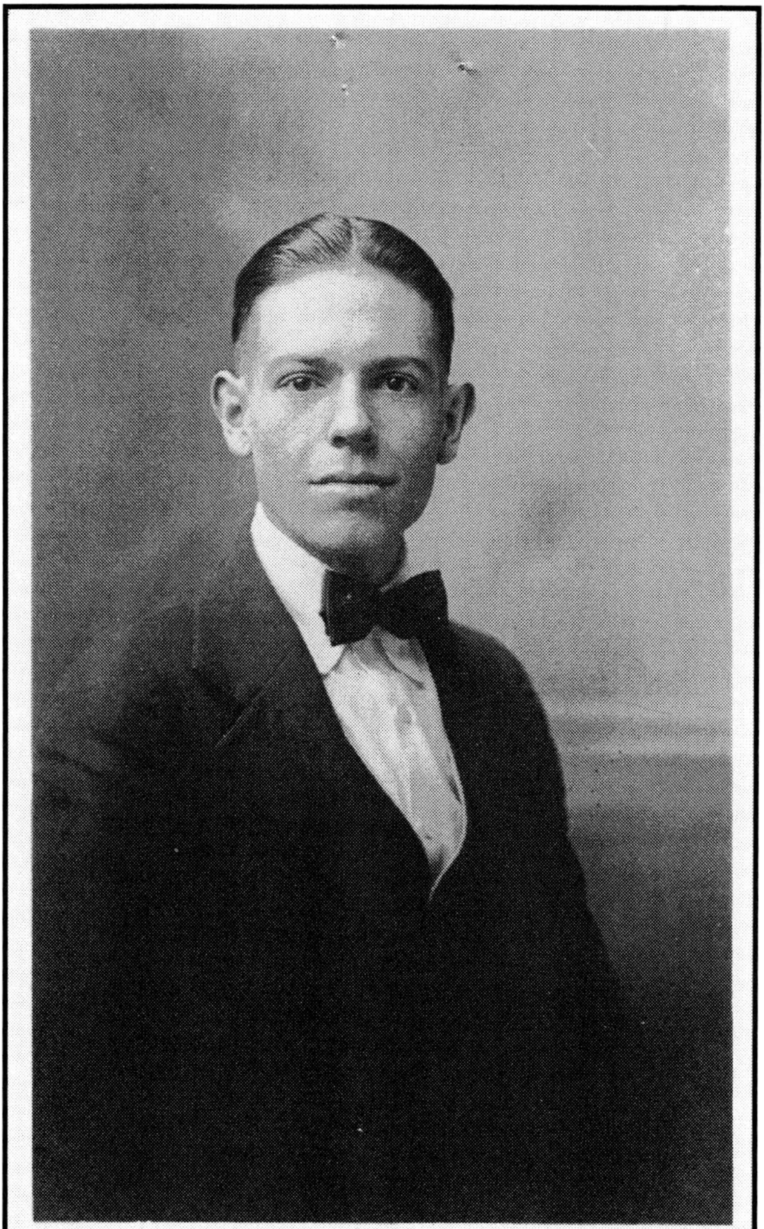

Near Miss

As a young man I had just finished my training at one of the Marconi wireless schools after being a telegrapher for nearly two years. I graduated at the top of my class and was ready to see the world. My plan had been to apply to the White Star line in hopes of being assigned to the *Titanic* for its maiden voyage. The competition was fierce and since I'd just passed my course I was not even considered. That was fortunate for me in retrospect.

I also applied to the Cunard line around the same period, those two being the largest of the luxury liners. I must have set my hopes too high. Neither White Star nor Cunard was looking for an unseasoned Marconi operator.

It was a conundrum; I needed experience to get the job but needed the job to get experience. I began to look around to see where I might find work in my field. It was either that or go back to being a telegraph operator. That would keep body and soul together but wouldn't let my spirit soar like traveling the sea would.

I finally got a position of assistant telegrapher with the *RMS Empress of Ireland* run by the Canadian Pacific Railroad. I stayed on from the summer of 1912 until the summer of 1913. I left with a letter of reference from Captain Henry Kendall.

I once again applied to the White Star and Cunard lines. This time I was rewarded with an interview for assistant telegrapher for the *RMS Lusitania*. I was awarded the position I think due to the letter of recommendation as well as my high marks from my Marconi class.

The *Lusitania* was a huge step up. It was nearly the largest luxury liner afloat, second only to its sister ship the *Mauretania*.

Though just being assistant telegrapher, my quarters were small and windowless, but I was on the high seas. I was one of the deck crew and this alone carried some prestige.

I'd been making the run between New York and Liverpool for about ten months. It was at the end of May of 1914 that I hear the *Empress of Ireland* had collided with another ship and sank. Of the nearly fifteen-hundred people on board, over one thousand perished. Had I stayed on with her, I could have been one of them. Luckily I was on one of Cunard's safest ships.

In late March of 1915 I was offered a promotion to telegrapher. The catch was I would have to transfer to the *Mauretania*. I was young and had no real ties to anyone or anywhere. I jumped at the chance. I would miss my friends, but a larger ship and a larger paycheck were too much to pass up.

I was to begin in mid-May and would miss another round trip on the *Lusitania*. She was to leave at the end of April for Liverpool, so I found a room for a couple of weeks and went out to see the sights of New York.

It was odd being on dry land, as I'd been on board ship for so long. Even after a few days I could feel the roll of the sea under my legs, but it was good to have the freedom to roam where you will.

It was unseasonably hot in New York that spring. The temperature had already reached ninety-one degrees. Walking through Central Park was a bit of a cool oasis and a welcome relief to see trees when you have been used to nothing but a flat horizon.

I had nearly exhausted my time and funds when I saw a newspaper boy hawking the big story of the day.

"*Lusitania* sinks! Germany sinks the *Lusitania*! Read all about it!" he bellowed.

I took a paper and began to read, dumbstruck — my friends,

all of those innocent passengers. How dare they sink a ship that was not a military vessel? My rage and impotence to do anything about it were nearly equal.

It was then it struck me how narrowly I had escaped being on another ship that had sunk and made me begin to wonder. Was I just lucky? Was God saving me for something special? Would those two ships have sunk if I had been on board? All these crazy thoughts began to swirl about in my head.

I found the nearest bench and sat down still grasping the paper, but now it was shaking violently in my hands.

I went into a bar and had a drink to calm my nerves. The bartender, an older gentleman, looked me in the eye and said, "You OK? You look like you've seen a ghost."

I told him my story, even my crazy thoughts. I felt better after I'd voiced them because they sounded a little less crazy out loud.

The bartender looked me up and down then said, "Maybe you're a jinx." I paid for my drink and left. Just what I needed, a bartender telling me that I'm a jinx. The more I thought about it the more I thought he might just be right. I saw a palm reader's sign up ahead and so I went into Madame Rose's. Her sign said, "She sees all and tells all."

I walked in and asked to see Madame Rose. I guess I was expecting someone in a flowing robe with lots of jewelry and a thick accent. The diminutive lady behind the counter was wearing a plain dark dress, no jewelry with the exception of a gold cross, and had no discernable accent. She held out her hand and said, "I am Madame Rose."

The way she said it broached no argument. I told her I wanted my palm read so she led me into an adjoining room. She motioned me to sit down and she did the same across the table from me. She took my hand and began to examine it.

"You have had much death in your past."

I began to tell her about the ships, but she stopped me.

"You are at a cross roads and don't know which way to go. Your lifeline is long but your love line is broken, maybe from long periods of separation. Your employment prospects look good and you should continue in your current line of work.

This did much to allay my fears. I paid her and left, never explaining why I'd come or what I was looking for. She just seemed to know.

I took my position as telegrapher on the *Mauritania*. Two years later we became a troop transport ship. We made it through the war without a scratch. I stayed with her until I retired from Cunard in 1935. It was that same year they sold her for scrap; I just couldn't bear seeing that.

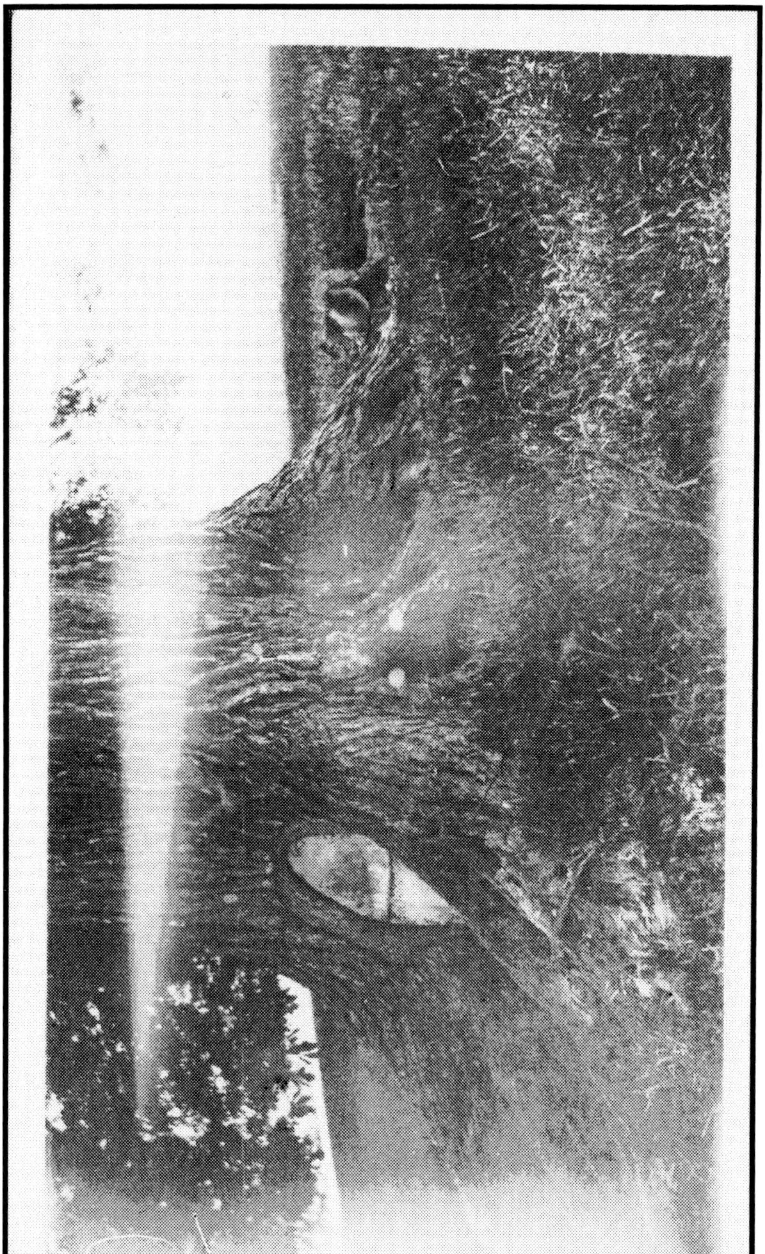

A Little Bit of Sunshine

This tree fascinated me as a child. I always imagined elves or gnomes or fairies living inside of it. I could envision in my mind's eye the crack in the knot hole sliding apart and an entire community of creatures pouring out. I guess that is why now as an adult I am still drawn to it if for no other reason than to take a photograph. If anyone comes along, I'll tell them I was trying to get a good picture of the squirrel. After all, who in their right mind would drag their camera equipment out in the middle of nowhere, set up a tripod and shoot pictures of a tree. Well maybe Ansel Adams, but I'm no Ansel Adams, the above picture being a case in point.

Between the drive out and the prep time, I'd wasted about half the day getting what turned out to be a not-so-great picture. The interesting part came when I had broken down the camera equipment and packed it up. I was headed down the hill to the car when I heard what sounded like a large limb breaking on the tree. I looked back and was astonished to see the hole in the tree was wide open and small creatures were emerging from it. I rubbed my eyes in disbelief, but they were still there. Either they didn't see me or didn't care that I was there.

As far as I could tell they were around a foot tall, dressed in muted grays and greens. They had no shoes on and seemed to have either very long toe nails or claws. They were gnomish in their look with long hair and beards as well as very bushy eyebrows. They seemed very intent on the squirrel. The squirrel on the other hand didn't seem to notice them until it was too late. Several of them had circled around behind the squirrel and by some unspoken command they began to advance on it. When the squirrel took notice of them, he began to run to and fro as squirrels do, with every fiber of its being twitching. After weighing all of the options in his little squirrel brain, he made a mad dash up the tree. He found four more of the gnome creatures waiting for him there with a net.

They sprang at the squirrel as he ran up the tree. Suddenly a large gray, green and furry object came tumbling out of the tree. At this point there were four of the gnomish creatures and a squirrel all tangled in the net. The squirrel was nearly as large as the creatures and it was biting and clawing at them.

One of the gnomes (for that is what I'd begun to think of them as) that had chased the squirrel up the tree came forward with a club. He raised it over his head and brought it down with great force. His target was the head of the struggling squirrel, but at the last second the animal jerked and pulled the hand of one of the gnomes into the path of the club. This instigated an altercation that required four other gnomes to break up and begin to calm down both sides.

All of this took place in a matter of moments, but it seemed like time had slowed down as I watched, dumbstruck. Coming to myself, I put down my camera equipment ever so slowly. I didn't want to alert them to my presence. When I opened the camera case latches they sounded like gun shots to my ears, but didn't seem to faze the gnomes. They continued their argument.

I pulled out the camera and decided not to waste the time of putting it on the tripod. I steadied it the best I could and began taking shots. Every time the shutter clicked, I winced thinking they had heard it. They seemed oblivious to me and more focused on the squirrel.

One of them was gesticulating at the squirrel, his hand and the club. The other just shrugged and this just set the first one off again. He grabbed the club and whacked the second gnome on the foot and the fight began anew. All the while I was taking photos. I may not be Ansel Adams, but I could see my fortune being made with these pictures.

Well somehow the fight was resolved and the gnomes turned their attention back to the squirrel. It was gone. It had apparently chewed through the net and squirmed out while nobody was paying attention. Now they began to argue again and I was thinking it might be a good time to pack up and go. I would get just one last picture. This was nearly my undoing; the sun chose that moment to come out from behind a cloud and reflect off of my camera lens. That momentary flash of light caught their attention. They all turned and looked at me, and not in a friendly way.

I'm not sure where all of the clubs came from, but they all had them. There must have been a dozen of them and they were all headed my way. I didn't have time to pack up anything. I just took off running with the camera in my hand. Seeing that I was outrunning them, they began throwing their clubs at me. They all fell short except for one and it hit my camera. I jumped into the car and left in a spew of gravel and dust.

Fame and fortune were not to be mine. It seems the club that hit my camera didn't do any real damage, it only jarred the housing open and exposed the film. The only photo that turned out was the first one on the reel.

I've driven by that spot many times since then and it always looks the same. I've never seen the gnomes again, nor any of my camera equipment. The only souvenir I have is a small dent in the housing of my camera.

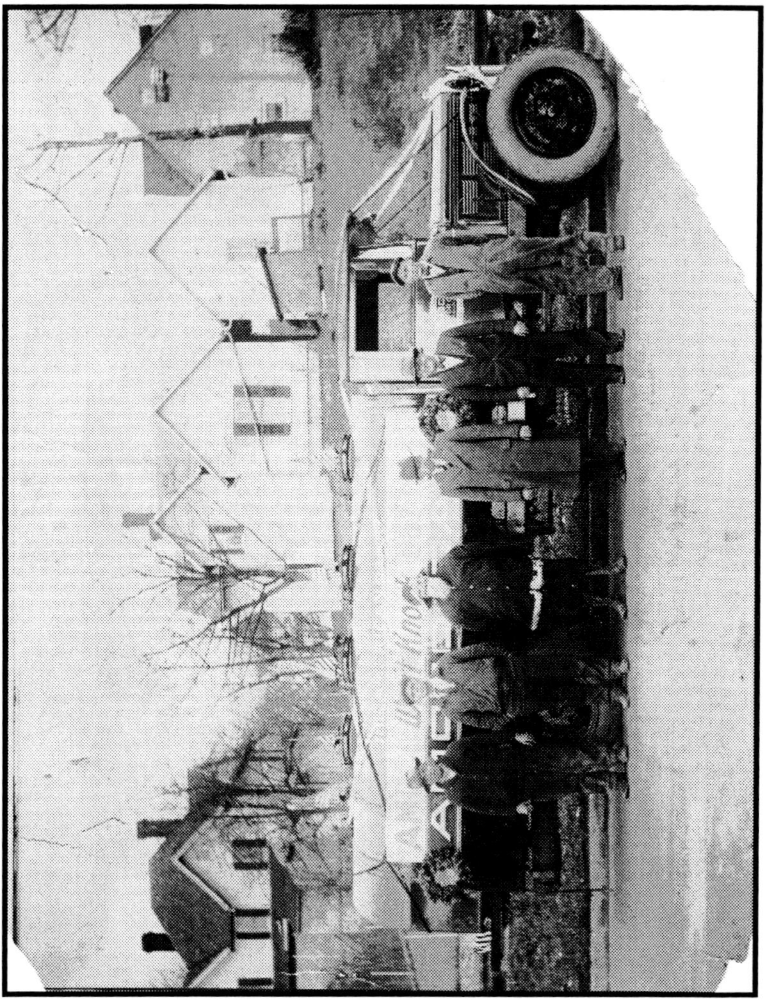

Ho, Ho, Ho,

From left to right: Bob Knolls, Rick Webster, Me in the Santa suit, Mr. Norton, Mr. White, and Buzz Hackett

This picture was taken on Christmas eve 1940. Buzz and I were going to take the truck around to our customers' homes and I (Santa) was to give out candy canes to the children and calendars to their parents. This sounds innocent enough, but you'd be surprised how much trouble two grown men can get into.

Even though the government said that the Depression was over, they didn't live in our neck of the woods. There were people just scraping by. Mr. Norton and Mr. White owned the oil company I worked for and thought it would be nice to give a little something back to our customers. They had also given us a list of those customers who owed us money. We had about a hundred customers and the list only had about twelve names on it. They wanted us to "just mention" the past due bills and see if we could collect a bit. So much for good will to all.

Just as we were all to go our separate ways, me and Buzz to deliver candy canes and Bob and Rick to head home to their families, Mr. Norton came around. He shook our hands and as he did said, "Merry Christmas." He placed a twenty-dollar gold piece in each of our hands and told us it was our Christmas bonus.

All the boys were thrilled with the windfall. I may have been the least enthused; since my wife ran off I had nobody to buy gifts for but it would fund a good two day drunk. I pocketed mine like everyone else and thanked Mr. Norton and Mr. White.

Buzz was the new kid on the block, having only been with the company since August. I was supposed to be taking him around and showing him the ropes. So Santa and his helper jumped in the truck and were off.

The first few stops were pretty uneventful. I'd get out and do my Santa thing. The moms would take the calendars and usually hand us a tin of homemade goodies. We had made our circuit of most of the houses on our list, but saved the slow pays for last. Neither Buzz nor I wanted to talk about what people owed at Christmas time and I'd pretty much decided not to mention it at all.

Buzz swung the truck around the corner and headed into the less desirable end of town. You could see the yards weren't kept up quite as well. Many of the houses needed a fresh coat of paint. Some yards had cars up on blocks in the midst of a repair. Nevertheless, Santa was there to spread good will.

At the first stop three children wearing threadbare clothes came running out followed by their mother. You could see she was happy for the children but there was some underlying burden she was carrying. I went over to hand her a calendar, determined not to say anything about her past due bill when she surprised me by bringing it up.

She looked me in the eyes and said, "Santa, I know we are a bit behind in our payment but they cut my husband's hours back at the mill. Is there any way you could let us have just twenty gallons of oil to get us through until the New Year? My husband is supposed to go back full time next year."

I looked at her and the kids and the house then said, "Buzz, put twenty gallons of oil in this lady's tank."

I could see tears welling up in her eyes and I had to turn away. You can't let the kids see Santa cry.

Buzz said, "But Santa, I thought—"

I cut him off mid-sentence. "Ho, Ho, Ho, Santa knows what he's doing."

Buzz just shrugged and pulled out the hose and gave her twenty gallons. I dutifully wrote it down in the log book.

Then the kid's mom said, "God bless you Santa."

Well that's kind of how it went for the last twelve stops. Only two of them didn't ask for more oil.

It was just getting dark when we rolled back up at the office and I could still see a light on in Mr. Norton's office. I told Buzz to take off and I'd handle telling Mr. Norton. I'll tell him I made you do it and I am totally responsible.

Mr. Norton's door was open when I came in and I pulled off my Santa hat and mask. I cleared my throat and Mr. Norton looked up.

"Well how'd it go?"

I handed him the log book and he looked it over.

"That's two-hundred gallons of my oil you have given out on credit and to the exact people I wanted you to collect from. What's the meaning of this?"

"Well sir, some of these people have fallen on hard times. There's been cutbacks at the mill and... you should have seen some of them. Those women looked like they had the weight of the world on their shoulders. All they needed was a helping hand."

"I run a business here, not a charity!"

"I know sir."

I handed him the twenty-dollar gold piece that had briefly resided in my pocket.

"I think this should cover all the oil from today and then some. Please split whatever is left across all of the outstanding debts."

"But, why would you do this?"

"Well I've got nobody to buy gifts for and I'd have just blown it anyway. It's just me and the cat so there's not much to celebrate. But if you could have seen the way those kids' eyes sparkled just from getting a candy cane, and it was the same way with their moms. Twenty dollars is a cheap price for all of that."

I could see the boss was thinking hard on what I just said and thought it might be a good time to make my exit.

"Good night Mr. Norton, and Merry Christmas."

I began to edge my way toward the door.

"Hold up there. Why don't you come and have Christmas dinner with my wife and me? My son and his wife will be there and a couple of rambunctious grandkids. There is always plenty of food. I won't take no for an answer."

"What time?"

"5:00," he said as he flipped the twenty-dollar gold piece my way.

I caught it in mid-air and looked at him inquisitively.

"I think I can absorb a twenty-dollar loss better than one of my employees. See you tomorrow."

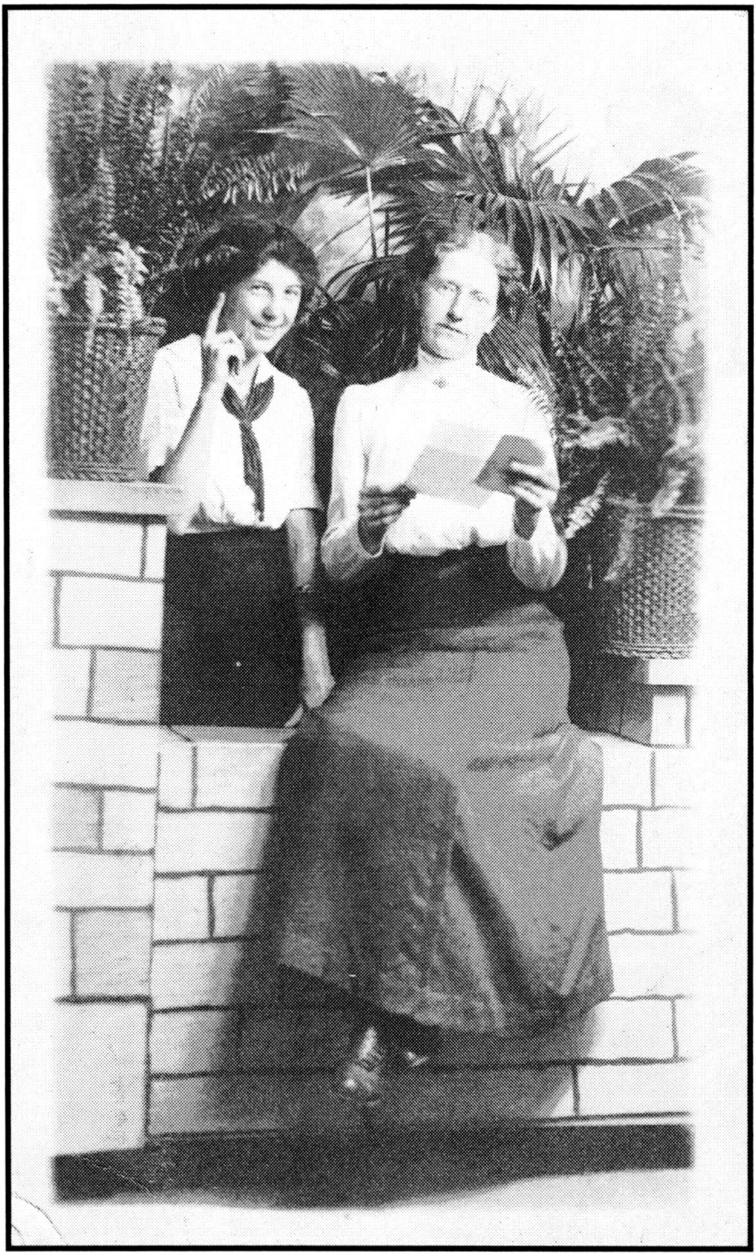

This Year I Resolve...

Ada had just finished writing her New Year's resolutions and was letting Aunt Mae look over them.

Mae was amazed that it was only one page. On past years they had run to three and four pages and none of them ever were accomplished. Mae, on the other hand, never wrote any of hers down. She felt they were nobody's business but her own. She had no such qualms with her niece. She was actually more than her niece; she was also her God-daughter and as such Mae had a moral responsibility to assist in raising her. Lord knew her parents did very little in that area. They either turned her over to the nanny or let her run loose like a heathen.

Nobody could figure out if Ada was just precocious or a bit addled in the head. She always seemed to lean towards the latter.

The first resolution was to take in all the stray cats from the neighborhood.

"Ada, you already have ten cats and two of them are pregnant. Why on earth would you want more?"

"Well Aunt Mae, they just wander around looking for food and their fur is all matted. They need a good home."

"That may well be, but they don't need a good home here. Besides, you don't have room for more cats. We'll just strike this one off."

Ada's shoulders slumped and her lower lip began to quiver.

Aunt Mae seeing this said, "What if we modify it to say you will help find good homes for the stray cats?"

Ada perked up at this and nodded her head vigorously.

"Alright, what is this next resolution? Become a vegetarian. A vegetarian? Ada, you don't even like vegetables and you know what this would do to your Father and Mother, not to mention the cook. This one we definitely have to strike."

"Alright."

"Wait, do you even understand what resolutions are? They are something that you feel strongly about changing in your life."

"I did feel strongly about it until you reminded me I didn't like vegetables. At that point it didn't seem too important."

"Resolution number three – try to take more walks. I don't see anything wrong with that one, it can stay."

"Look at number four; I think you'll like that one."

"Learn Esperanto. Ada you already know German, French and a smattering of Latin. Why do you want to learn Esperanto?"

"Well, Aunt Mae, Esperanto is going to be the universal language one day and if I already know it I'll be that much ahead and be able to talk to anybody about anything because we will have a common language."

"Well do it if you want to; I think it's a complete waste of time."

Mae read down the list. There were a few throw away resolutions like be nicer to Mother and Father, write to cousin Edith more often, innocuous things like that. Towards the bottom of the page she saw, "Become a suffragette."

Mae pointed to the offending line and asked, "Do you really think that women should be able to vote?"

"Don't you?"

Mae was taken aback by the directness of the question but then stammered out, "No, of course not; we never have before."

"Times are changing Aunt Mae. Men fly through the air, we talk over vast distances with the Marconi, we have refrigeration and no longer rely on the ice man. We even have indoor plumbing."

"I don't see what any of those has to do with women voting.

Women need to remember their place. No man is looking for an uppity wife."

"Or opinionated old biddies," she said under her breath.

"What was that?"

"I just said I suppose you are right."

"We'll just scratch this one off then."

With a swipe of her pen it was gone.

"The rest of your list looks fine to me. Why don't you go to the study and write it out fresh; it's quite a mess now."

"Yes, Aunt Mae," she said with a smile.

How many times had she pasted that smile on her face for her aunt? Too many to count, but this was the last year she would have to put up with her. This year she would turn eighteen and come into a quarter of her trust fund. The day after her birthday she was leaving for Europe. She could see the scene already. Aunt Mae would have a fit because she couldn't see an unaccompanied girl traipsing around Europe.

It was actually going to be her and her cousin Edith, but Aunt Mae didn't need to know that. It would cost her two first class tickets and some luggage, but it would be worth it to get rid of her.

It was a simple plan – two sets of luggage, one with her clothes and one empty... two sets of first class tickets, one set for Ireland and the other set for England. The timing was going to be the hard part unless she drugged her aunt. That would make sure her aunt was well out to sea before she could stir up any trouble. A little laudanum in her tea and then Ada could slip off of the ship and catch up with Edith and head for England. By the time her aunt woke up they would have gone their separate ways.

Ada went to study and crumpled up the list of resolutions.

She knew that suffragette one would get to her. She patted her skirt pocket that had her real list. It only had one item on it. Get free of the old biddy at any cost.

She sat down and began to write a letter to Edith and outline the plan. She smiled that secret smile, knowing that Aunt Mae thought her a half-wit.

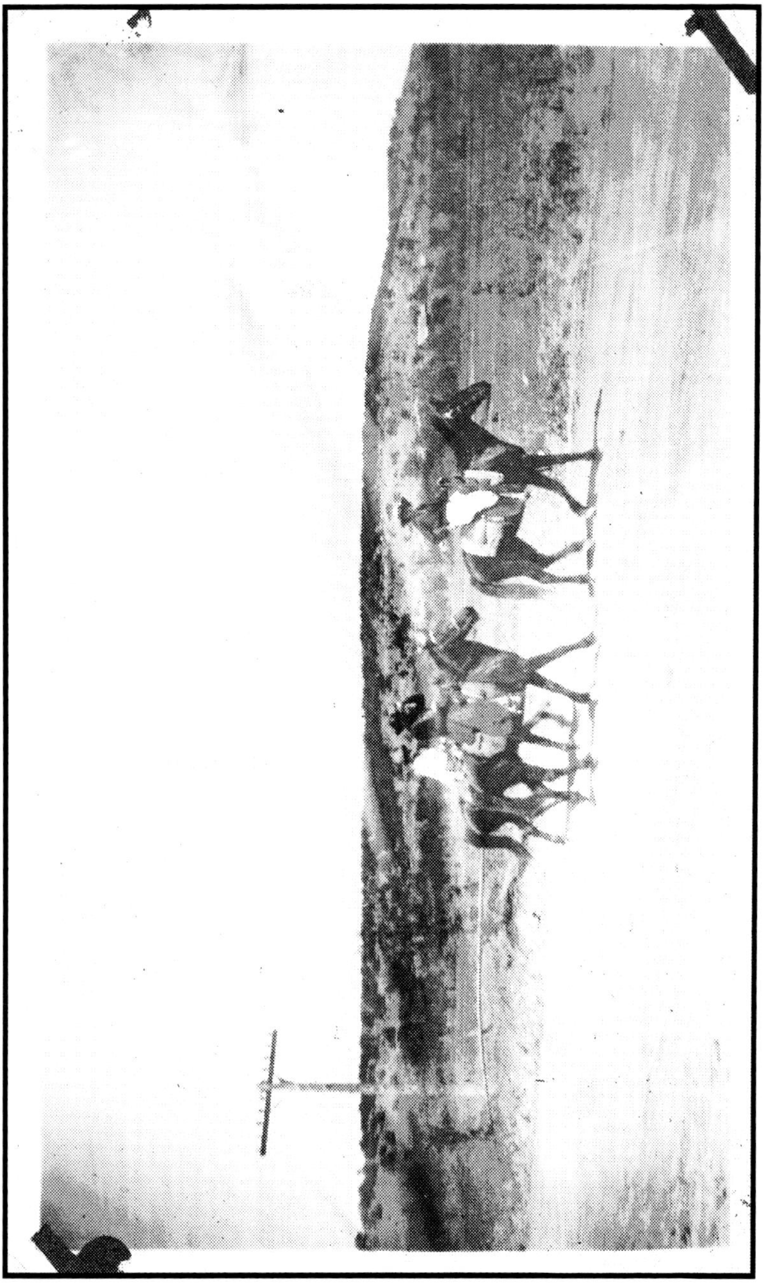

The Hunt

Well I'm old now and the doctors don't give me much longer so I wanted to get this off of my chest before I move on. I've left out names intentionally.

We were a small party, only the three of us. We needed stealth more than numbers. The creature we were after was one of the most elusive in the world. We had no qualms about bringing one back dead, but the big money would be if we could trap one alive. To date nobody had ever been able to capture the rare Lepus antilocapra, commonly known as a jackalope.

We'd had discussions with Barnum & Bailey's, Ripley's and various zoos around the world. Nobody would go on record with an actual price they would pay, but they all hinted it would be in the tens of thousands.

We had provisions for several days. One of our party was an experienced tracker and guide while the other two of us had tracked and captured big game in Africa. How hard could it be to track down and capture a jackalope? We were about to find out.

The first day out we began to see possible signs of jackalopes. We found scat that may have been jackalope or jack rabbit. The problem was that they were so closely related that it was hard to distinguish between the two. Following up on the tracks we came across some jack rabbits. To say we were disappointed was an understatement.

It was getting late so we made camp for the evening. There were occasional flashes of heat lightning in the sky, so there may have been a thunderstorm brewing. As we were sitting around the campfire we began to sing some cowboy songs. As we were singing, we thought we heard in the distance the sound of voices singing along. If we stopped, they would stop. We couldn't decide if it was some weird echo or if it might be jackalopes. It was known that they could mimic the human voice. There were stories of cowboys hearing them in the night — before a thunderstorm, singing along with the campfire songs.

The next morning, we investigated in the vicinity of the singing and found more scat similar to the previous day, but this we knew belonged to a jackalope. We followed the tracks as far as we could and then they seemed to just vanish. This was not unusual with the hard packed earth and the winds that kick up.

Although we had lost the tracks, we knew jackalopes had been here recently. We figured this was a good place to set our trap. We dug a hole approximately three feet around, five feet deep and lined it with a net. Then we scrounged up some thin mesquite branches and some sagebrush. We covered the hole with this and threw some sand on top for good measure. In the middle of this we put the bait, a bowl full of whiskey (purported to be an effective lure). We also attached a long string to one of the mesquite branches in the middle. This we ran all the way back to our camp and attached a bell to it. That way if the trap was sprung we would hear the bell and could capture the jackalope.

We settled down for the evening, tired from our work. We had been asleep several hours when we heard the bell ring. With no moon out it was inky dark. We lit a lantern and went to investigate. That was when everything went bad in a hurry. You need to remember we were experienced big game hunters. This was only a jackrabbit with antlers after all. We were not prepared for what we found.

One of our party held the lantern out at arm's length over the hole so we could see down into the bottom. What we saw was a very agitated jackalope at the bottom of the hole. We began to reach for the ropes to close the net when the jackalope, spotting the light from the lantern, cocked its head upward. In an instant it had jumped out of the hole, knocking the lantern back down in the hole. The whiskey soaked dry branches and sagebrush burst into flames, licking the top edge of the hole.

Meanwhile the enraged jackalope began to charge the two men closest to it and managed to gore one in the calf. He fell over and nearly stumbled into the blazing hole. I caught him before he fell in. As the jackalope was looking around for a second victim I had the presence of mind to pull out my revolver. I took aim as best I could but it was on the far side of the inferno and the heat waves made it hard to get a clear shot.

My first shot missed, but just barely. It hit the ground right in front of the jackalope. This only served to alert it to my presence. The fact that it was on the other side of a burning hole in the earth didn't seem to come into its calculations. The only way I can describe the look that it had was malevolent. Its eyes gleamed red in the fire light and with the horns glowing red it seemed like a creature from Hell.

It took three bounding leaps and then was airborne, flames licking the underside of its belly. It was headed straight for me. I had one chance to stop it. I raise my revolver and pulled the trigger. If I missed at this range, I deserved whatever I got. My aim was true this time. The shot caught him in the head and flipped him over backwards as he tumbled into the fire. There was a plume of sparks and the smell of burning fur.

I patched up my fellow big game hunter; luckily it was a flesh wound in the muscle. He still has a slight limp to this day. We packed up our gear and headed back the next day. We all decided to agree on a story about how the injury occurred and to never speak of the jackalope again.

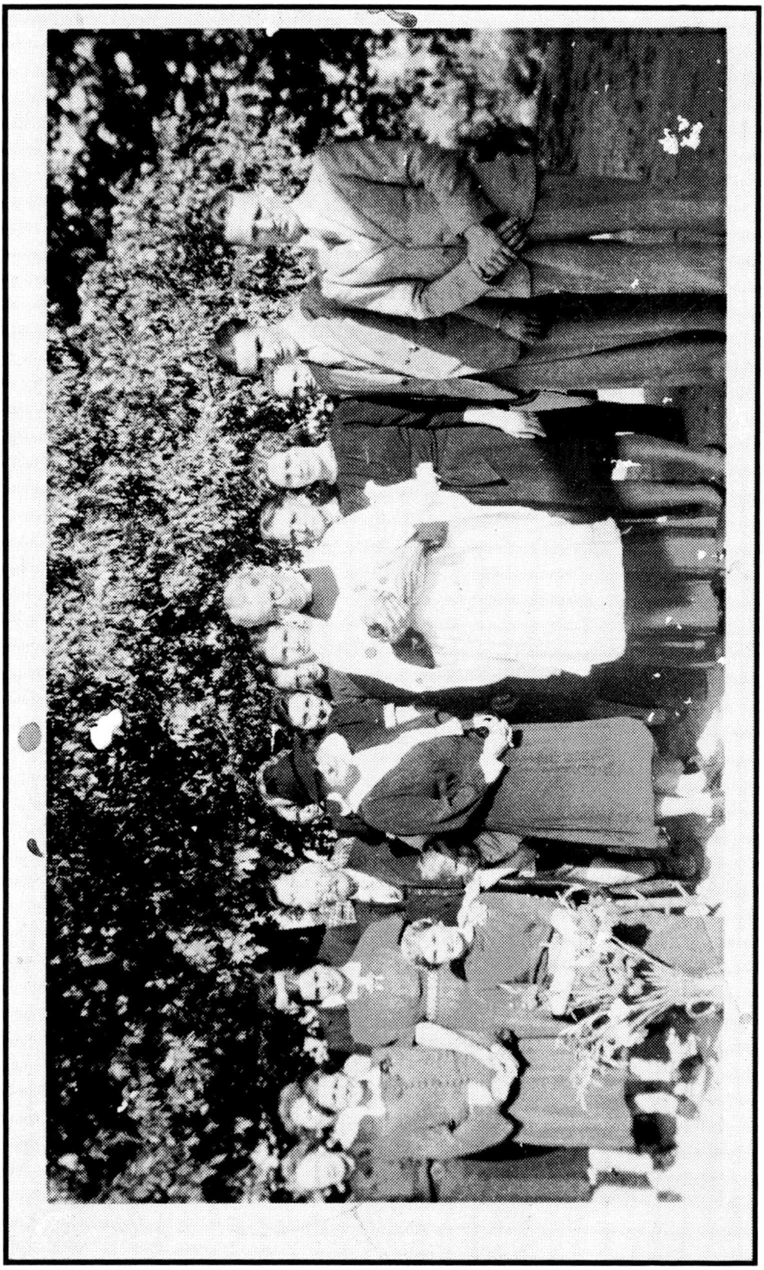

More to a Name

"This is my last official act as a minister," thought Rev. Harold Cleveland.

He'd seen them come into this world, like the one he was holding, and he'd officiated when they were laid to rest. For fifty-two years nothing but sermons, marriages, and funerals. He needed a rest; he deserved a rest. It was good that this was to be his last hurrah. Alpha and Omega, the beginning and the end. It was a glorious spring day. Family and friends of the parents had driven in from all over. Everything was perfect.

Now if he could just remember how the ceremony went. How many times had he performed this ritual and now he was drawing a blank. That was the trouble nowadays; something he should be able to do in his sleep just eluded him.

It probably began with dearly beloved, but didn't they all? he thought.

"Dearly beloved, we are gathered here today for this most important ceremony."

I wish I could remember what the heck it's called; if I could just remember that I'm sure the rest would come back to me.

"But first, this is a doubly auspicious occasion because this is the last time I will be performing this ceremony in my official capacity as Reverend. You see, tomorrow I retire. I plan to have a small vegetable garden and maybe a few chickens. Fresh eggs in the morning and a good strong cup of coffee – it doesn't get much better than that. But I digress. I hope I have been a good shepherd to my flock. I say flock, but it has been several flocks over the past fifty-two years. I've preached many sermons, conducted many marriages, and quite a few funerals as well. This ceremony we are about to conduct reminds me of a wedding."

This drew a few strange looks, but the good Reverend soldiered on waiting for the words to come back to him.

"It reminds me of a wedding in this respect: we come into this world and take it on for better or worse, for richer or poorer, in sickness and in health and don't leave it 'til death do us part."

My God I'm just rambling — these people didn't come all this way for this. This is supposed to be ... damn, it was right there on the tip of my tongue. Just take a deep breath and keep talking. It'll come back to you, it always does, or it has so far.

"But let's not talk about death on such a vibrant spring day. This young man has his entire life ahead of him. The possibilities are limitless. He can be anything, a doctor, a lawyer, a professor, even President of the United States, or maybe just a humble Reverend such as myself."

The crowd was beginning to get restless and Rev. Cleveland didn't blame them.

I should just confess, tell them my memory isn't what it used to be and I can't remember the ceremony, let alone what it's called. I guess I still have too much ego to show weakness before my flock. This ceremony will be the last thing they ever remember about me. I don't want it to be "Oh yes Rev. Cleveland was good right up until the end and then he screwed up the ..." Damn, almost had it again. I've got to stop thinking about it and then it will come to me.

It had begun to get warm in the parish garden. All the dew had evaporated and the sun was beaming down from a cloudless sky. Most of the men were fidgeting with their ties and trying to loosen their collars as inconspicuously as possible. The women on the other hand were fanning themselves openly.

Rev. Cleveland looked down and noticed as if for the first

time he was holding a baby.

Looking around he caught sight of the parents and he said, "This is a fine looking baby boy you have here. What's his name?"

Mr. and Mrs. Jones just stared at Rev. Cleveland. Then Mrs. Jones found her voice and said, "Jimmy, I mean James, but it won't be his Christian name until you christen him."

Christening ceremony. That's what I'm supposed to be doing. I could almost kiss her!

"Why of course, that's why we are all here on this fine day. So let us begin. Dearly beloved, baptism is an outward and visible sign of the grace of the Lord Jesus Christ. It is through this grace that we become partakers of His righteousness and heirs of life eternal."

Rev. Cleveland conducted the christening ceremony without a flaw. It was one of his finest, if not the finest he'd ever given. Once he got started he was on auto-pilot; the liturgy that he'd repeated so many times, once it began to flow, was as unstoppable as Niagara Falls. The heat was forgotten and the babbling on about retirement was forgotten. All that anyone remembered was the child was christened James Warren Jones.

Beaming, Rev. Cleveland said, "There are light refreshments and punch to drink in the reception hall."

He was exhausted and went to sit on a bench in the shade of a tree. Someone brought him out a cup of punch that he sipped on before setting the cup aside. He needed to close his eyes for just a moment and then he would join the christening party. Such a glorious day it had been, a day of endings and new beginnings. He closed his eyes and slipped away with a satisfied smile on his face.

The christening party left, not wanting to wake the old Reverend, not that they could have anyway.

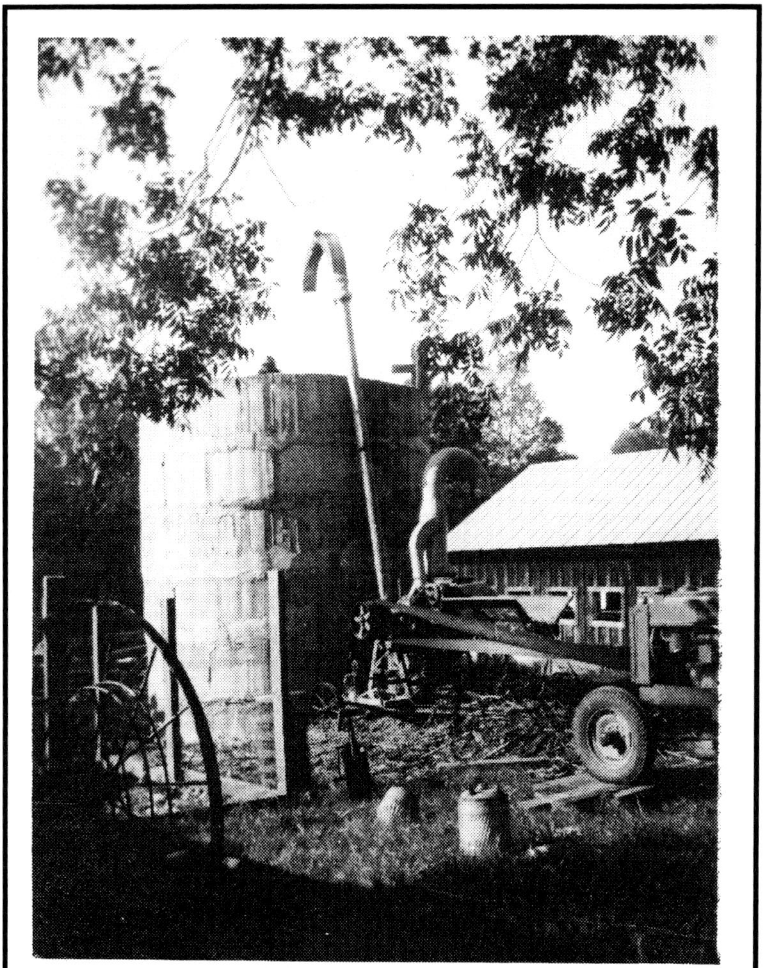

Still, It Was a Nice Farm

This was one of the final pictures of the old farm. After we inherited it from my great Uncle Pat, we farmed it for about ten years. We were barely scraping by from one year 'til the next. One day me and the missus were going over the books. We were trying to figure out how Uncle Pat had been able to make a go of it for so many years. We were sitting there praying to God to help us figure out where we could cut back to make ends meet. It was then we heard a knock on the front door. We knew it had to be somebody selling something because those were the only folks that used the front door.

I went to the door with my speech prepared to move the salesman on down the road. When I opened the door there stood a man in a crisply ironed brown suit, wing-tipped shoes, and a fedora. He was also carrying a brief case, one of those skinny jobs, not a regular sample case like most of those salesmen.

I opened my mouth to tell him that we didn't want any of what he was selling when the young man surprised me and asked if I was Mr. Melson. Most salesmen don't know you from Adam.

I said, "Yeah my name is Melson, what can I do for you?"

I still thought he was selling something.

"Well Mr. Melson, my name is George Turner and I represent Grange Realty."

As he said this he pulled out what looked like the smallest wallet in the world and opened it up and handed me a business card. It was nice stiff paper and all raised lettering. I looked it over and then looked him in the eye.

"Well Mr. Turner, we're not in the market for any more

property; we can barely keep what we've got afloat. You might try Mr. Hendrickson; he's down the road about half a mile. Good day to you."

I said this as I was backing back into the house and closing the door.

"Mr. Melson, I think you have misunderstood me. I'm not selling anything. My firm is interested in buying your farm. The plats in the courthouse show it to be around twelve acres."

"Yeah, that would be about right. Why don't you come in for a minute? Ma can you bring us some iced tea, and you come in here too. Now why do you want to buy our farm?"

Mr. Turner stood up when Ma came in with the tea, so at least he had good manners.

"Well with all the servicemen returning from the war, there is a shortage of houses that they can buy. Our firm plans on subdividing your property into twenty lots of a half acre, more or less, and then building homes on them."

"So what would happen to this house?"

"We'd eventually tear it down, but would probably use it for the field office during construction."

Ma chimed in, "Why do you care? You never liked this place to begin with."

"I just gave her one of those looks and said, "Hush, I've grown pretty fond of this place over the years. So Mr. Turner, how much is this farm worth to you?"

"My firm has authorized me to offer you substantially more than it's worth as a working farm."

"How much is substantially more?"

He pulled a pad out of his pocket and wrote a number on it and slid it over to me. I showed it to Ma all the while giving her a look so she wouldn't give anything away. That number was more money than we would make if we worked this farm for the next twenty years. I have learned a thing or two about horse trading over the years and one thing is you never offer your final price to begin with. So I was thinking how much further he would go. I wrote a number that was ten percent over his initial offer figuring we'd meet in the middle at around five percent after much back and forth.

He picked up the pad and looked at the number and then did something I was completely unprepared for.

He said, "That's a reasonable amount, so do we have a deal?"

I am not a man that likes to be hasty so I asked him if we could sleep on it and he could stop back by tomorrow.

"I'll come back tomorrow and have all the paperwork drawn up, just in case."

"That's fair enough," I said

We shook hands and he left.

I looked at Ma and said, "I think the Lord has answered our prayers."

She just looked at me and asked, "What will we do if we aren't farming?"

I just smiled and said, "With that much money, anything we want to. We could get one of those travel trailers and go explore the United States. We could see the Grand Canyon, the Pacific Ocean, go to the Mardi Gras, whatever you want."

She looked doubtful, but by the following day the deal was sealed and we were on our way.

We'd been traveling around the country for almost a year when some mail caught up to us. One piece was a package with a letter attached from Mr. Turner:

Dear Mr. Melson,

I hope this letter finds you and your wife well.

The housing development is nearly complete and I wanted to tell you something was discovered on the property. When we were tearing down the silo we were expecting to have a bunch of dry corn to dispose of. To our surprise the silo was empty. Well not entirely empty. There had been a door cut into the base of the silo and camouflaged to just appear as a patched area in the sheet metal. I don't think we would have found it except we were trying to salvage it because we had a buyer for the silo.

Let me get to the point. We found a very elaborate moonshine still inside. There were even a few jars of the product on a shelf. I have enclosed one of the remaining jars. We scrapped the still and didn't mention it to anyone. I can only assume you were unaware of it.

Sincerely,
George Turner

I looked at Ma and pulled the jar out of the box. It looked like a jar of water. She got out a couple of juice glasses and we put about a thimbleful in each. Then we toasted Uncle Pat, and downed the moonshine.

Once she had her breath back she said, "So now we know how Pat made ends meet."

I just nodded, still unable to speak.

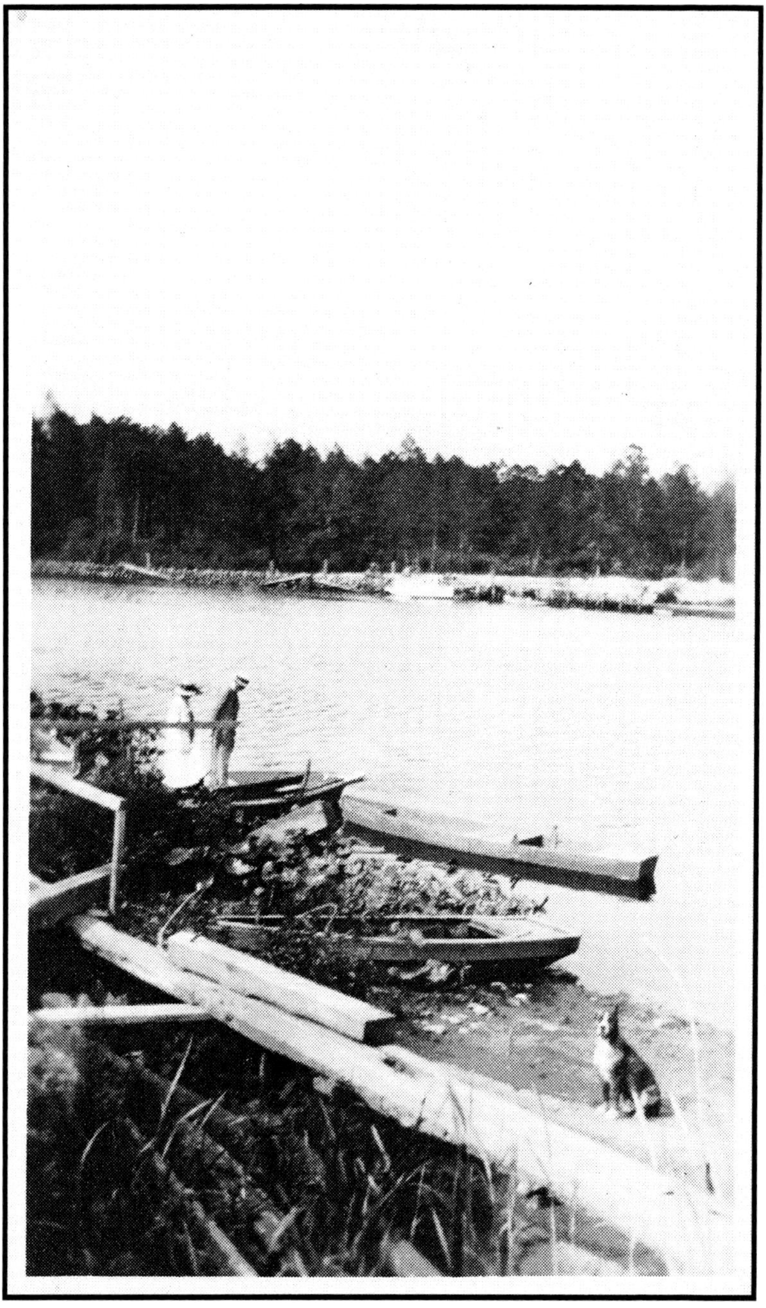

Not Man's Best Friend

Skipper was Margaret's dog and he'd followed us out to the edge of the water where we had the little boat tied up. I guess he thought he was going along with us, but that wasn't part of my plan. Margaret on the other hand couldn't say no to the mutt so he jumped into the boat with us. Skipper and I have never seen eye to eye; I think he is jealous of me.

I'd planned on rowing to the far side of the lake and having a quiet picnic lunch, just the two of us. I could see that wasn't going to happen.

It was mid-morning when we got there and there was hardly a ripple on the water. The weather was comfortable for the beginning of June and it promised to be a glorious day. I also had a surprise for Margaret, tucked away in my coat pocket. It was an engagement ring. I'd just gotten a promotion at the bank and was now an up-and-coming financier; well at least I was senior teller. Her parents had taken to me favorably and I'd asked her father privately for her hand in marriage.

So, I rowed us across the lake, Margaret in the stern and Skipper in the bow like the proud masthead of a ship from bygone days. We found a sandy beach to pull the boat up on. We tried to unfurl the picnic blanket but the entire time Skipper was grabbing it trying to play tug of war. I was not amused. Margaret threw a stick for him to chase so we could get the blanket settled and spread out all of the food. I'm not sure who she was cooking for, but there seemed to be enough food for about six people.

Luckily for us Skipper had found something further down the beach that was more interesting than we were.

"Margaret, I have something to ask you."

"What is it John?"

I was about to pop the question when Skipper came running up with something disgusting in his jaws.

Margaret said, "Ew, what is that? Take it away from him John."

As I tried to get whatever it was away from Skipper I could hear some deep throated growls and knew that they weren't playful. Thinking quickly before I got bitten, I picked up a fried chicken leg and waved it under his nose. This got his attention. I threw it as far as I could and he dropped the disgusting thing and ran after it.

"There you go," I said.

"But John, what if he chokes on that chicken bone?"

I could think of no better end for the mutt but held my tongue.

"Margaret, sometimes I think you love that dog more than you love me."

"Don't be silly."

Those were the words that came out of her mouth, but there was a bewildering puzzled look on her face. It's like she'd never given it much thought but now that she had, she wasn't sure.

"Can you go and check on him and make sure he's alright?"

I trudged down the beach and saw Skipper. He saw me at the same moment and I heard that same low growl as he gnawed on the chicken leg.

"He's fine," I shouted back down the beach.

When I got back Margaret was packing up the picnic and she looked as if she were mad at me.

"What's the matter? Have I done something to make you mad?"

"You don't like Skipper."

"I think the feeling is mutual."

"So, you admit it."

Well I'd kind of put my foot into it and couldn't back out gracefully.

"He hasn't liked me from the start. It's kind of hard to like a dog when he doesn't like you."

"You haven't even tried. I thought that if he came out with us today, you might play with him a bit and get to be friends."

I opened my mouth to say something, but thought better of it. It was then we heard the distant rumble of thunder and thought it was time to go.

We were about halfway back when the sky grew dark and we heard thunder. The last place I wanted us to be was out in the middle of the lake during a thunderstorm. It seemed to be one of those squalls that pops up out of nowhere. Before we knew it clouds had completely obscured the sun and the rain was pouring down. I was rowing for all I was worth towards the shore. Just as we made landfall as if on cue the storm passed and the sun came back out. Margaret, Skipper and I were all soaked to the bone. Skipper smelled like a wet dog of course.

We managed to unload the boat and get everything loaded into the car.

Margaret looked at me and said, "John, I don't think I can see you anymore. Any man who can't get along with my dog probably wouldn't get along with me before too long. I'm sorry John."

I just stood there, flabbergasted. The whole reason behind this picnic was so that I could propose marriage and now she was breaking up with me.

Then she looked as if she'd just remembered something and

said, "You wanted to ask me something… what was it?"

"Oh … it must not have been too important because I can't seem to remember what it was.

"Oh well," she said.

Skipper sat there beside her wagging his tail almost saying, "I've seen them come and I've seen them go."

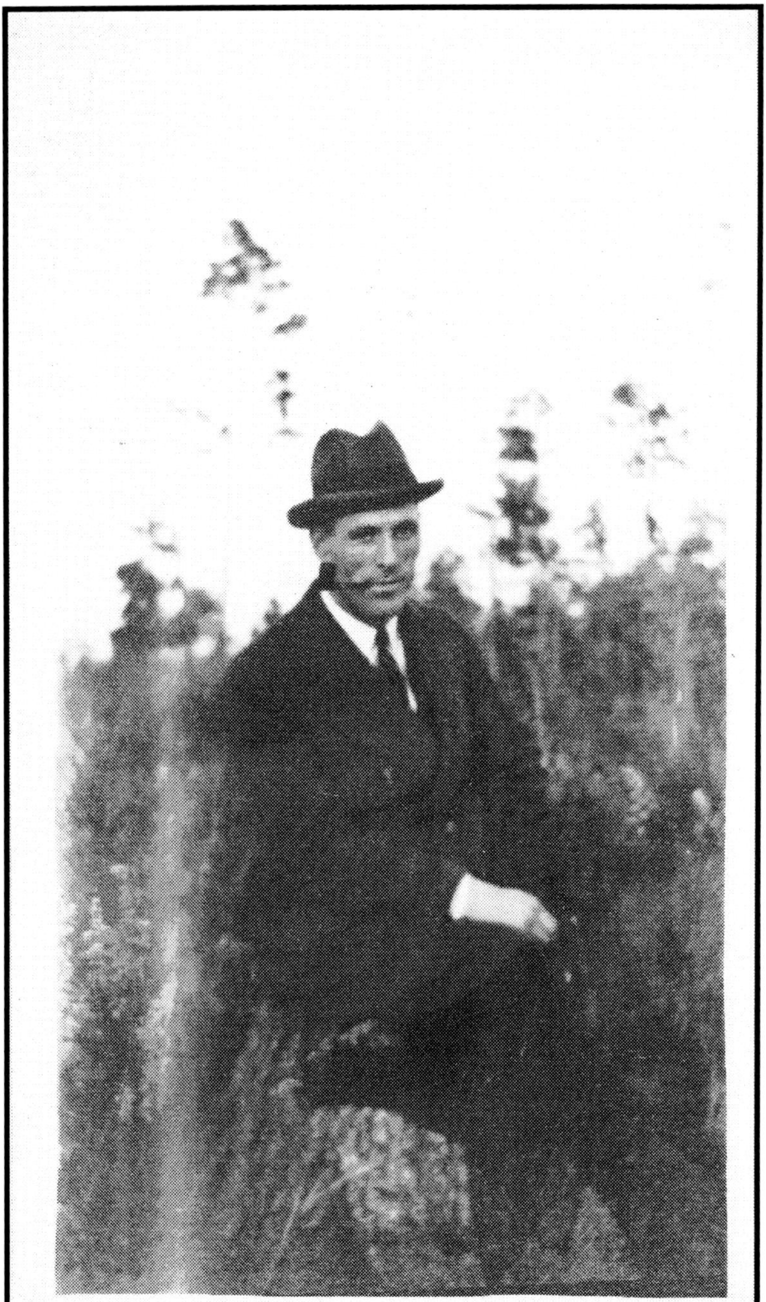

The Arbitrageur

Well, it was done. Twenty-six acres of hardwood cut and taken to the mill.

Elias Hopewell had been doing this for more years than he could remember. As a boy he'd grown up poor in all but mother's love. His father was a lumberjack and was seldom home and never sent back enough of his pay. On one of his infrequent visits home he devoted a bit of time to young Elias.

He took him out in the woods and began to tell the boy all the different species of trees. He'd point out the ones that brought the best price such as walnut, oak and hickory. He then began to explain how to figure out the board feet in a standing tree. This was something that took grown men years to learn, but young Elias seemed to pick it up like it was second nature to him.

The next lesson his father was to impart to him was how to estimate how many trees there were per acre. Even though Elias was just average at math, he picked up on this in no time. Once his father had seen how quickly Elias had grasped the concepts, he posed him a question.

"Now suppose you have four acres of mature oak trees — how many board feet would that be?"

Elias scratched his head for a minute and then picked up a twig and began to scratch some numbers in the dirt. Then he shook his head and wiped it all out with the toe of his shoe and started over. This time he was more satisfied with his answer. He showed his father what he'd come up with. For all other purposes his father was devoid of math skills, but he seemed to have some innate ability to do this type of estimation in his head. He looked at his son's final total and nodded his head in approval.

"That's about what I came up with give or take fifty board feet."

He then squatted down to be at eye level with the boy and began to give some fatherly advice.

"Elias, you are a smart boy, too smart to become a lumberjack. Being a lumberjack is hard and dangerous work and if I could do something else I would, but it's all I know. It keeps me away from you and your ma. I want you to promise me that you'll work hard in school. I want you to have a better life than I had and a good education will help do that. Will you promise me that?"

Elias promised him. He was thirteen years old at the time. It was the last time that he saw his father alive. The next year Elias' father was killed when the top of a tree he was felling came crashing down on him. Luckily the logging company had insurance on all the lumberjacks and it was enough to cover the funeral expense, but not much more.

Now at age fourteen he had to break his promise to his father. He quit school and got a job at the saw mill. He started out shoveling sawdust, but it was a job and the money was enough to keep them fed and clothed and a roof over their heads.

He was a good worker and the foreman had taken note of him and was grooming him for a better position. As a large tree was being loaded to be sawn into boards Elias said to the foreman, "I bet that comes out to eight-hundred and sixty board feet."

The foreman looked the kid over and said. "What'll you bet?"

"I'll bet two bits."

Since he was only making two dollars a week, that was a grandiose bet.

"You're on."

They shook on it and Elias stopped shoveling while the board was being cut. When it was done the board feet came out to be eight-hundred and fifty-eight. Elias hung his head, he'd just lost an eighth of his weekly pay on a stupid bet.

The foreman looked at the boy with new eyes.

Elias told the foreman he'd have to take it out of his pay because he only had a nickel in his pocket.

The foreman laughed, "It's me that owes you, I didn't think you'd come anywhere close and decided if you were within ten feet I'd call you the winner. You were only off by two feet. Do you know how hard that is to do? No I guess you don't. Let's see if you just got lucky. Here come three more logs. Give me your best guess on them."

Elias told the foreman what he thought they'd be. After they'd been cut he was only off by a total of twelve board feet.

He soon became the youngest estimator of standing timber that the company had ever employed. Although he was making better money as an estimator, it was a bit boring. He did get to go out and wander around the forest, but that was the only fun part. Coming back and filling out all of the paperwork was tedious.

Elias was stepping out of the woods one day and noticed an older man doing the same on the other side of the road. They struck up a conversation and Elias found out they were in the same line of business except that this fellow worked freelance. He'd find a stand of good looking timber, find out who owned it and how large it was. He'd then walk it off and get an idea of the board feet and then he'd go find a buyer for it. For his trouble he would take five percent of the sale.

Elias couldn't believe it. This man was doing the same thing that he did and getting paid about ten times what he was making.

Elias asked, "Could you teach me to do what you do?"

"Well, I've been thinking about retiring anyway. I'll let you apprentice with me for a year. I'll give you one percent of all the sales we make and turn it over to you after a year. They shook on it and Elias quit his position that very day.

After a grueling year, he had done all of the work. He wasn't complaining because he'd learned all he needed to know. He was now an arbitrageur — a word he'd never even heard of a year before.

That was many years ago and hundreds of thousands of board feet of lumber behind him. He sat on a stump and smoked his pipe and thought, "Thank you, Dad."

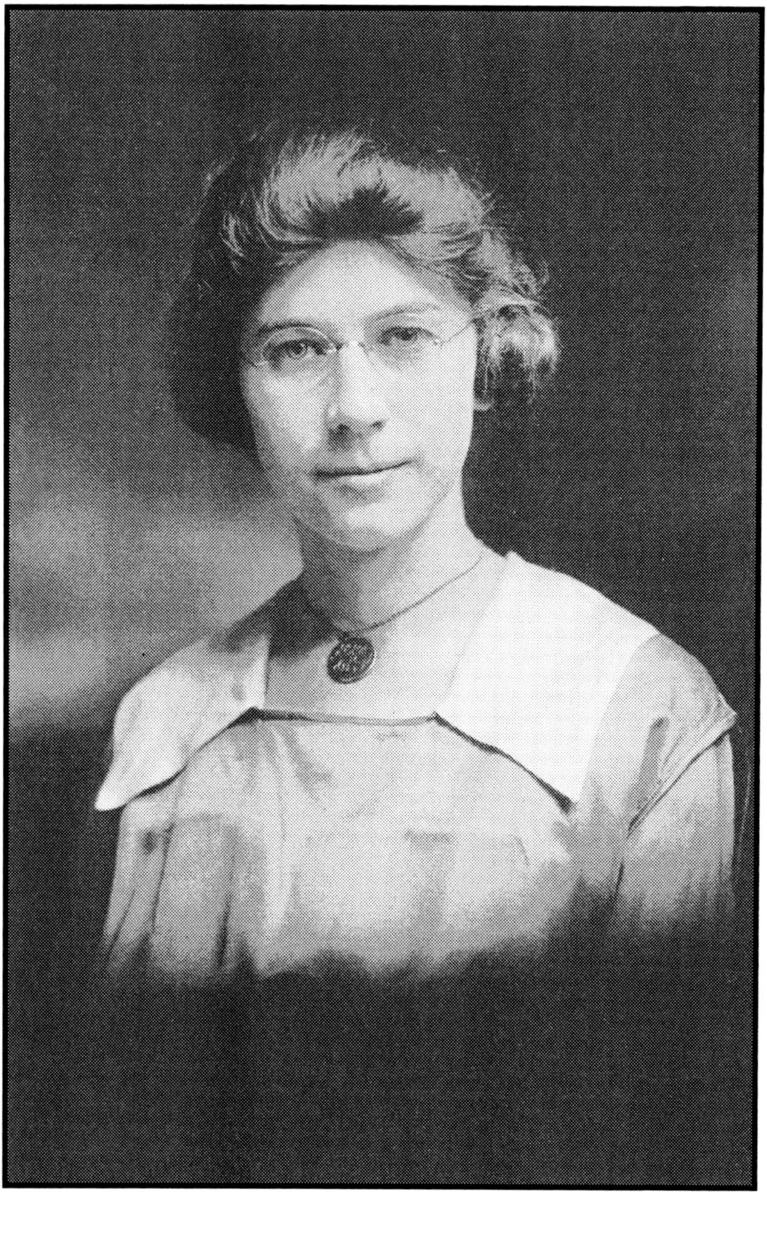

More Than Meets the Eye

The year was 1910 and Miss Alma Richards came to work in Ruxton as the first fulltime school teacher. The school house was only one room with a row of pegs on the wall for us to hang our coats on. There was a potbelly stove in one corner for when it got cold in the winter and there was an outhouse behind the school.

I must have been in what would have been the third grade had those distinctions been made at the time. Miss Richards was fresh out of state teachers' college when she took the position with us. There were about thirty of us in all ranging in age from five to fifteen years old. The first year she was just sorting us all out. By the end of the year she had about nine grades and a clear idea of where we would be going for the next year.

Everyone loved Miss Richards, the children and parents alike. All of the boys had a crush on her and would bring her apples to get into her good graces. She also had no lack of gentleman callers, but none of them seemed to last very long. Nobody could understand why Miss Richards wasn't married yet since the social norm had changed about teachers being married.

When I left school for the last time, I was nearly sixteen. I had tried to learn everything that she had taught us. I don't think I was a star student but I had learned enough in my eight years to read and write pretty well and to do any of the math I'd ever need on the farm.

Two years later I'd gotten married and built a small house on some of the family land. Miss Richards by now had seen an entire generation of students pass through her domain. She had moved out of her rented room and was living in a small bungalow at the edge of town. She was still unmarried, in her mid-thirties, and people were beginning to whisper behind her back. She had fewer and fewer suitors calling, but there was one who had been persistent from the beginning.

Nobody knew who he was; he'd drive into town and call on her. Sometimes they would go out to dinner or a movie. Tongues would wag every time he was in town, but then he would leave and everything would settle down until he showed up again.

I was busy with the farm and my wife and raising a son and a daughter and didn't think too much about Miss Richards until it was time for our children to go to school. There she was on the first day of school to greet the children with that same smile she'd always given us. She'd been with us for twenty years and had become a fixture in the community. For all that, nobody really knew her; she kept herself to herself as they say. She would occasionally leave town for the weekend, but was always back Monday morning for class. She would also leave for Christmas break. Everyone assumed she went back east to visit her parents, but nobody really knew. Now that she was teaching my children and not me, I guess I'd become a little more interested. When I asked my wife about it she said, "That's none of our business." So I left it at that.

This went on for about another ten years — visits from the mysterious man, weekends and Christmas vacation off to who knows where.

The year that my daughter was going to finish school Miss Richards announced that she would not be coming back the following year. There were many tear-stained cheeks and long goodbyes on her last day. She had been with us for almost thirty years so we all guessed it was time for her to retire.

She was picked up by the mysterious gentleman in a shiny

new car and driven out of town. That was the last we would see of Miss Richards, or so we thought.

A few weeks later I was looking through the newspaper and saw a picture of Miss Richards and the mysterious gentleman so I began to read the caption.

Miss Amanda P. Goodweather announces her engagement to long time friend and family lawyer Ernest Oberlin.

The article went on to say:

Miss Goodweather, heiress to the Goodweather rubber plantations will be married in a private ceremony at St. Patrick's Cathedral on March 22. The couple will be taking an extended honeymoon in Europe.

This didn't make any sense. Why were they calling her Goodweather and not Richards and if she was so wealthy why was she working as a school teacher?

The answers came the next week in the form of a letter to the town.

Dear Good Citizens of Ruxton,

By now you know I am not who I said I was, and for this I beg your forgiveness. I was a fully qualified school teacher, but my name was Amanda Goodweather. I perpetrated this hoax because I had to. In order to inherit any money at all from my father, I had to be self-sufficient until he had passed away. He felt that since he had started with nothing and had to work for all he had, then his only daughter should have to make her own way as well in order to learn the value of money. The gentleman you have seen come and go over the years was my father's attorney. He was sent periodically to check on my status to be sure I was abiding by my father's terms. Although I was here under false identity, I nevertheless came to know and love all of the children in my care. It was with a heavy heart that I left Ruxton. I regret that I couldn't get to know my fellow townspeople for fear of letting something slip out about my background. Since I will not be around to teach the next generation, I wish to help them along with their studies. I am enclosing a check for twenty-five thousand dollars to build a new school and library for Ruxton.

Yours Very Sincerely,
Amanda P. Goodweather

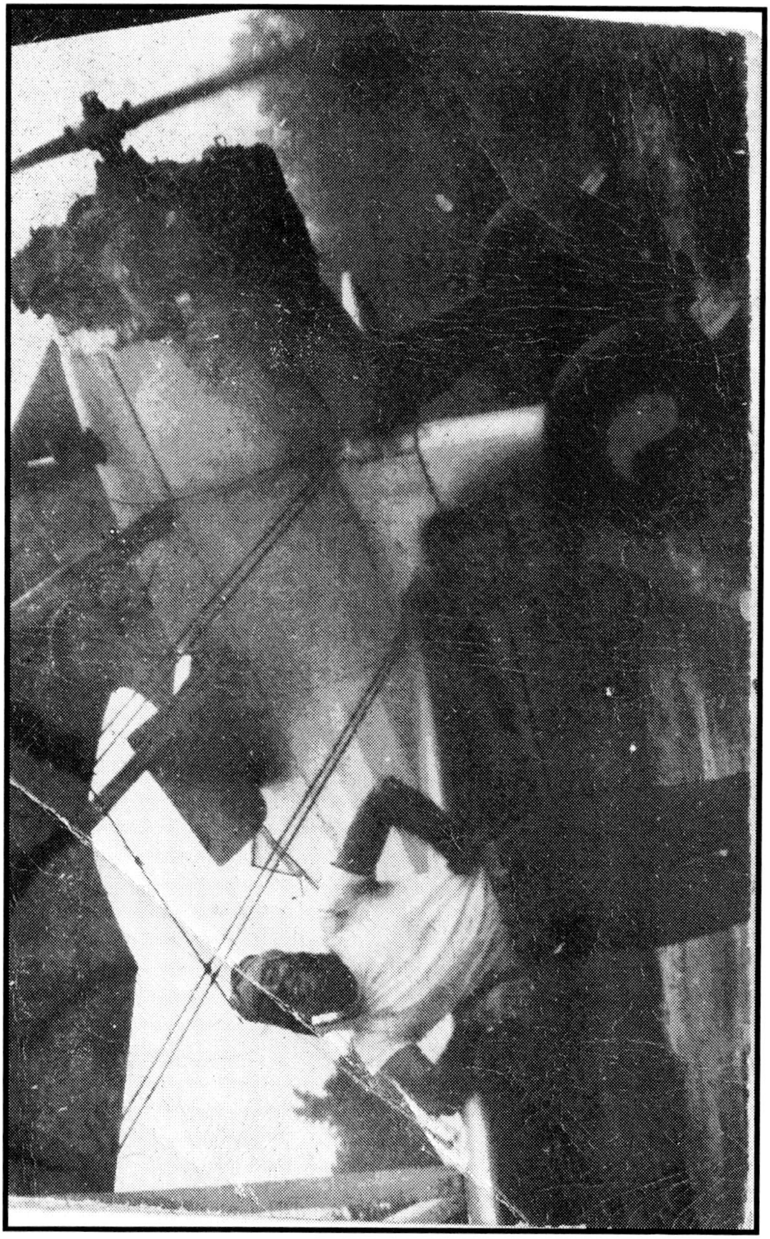

Maybe Next Time

Jim "Speedy" Enright was always up for a challenge. He'd done some barnstorm flying back in the day and some wing walking too. He'd always been working for somebody else though because he never had the cash to purchase his own plane.

He'd tried many schemes to get the money together. He'd tried to get nine other guys to go in together on a plane, but that plan just didn't seem workable. He tried to win enough money playing poker. Speedy was a good poker player and might have been able to make that scheme work except nobody played anything but penny-ante poker in the circles he moved in. He even went to the bank and pitched the idea to them. It seemed like a good investment to Speedy because with a plane he could possibly secure an airmail route. There was good money to be made delivering air mail. The bank manager agreed that there was good money to be made with air mail and as soon as he'd secured a contract he should come back to the bank and they could discuss it.

Speedy had run into a conundrum; he couldn't get the contract without the plane and he couldn't get the money to buy a plane without the contract. It made his head hurt. He was back to square one.

He decided that playing poker was his best option. He began asking around about games that had higher stakes than the local games. Nobody knew anything about any big games anywhere, but the word got around. One night after work Speedy was in the local bar having a beer when a stranger approached him. He stood out in the bar of working class stiffs. He had on a dark pinstriped suit, black and white wing tip shoes and a fedora.

"Are you Speedy Enright?"

"Yeah, who are you?"

"My name isn't important, but I hear you are looking for a poker game."

"Maybe," said Speedy, not wanting to seem too anxious.

"Well maybe you ain't the guy I'm looking for then." He said turning to go.

"No wait, I *am* looking for a game that's more than penny-ante poker."

"You know where Jefferson is don't you, about thirty miles south of here?"

"Yeah, I know where Jefferson is." He'd never been there, but he knew where it was.

The stranger proceeded to give him directions to a house and told him it was a hundred-dollar buy in, cash money. It was every Friday night, by invitation only. The stranger handed him a business card and told him to show this at the door and they'll let you in.

As he left the stranger said, "Don't forget, one-hundred dollars cash money, and tidy yourself up."

With that he was gone.

Where was Speedy going to get one-hundred dollars? He had a little over forty dollars in savings. If he cut back he could save five dollars a week. At that rate it would take him three months; he couldn't wait that long. In fact, a deal had fallen into his lap on a crashed plane. The engine was good, the prop was busted, one wing was busted and the tail section was missing but it was salvageable. The guy who crashed it had other planes and didn't want to fool with fixing this one. He was going to let Speedy have it for the unheard of price of two-hundred and fifty dollars, but it might as well have been two thousand. He had to give the guy the money in two weeks or he'd sell it to somebody else.

The only way he was going to be able to come up with the money for the poker game was to sell off his beloved 1923 Triumph Ricardo motorcycle. One of his buddies had been trying to get him to sell it for years, but he'd always said no, until now.

He offered to sell it to his buddy, George, for two-hundred and fifty dollars. If he could get that for the motorcycle he wouldn't even have to play poker. George just laughed and told him he could give him one-hundred dollars for it. Speedy accepted with the condition that he could borrow it on Friday night. They shook on it and headed to the bank.

Friday night rolled around and Speedy showed up at the house. He got off of his former motorcycle and peeled off a set of coveralls to reveal a not too shabby brown suit. He knocked on the door and presented the business card and was ushered in. It was a modest house but the living room had been outfitted as a poker parlor — a six-sided table with chairs in the center of the room and chairs lining the wall. A full bar with a bartender was on one side and a haze of cigarette and cigar smoke hung in the air.

He took a seat at the table and handed over his cash and got a small stack of chips. It consisted of twenty white one-dollar chips, eight red five-dollar chips and four blue ten-dollar chips. This was the big league and you could lose your stake in no time flat if you weren't careful. The ante was one dollar; the game was five card draw, nothing wild.

The game went on for a several hours and his chips ebbed and flowed, but he never seemed to have any more than he started with. He knew it was bad form to count your chips at the table, but he had a good estimate. It was nearing midnight and Speedy thought it might be a good time to cash in and go home. He could always come back next week and try his luck again. On his final hand he was dealt jack, queen, king of hearts and a couple of junk cards. He anted up, discarded the junk and drew two cards. He couldn't believe his eyes — he drew the ten and ace of hearts. He was holding a royal flush, an unbeatable hand. He had to stay composed though. It all hinged on how he played out this last hand. The bet went around and was at twenty dollars when it got to him and he raised it to forty. It went around a couple of more times being bumped each time. On the last pass, three of the six players folded. At this point Speedy slid all of his chips in; it was all or nothing. One of the remaining players did the same and the third folded. There was over four-hundred dollars worth of chips on the table.

Speedy lay down his winning hand and got up to leave. Everyone complained, wanting to get some of their losses back. Speedy just smiled and said, "Maybe next time gents."

There was no next time. Speedy never went back again, but always loved to say he won his airplane in a poker game.

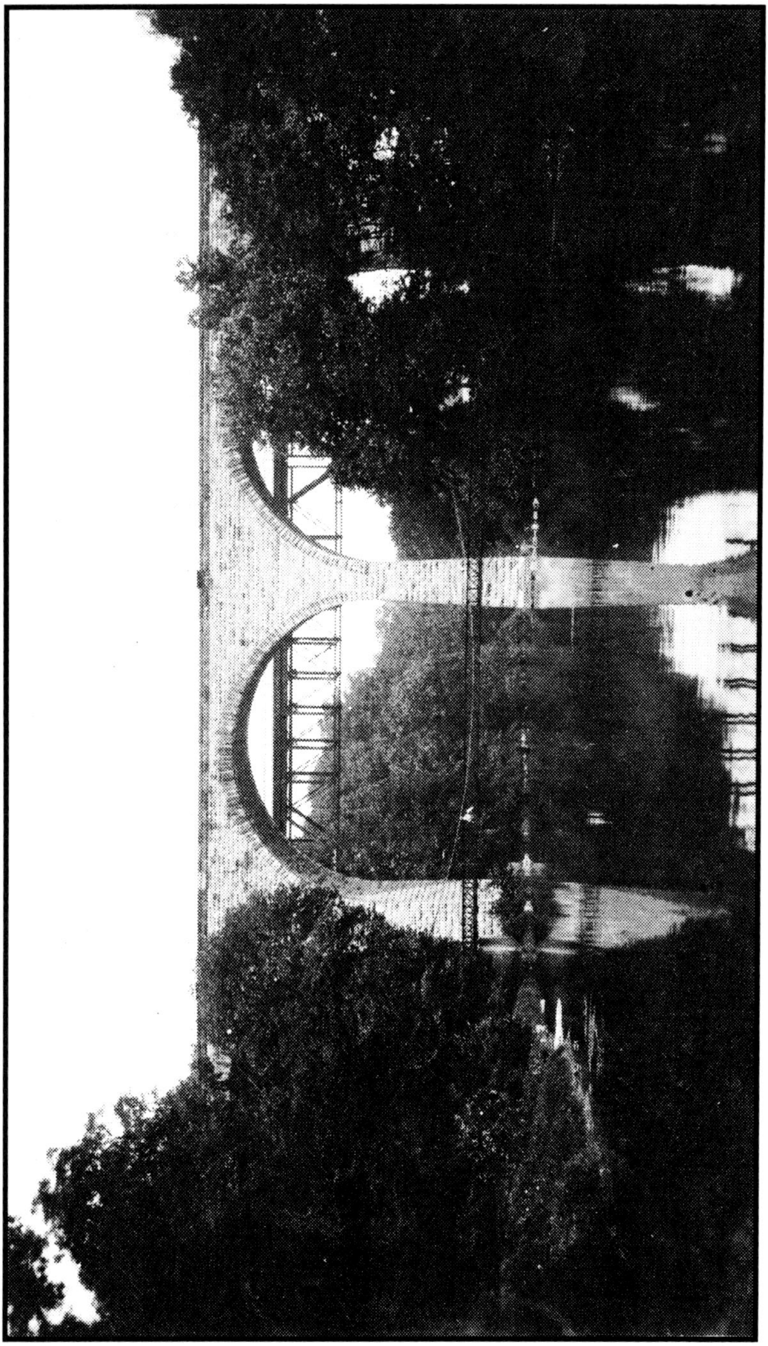

The Impossible Bet

There were three bridges that spanned the river – one for cars, one for trains, and the last for foot traffic. I'd taken on a bet that all three bridges couldn't be crossed both ways in twenty-four hours. I was certain I could do it and my girlfriend Martha was game too. She thought it would be a lark.

The wager was one-hundred dollars and having to act as butler for a day for the winner. My best pal Winnie, his actual name was Winston, had made the bet and I'd accepted. Winnie was aware of a fact that I was ignorant of at the time. Apparently the train didn't cross the bridge both ways within twenty-four hours.

Winnie laughed as he pulled out the train time table and slapped it on the table between us.

"You see, it can't be done. It's physically impossible."

I said, "Give me the weekend to think this over before I give up. If I don't have an answer by Monday, I'll concede."

"You have until Monday at lunchtime. I'll meet you back here then." Winnie took his leave and I began to make some notes on a napkin. The train schedule was the limiting factor, but there must be a way around it. I asked Martha if she could talk to her father; he was one of the owners of the railroad.

She said she would call him right now and ask. She went off to use the phone in the lobby and I went back to scribbling my notes. She came back about ten minutes later and I could tell from her expression that I would get no help from that quarter, but to my surprise there was a glimmer of hope.

"Daddy says he won't re-route a passenger train for some cockamamie bet. He did say that there was a hand car on the siding that was about ten miles from the bridge just behind the train station in Farnsworth. He has alerted the station master to turn a blind eye if it were to be "borrowed" in the next couple of days."

After a few hasty sketches and looking at the train timetable I had a plan. We'd get on the train in Ellingham at eight o'clock in the morning and arrive at Farnsworth at nine o'clock. We'd take our picnic lunch with us and we'd "borrow" the hand car. I think we can cover the twenty-five miles in five hours. So around two o'clock we'll roll back into Ellingham and get the car and drive across the bridge and back. Since it's only fifteen miles to the bridge and a mile back, we should be able to do that in thirty minutes. So by two-thirty we should have the car parked on the side of the road and be taking a leisurely stroll back and forth across the foot bridge. By four o'clock we'll be back on the road and home in time for cocktails.

Well you know what they say about the best laid plans. All went according to plan until we were about a quarter of the way across the foot bridge. All of a sudden Martha just stopped walking.

I said, "Come on Martha."

She said, "I can't. I'm afraid to move."

I'd heard of being scared stiff, but just thought it was an expression.

"Come on, stop kidding around."

"I'm not kidding," she said and I saw the tears running down her cheeks.

"What's the matter?"

"I don't know, I just looked down and suddenly I had a fear grip me that if I went any further the bridge would collapse."

I saw her white knuckles gripping the sides of the bridge and knew it was pointless to try to talk her out of this.

"Stay where you are; I'll go across to the other side and come back and get you."

"No! Don't leave me here," she wailed.

What could I do? I went back to her and she threw her arms around me like a drowning man clutching a life preserver. I began to take very small steps back toward the shore.

"No! We can't move or the bridge might collapse."

I told her to close her eyes and we could back up just a little at a time. We were only a few hundred feet from terra firma, but she'd have no parts of it.

"We can't just stand here forever you know."

"I know, but I'm too afraid to move."

At that point I grasped her around the waist and lifted her up and proceeded to carry her back. She began to shriek, to pound my chest with her fists and kick me about the shins. Through all of that I didn't let go until I had her on firm ground. By this time, she was in full-blown tears, but tears of rage because I'd carried her off of the bridge. She was still full of the irrational fear that the bridge was going to collapse and was running all of the what-if scenarios by me. I listened until she was finished and calmed down and then pointed out that none of those things happened and that she was safe here on the bank. This only allayed her fears momentarily. As soon as I made my intentions to go across alone and then come back, she began to sob again in earnest. She knew I'd never make it and if I attempted to go it was because that stupid bet meant more to me than she did. I was in a no-win situation.

I got her back to the car and we did make it back for cocktails. We both needed one after the day we'd had.

On Monday I was at the club bright and early thinking I'd

miss Winnie and just leave the hundred with the bartender to give to him to collect later. I was not so lucky. There sat Winnie with the morning paper and a cup of coffee. I went over to him and explained the circumstances of my loss. He seemed unfazed. As I turned to go, Winnie cleared his throat.

"I think you forgot the other part of the wager."

He handed me his coffee cup and said, I'll have another of these. I stared at it for a moment and then realized what he meant.

"Yes, sir. Very good sir. Will there be anything else?"

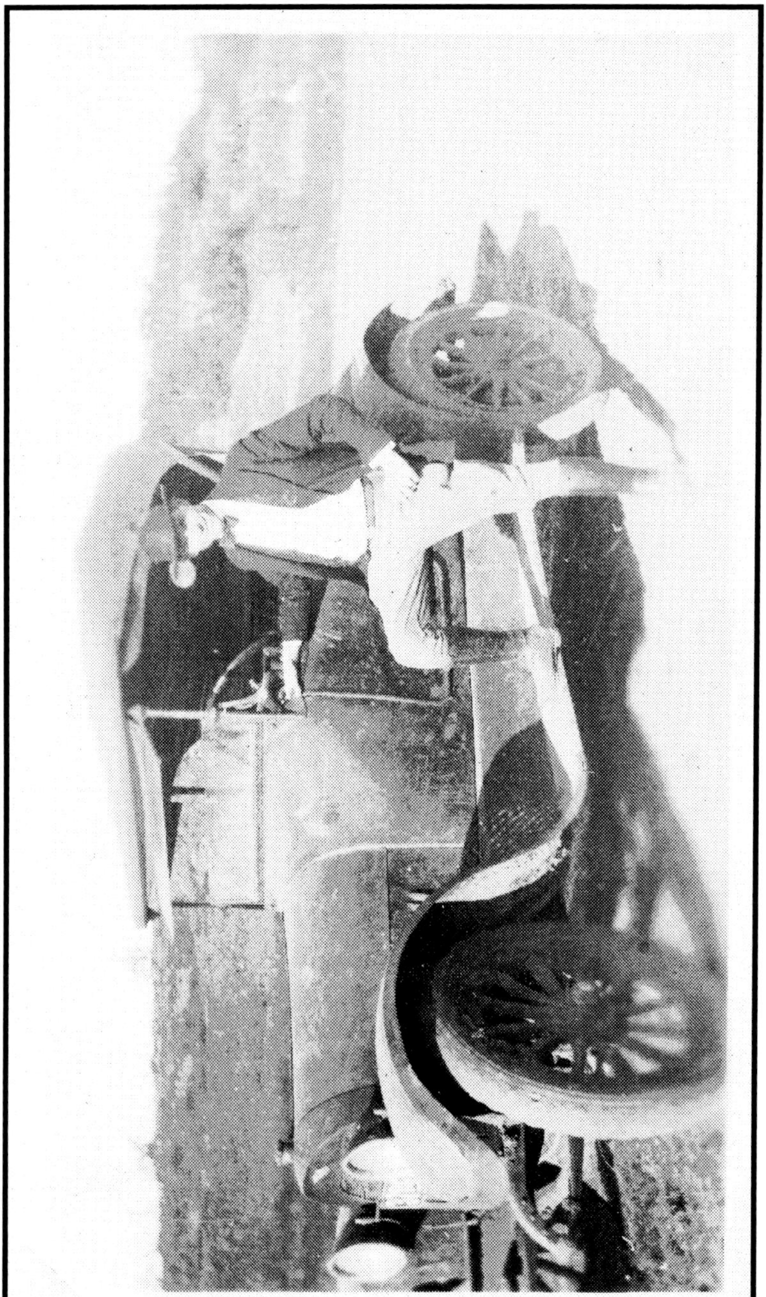

Dowsing For Oil

My old car might not have looked like much considering the coating of dirt, but what she lacked in beauty she more than made up for in reliability. We'd put well over five-hundred miles on her this week. We'd scouted nearly seventy-five sites and had come back to town to file the claims for oil rights on two of them.

They call me "Doc" and my fellow traveler and part time photographer's name is Pete McNairy. His true vocation was an oil dowser. We'd find a likely area and set up camp and then he would get out his tools. They consisted of two copper rods that were bent at a ninety-degree angle, the longer end being about two feet long and the shorter being about six inches. The six-inch pieces had hollow wooden handles that the rods would swivel in.

What he did with them was to hold them out in front of himself so that the rods were parallel. He would begin to wander the site we'd chosen and wait for something to happen. The something was the two rods were supposed to swivel and cross when he was over oil. If this happened, we'd mark the spot and then go get the survey equipment to get all of the measurements for the claim form.

It was good for us that we were essentially in the desert, otherwise he might have been picking up on water deposits. He told me he could tell the difference.

He said, "The rods have a different feel to them when you get over water."

Who was I to argue with him; it was all black magic to me. I just drove the car, did the surveying, and filled out the paperwork for the claim. Although it seemed like I did more, the expertise came in finding the oil, and that was Pete's area. His track record wasn't perfect, but his dowsing found oil six out of ten times. I'd take sixty percent odds any day especially if the payoff was big enough. If you sank a well and hit oil, it could be worth hundreds of thousands of dollars. It would also cost thousands of dollars to drill a well and set up a pump before you ever saw the first drop of oil.

That's why Pete and I weren't oil men. We called ourselves oil prospectors, but unlike gold prospectors we never planned on working our claim. That was too risky and cost too much money. No, what Pete and I would do is go out for about a week and see if we could find some prospective sites. We'd map them out and then come back and file the paperwork for the claim. It was a nominal fee to file the claim, then we'd wait. Once the word got around that Pete had dowsed the claim there were multiple offers. We could easily make over a thousand dollars each, but I never told Pete that. I was the one who handled all the paperwork and received the payments.

Pete was one of those guys who couldn't hold on to a dollar if it was glued to the palm of his hand. He'd eat fancy dinners with even fancier women, drinking champagne and occasionally get fleeced in a card game. I'd know when he'd run through his share of the money because he would be knocking on my door looking for another prospecting trip.

What Pete didn't know was I only gave him half of what he earned; the rest of it I put into a bank account in my name and his. I knew one day the dowsing rods would fail him or he'd just get too old to do it anymore and this way he'd have a nest egg that he would have never saved.

One day Pete came by because he was very nearly out of funds.

He said, "Doc, I don't get it. We make the same money but I never see you spending any except on necessities, like that old clunker out there. Why don't you get a new car?"

"Well, Pete, that old car is the most reliable car I've ever owned. It's easy to work on and get parts for and she has never left me stranded."

Pete stroked his chin in a thoughtful way and said, "I guess you have a point, so what do you do with all your money?"

"If we weren't such good friends I'd tell you it wasn't any of your business, but I put most of it in the bank and they pay me interest on it. That way when I retire I'll have something to live on."

"Ha, I don't plan on living that long. Are you ready for another prospecting trip?"

"Aren't I always ready?"

This cycle went on for a couple of years and I had put aside a good chunk of change for Pete, but I didn't see giving it to him any time soon.

The next time I saw Pete, he looked like a new man. He was clean shaven and had on a new suit of clothes.

"What's happened to you Pete?" I said this as I gestured at the new clothes and lack of facial hair.

"Well Doc, it's like this – I've fallen in love. She just moved into town and her father just opened a new general store. Doc, she's beautiful and smart and funny and—"

"Ok hold up there, I get the picture. What does this girl think of you?"

"Her name is Frances and that's the curious thing — she loves me too."

I gave him the hairy eyeball and asked, "How long has this been going on?"

"About a month, ever since Mr. Slocomb started opening the new store. I've been doing some odd jobs for him and a bit of carpentry, whatever he needs... just to be close to her. I haven't had a drink in a month. I even have money left from our last prospecting trip."

This last part amazed me nearly as much as Pete being in love.

"We want to get married soon. That's one of the reasons I came by was to ask you to be my best man."

"Of course I will. What's the other reason? You said that was one of the reasons."

I never knew Pete to look embarrassed, but he looked like a kid who got caught with his hand in the cookie jar.

"It's about that money you're holding for me." He said this almost apologetically.

Now it was my turn to act embarrassed. "How did you know about that?"

"Oh, I've known all along; I'm not all that stupid. Every once in a while I wonder how much it is, but then figure it's better if I didn't know. We want to buy a little farm outside of town and I thought it might be enough for a down payment."

I just laughed. "With interest you might just have enough to buy the farm outright. Congratulations Pete."

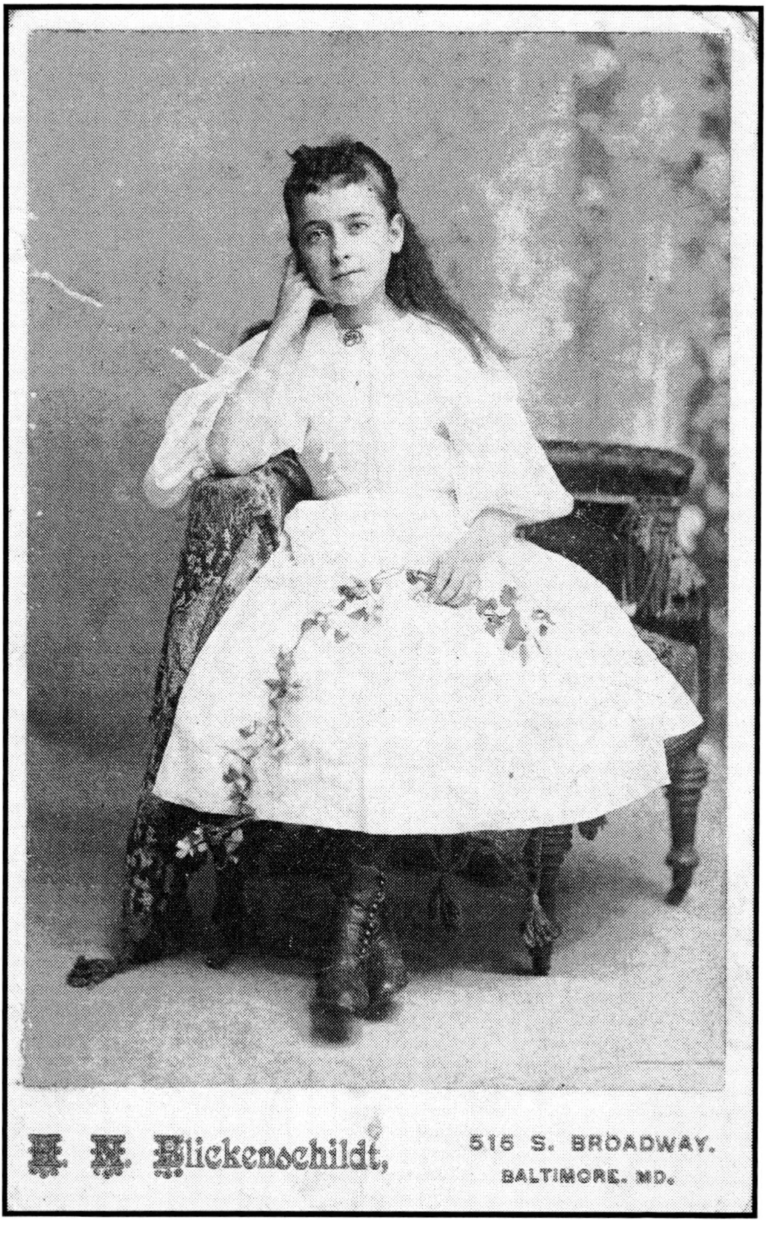
H. N. Blickenschildt,
515 S. BROADWAY.
BALTIMORE. MD.

Off With the Faeries

The business with Sir Arthur Conan Doyle and the Cottingley Fairies was still a few years in the future when Nessie Rogers first reported seeing faeries.

Nessie and her parents had recently moved to a tobacco plantation in rural Maryland. Her father ran the plantation and her mother the house. This left young Nessie at loose ends. It was the beginning of summer so there was no school and she hadn't made any friends yet. She had a lively imagination that came with being an only child and being left to her own devices. She would spend part of her time writing letters to the friends she'd left behind in Ohio, but this only served to punctuate how bored she was.

She would roam the grounds for hours investigating every path and forgotten trail. On one of these excursions she found a lovely meadow surrounded by trees. The meadow was full of wild flowers and she picked a few for her mother. She delivered the flowers and began to tell her mother of the wonderful meadow she had found.

Her mother just said, "That's nice dear. Now run upstairs and wash up. Cook will be calling you for dinner soon."

She reluctantly did as she was told, but didn't let this dampen her spirit. She felt that there was something magical about that meadow.

For nearly a month she returned to the meadow. Although it was now the heat of the summer, the spring flowers were still in bloom. It was always warm and sunny there too, but with a cool breeze wafting over everything. Today Nessie decided to lay down in a patch of springy grass. Within moments she had dozed off. She opened her eyes but thought she must still be asleep. She saw a couple of luminous beings staring at her. As she sat up, they backed up a step as if to flee.

She thought, "I won't hurt you," but before she formed the words to say it she heard a reply, but only in her head.

"And we won't hurt you either."

"I must be going mad," she thought.

Then just as before, she heard without the use of her senses, "You aren't going mad; we are communicating to you from our minds to your mind. You might know us as the faerie folk."

Nessie stood up and looked at them closely. They seemed to be girls, one about her age and the other a bit younger, but they also seemed to be older too. It was only a feeling she got and she couldn't explain it.

"My name is Nessie. Pleased to meet you."

The two beings looked at each other for a moment and then back at Nessie.

Nessie heard the older girl say, "You couldn't pronounce our names — just call me Summer and my sister is Spring. We have been watching you for quite some time now and have determined you possess a radiant soul and we would like to play with you. Would you like to play?"

"Oh more than anything I want to play."

They each took Nessie by the hand and played the day away.

When she arrived back home she was bursting to tell her mother the adventure she had that day. No sooner had she begun her tale than her mother cut her off with the usual speech about getting washed up for dinner. She couldn't bring it up over dinner because where her father was concerned she was to be seen and not heard. After dinner she was obliged to read quietly until bedtime.

That evening she drifted off to sleep recounting the day's events in her head.

Things went on like this for the rest of the summer and she was never able to tell her mother. The summer vacation was nearly over and she would be attending a new school and having to make new friends. She dreaded this. She had two good friends in the meadow and she didn't want to have to leave them. She knew she would have to tell them soon.

The next morning Nessie lingered around the house after breakfast and caught her mother in an idle moment.

"Mother, can I take you to meet a couple of my friends?"

"Why not invite them to come here and then I could meet them."

"Oh, please Mother. I'm supposed to meet them in the meadow where I pick you wild flowers. Please, please, please."

"Alright, I'd like to see this meadow where you can get spring flowers in the summer."

Nessie and her mother showed up at the edge of the meadow, but they were the only ones there.

Nessie called out, "Summer! Spring!"

No answer.

Her mother said it was a lovely place and she was sorry that her friend hadn't showed up, but she had to get back to the house because she had work to do.

She left Nessie and headed back to the house. As soon as she was out of sight Summer and Spring appeared.

Nessie said, "Why didn't you come out when my mother was here?"

"She wouldn't have been able to see us. She has lost all of her magic. Even if she did see us she wouldn't believe her eyes."

Nessie understood. Neither her mother nor her father had

any magic left and she felt sorry for them. She went on to explain that school was starting and she wouldn't be able to come every day like she had in the summer. This brought tears to the eyes of Spring and Summer and finally Nessie too.

Spring said, "Why don't you come and live with us? We'll take care of you and teach you the ways of the faeries."

"I can't," thought Nessie and then she thought, "Why can't I?"

She had a restless night thinking about living with the faeries. In the morning after breakfast she wrote out a note and left it on her pillow.

All it said was:
>I've gone to live with the faeries.
>Nessie

She met Spring and Summer at the meadow. They told her to take off her clothes because she wouldn't need them where they were going and they clothed her in the garb of the faeries which made her feel like she could fly.

She folded her clothes in a neat pile and left them at the edge of the meadow.

That was the last time that she walked among the mortals.

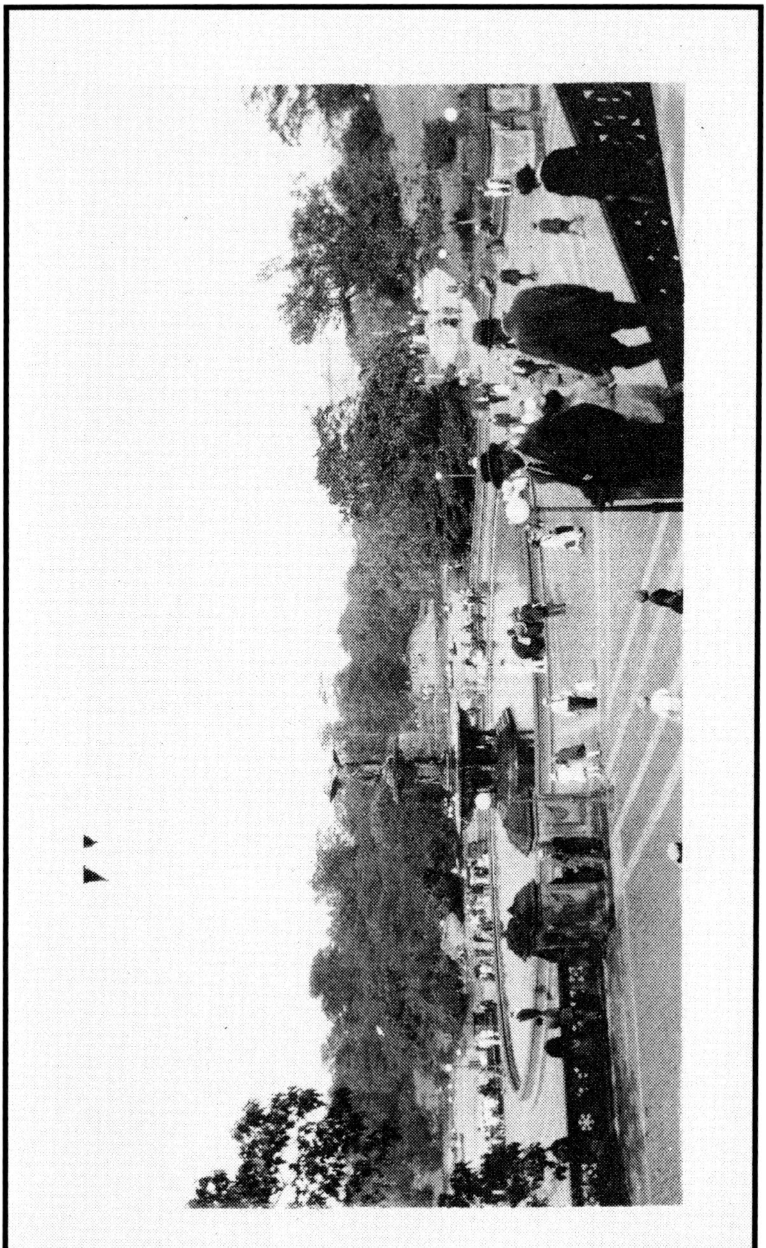

Father of Inventions

The year was 1959 when I went into a diner and saw a man sitting alone having a burger, fries, and a milkshake. I went over to his table and asked him if he minded me sitting down. He looked a bit put out but nodded.

"You don't know me, but if you'll listen to my story for a few moments I'll buy your lunch for you and might give you some information you can use later."

He said, "OK, let's hear this story."

I pulled out an old photo and showed it to him.

"Have you ever seen the man in the photo before?"

He looked at the photo and said, "There's a lot of men in that picture."

"The one looking at the camera."

"Nope, never saw him before. This looks like it was taken in the 20's. He'd be an old man now."

"We'll call the gentleman in the photo John Doe because you would have never heard of him. This snapshot was taken in 1922 to be exact, when men like John D. Rockefeller, Henry Ford, and Andrew Mellon were all billionaires and flaunted their wealth. John on the other hand could have bought and sold them ten times over had he so wished, but he didn't. He likes his anonymity."

"If he was so rich how come I've never heard of him?"

"Well as I said, he likes his anonymity. He goes from place to place and advises certain people. Some of these people have heeded his advice and accumulated great wealth."

"Are you saying that he was an advisor to those billionaires?"

"Oh, no. He finds your average person who may be making

a good living but who has never aspired to be a millionaire and then he may give them a small insight and if they act on it, it will bring them great wealth."

"Sounds like the Devil himself. What's this guy's angle? Why doesn't he use the information himself?"

"I can assure you that he isn't the Devil. It is hard to become rich and retain your anonymity — not impossible, but hard. As I said, Mr. Doe is extremely wealthy and has no need for extra wealth or publicity."

"OK so what's your point? I need to finish my burger and get back to the office."

"This is where it gets a bit strange. He is from the future and he travels in time. I'm not crazy."

I saw my lunch companion scooting his chair back preparing to make a hasty departure.

"Your name is Ernie Fraze and you own an engineering firm. You were on a picnic recently and forgot to bring a can opener and had to open your sodas on the bumper of a car."

He sat back down and stared at me, long and hard.

"How do you know that? I've never seen you before in my life."

"The story goes that one night, a few months after the picnic, you can't sleep and start thinking about the soda can problem. It's then that you come up with the idea of a pull ring that opens the can. You call it the pop top I think."

"What do you mean a few months after the picnic? That was just a week ago."

"Bear with me here; I'm trying to explain. I'm also from the future and I've been tracking John for the last twenty years. He seems to turn up here and there. In your case he would nudge you in the direction of creating a can that is opened without an opener. Even though the history books show that you did invent it, he seems to think he has a part in all of these inventions. He's not dangerous, just misguided. It would only take him putting the wrong idea into the wrong head at the wrong time and it could take centuries to correct the time line. It's like a row of... what do you call those black tiles with the white dots on them?"

"Dominoes?"

"Yes, it's like a row of dominoes. When the first one falls, the rest of them fall in sequence. It's like that too with the timeline; if one thing happens that isn't supposed to, it leads to the next and the next and soon you have a mess."

Ernie sat there for a moment just taking it all in.

"So are you a policeman?"

"Not exactly, but close. I'm with the department of Rogue Time Travel. There have been incidents but nobody knows about them because they were corrected and the timeline set back to where it should be, but the man hours to do something like that are astronomical. It is much more cost effective if we can stop it before it happens."

Looking a bit dubious he said, "OK, so what do you want from me? I've never seen your guy."

I pulled out a card case and handed him one of my cards.

"There is a local phone number on there. Call it anytime day or night. We have a secretary on duty twenty-four hours a day. If you see him, call. Don't wait until he approaches you because he may be gone before we can get to him. He may follow you for a couple of days to find out when is a good time to get you by yourself. Much like I did with you today."

"What if I don't see him before he approaches me?"

"Excuse yourself, say you need to use the rest room or something and then find the nearest phone booth and call. We will be here amazingly fast."

"What if he never shows up? Maybe I come up with this pop top thing all on my own. By the way it's a good idea."

"If he doesn't show up we have other leads. Thank you for your time."

He threw a twenty-dollar bill on the table.

"That should cover your lunch and your time. Good luck with the pop top."

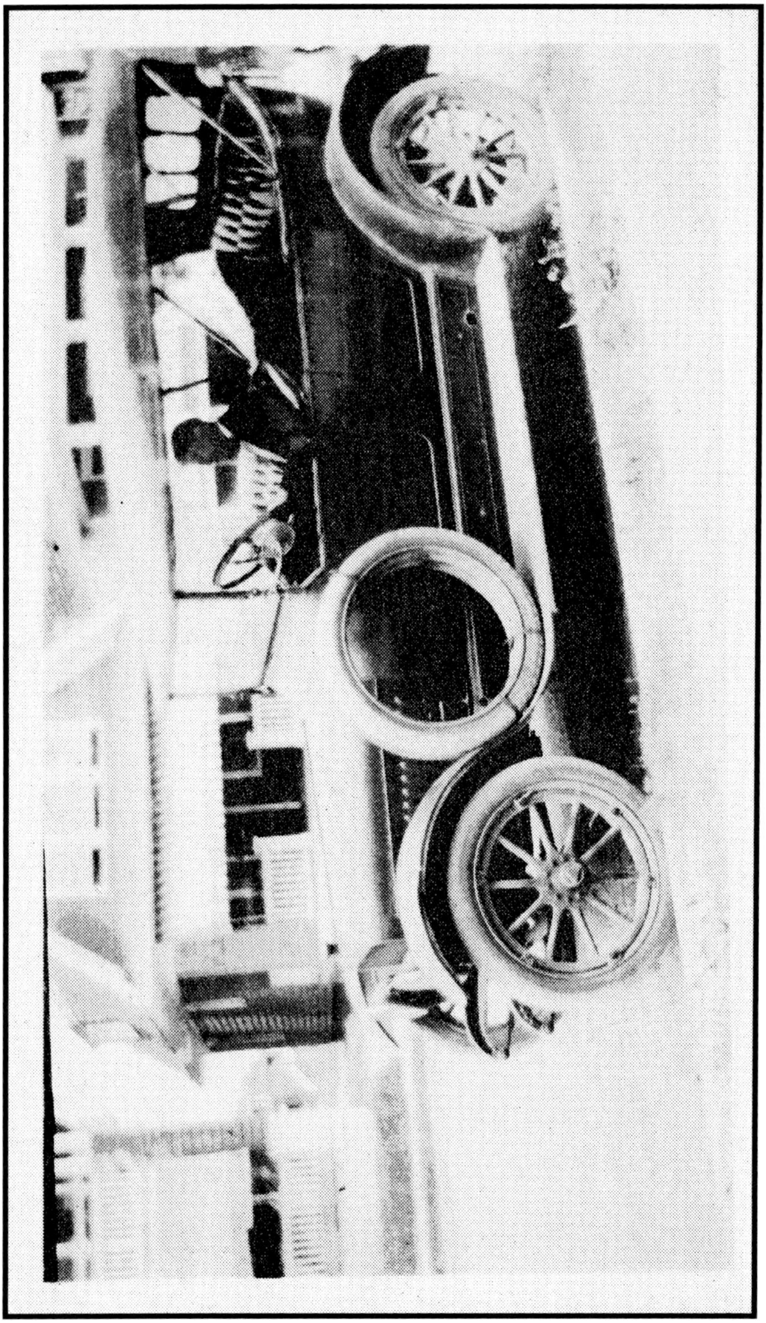

Mother Knows Best

Walter was as proud as a peacock when he drove up in his Hudson Six. It had been almost two-thousand dollars when it was new. It was now five years old but had been well taken care of. The original owner had kept it in the garage and only driven it on the weekends so it was like new. The odometer only had two-thousand and eighty-seven miles on it.

We all poured out of the house to come and look at it — even the neighbors came over. You would have thought that Walter was a car salesman the way he went on about all of its features.

"My friends, you have here an exquisite example of the 1914 Hudson Six. It has a hundred and twenty-three-inch wheel base and can seat seven passengers. You'll notice here on the dash is a gasoline gauge. The doors have hidden hinges for a sleeker look. The top can easily be raised and lowered by one man."

Walter proceeded to demonstrate this as he folded the top back and secured it with the attached straps. The whole operation took less than five minutes.

"Once the top is retracted, the rain-vision screen can also be lowered for unimpeded visibility. The upholstery is hand-buffed leather. The headlamps are dimmable and the horn is electric. The spare tire is mounted just in front of the driver's side door for easy access. There is also a full set of tools included in the trunk."

Everyone was nearly as thrilled as Walter was. He'd been talking about nothing else for almost a year. He knew his friend was going to be selling soon and Walter had been scrimping and saving and doing odd jobs all over town to get the money together to buy it. Of course, he only had about a quarter of the money, but he got a loan from the bank. He'd be paying it off for the next three years at eleven dollars a month. With a few hours overtime at the plant he wouldn't feel the pinch too badly.

Walter was concerned that he didn't have a garage to keep his new treasure in and knew that the weather would take its toll on the finish and the upholstery. His friend Oscar worked down at the shipyard and sometimes some rich fellow with a sail boat would have his sails redone. It was times like this that Oscar would find himself with yards and yards of canvas. Several yards of canvas would make a suitable car cover until such time as Walter had the funds to build a garage.

The neighbors had disbursed after congratulating Walter on his new purchase. It seemed that every child had to have a turn in the driver's seat. They all made motor noises and pretended to turn the wheel back and forth. None of them could see over the dashboard, nor could their feet reach the pedals. Walter knew they couldn't hurt anything so he let them have their fun and pretend to drive his car.

The family was all that was left to admire the car now.

Walter asked, "Who wants to go for a ride?"

His mother said, "I don't think we can all fit; I'll just stay behind."

"Mother, we can all fit. Come on."

"I have a pie in the oven; I can't just go riding off to who knows where."

"Mother, I'll just drive around the block. I wasn't planning on driving to Chicago."

"Oh, alright. First let me go check on the pie. I don't want it to burn."

While she went to check on the pie, we all piled into the car — three of us across the back seat, two of us on the disappearing seats that folded down, and that left room for Father and Mother in the front with Walter.

When she returned, Walter helped his mother into the front seat and then climbed into the driver's seat. He pushed the starter button and the Hudson roared to life. Walter disengaged the parking brake and let out on the clutch. The Hudson slowly picked up speed as Walter shifted gears. No sooner had he shifted to second than he had to down shift to stop at the corner stop sign. After indicating a right turn, he proceeded down Maple Street, never getting beyond second gear. A right on Fourth Avenue then a right on Ash Street. As he took the final right onto Third Avenue, he was a bit disappointed that he hadn't been able to show them what she could really do out on the open road. He knew he'd have plenty of time to do that later, but wanted to show off his new toy.

Walter was pulling up in front of their house when he heard a loud pop and then a hiss. Everyone got out and saw that one of the tires on Walter's new car had a puncture. Now he was glad he hadn't taken them out on the open road. If this had happened when he was going thirty miles an hour, they may have had a bad accident.

Walter's mother saw the disappointment in his face.

She said, "At least it happened close to home."

Walter agreed and said, "That's why they make spare tires."

"When you get that fixed, there will be a warm slice of pie waiting for you."

Walter smiled and said, "Thanks, Mother."

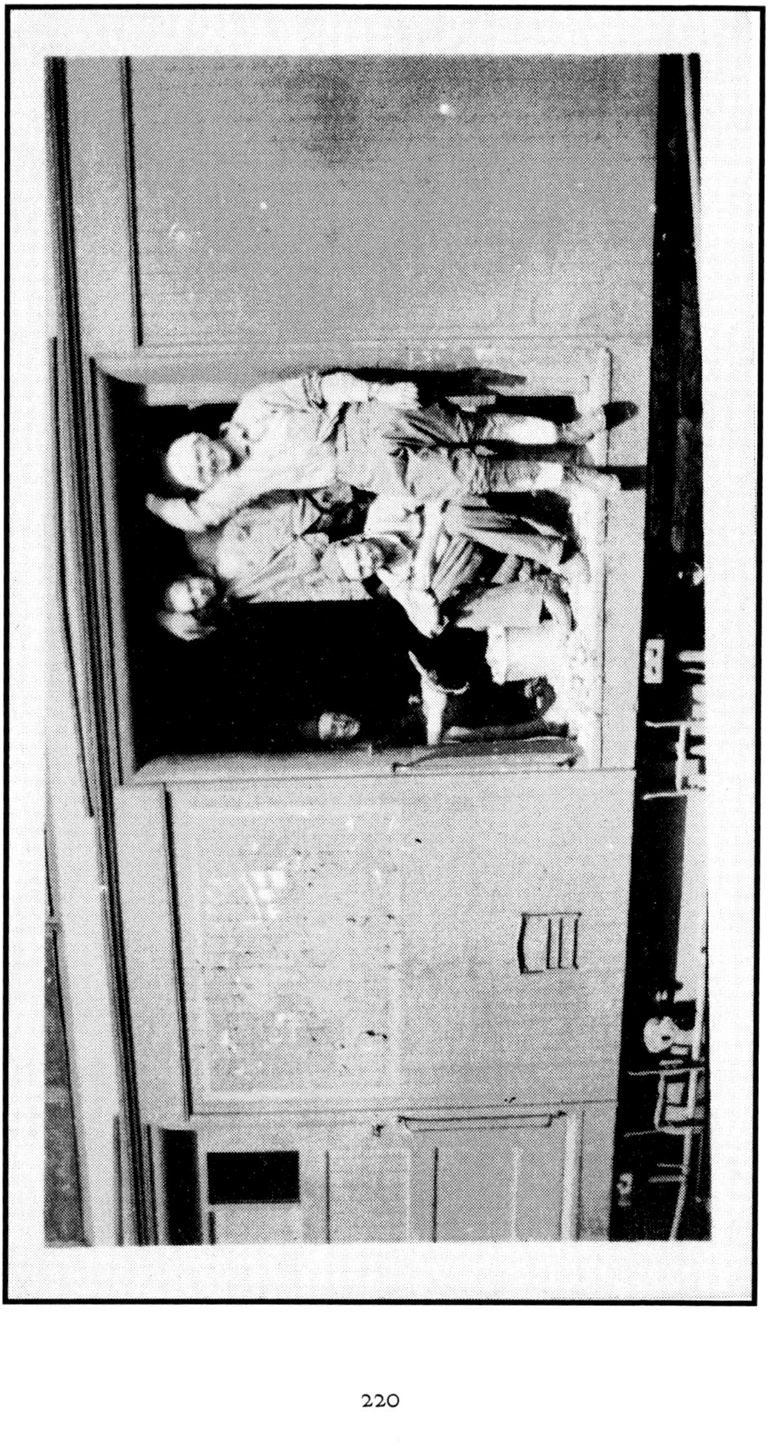

Private Plotnick

Left to right: George "Hayseed" Parker, Claude "Tiny" Muldoon, "Doc" Gordon and Gene Plotnick.

George was a farm boy from Iowa, hence the "Hayseed" nickname. Tiny was over six feet tall. Doc came to us with that nickname and nobody ever asked him where it came from. Then there's me sitting there peeling potatoes. They called me a lot of things, and I answered to most of them.

We were like the four musketeers of boot camp. If one of us was in trouble, it was fairly certain that the other three weren't far behind. We spent our fair share of time picking up cigarette butts, digging latrines and of course kitchen police.

The drill sergeant would wake us up at o' dark-thirty in the morning and expect us to be fully functional. Since lights out was at 8:30 p.m. we should have had enough sleep, but we were always up late playing cards or dominoes. In retrospect, the sergeant really didn't have it in for us, it just seemed like it at the time, like if anything was out of order. It was our fault. A day didn't go by that one of us wasn't doing some grunt work.

We were halfway through our basic training at Fort Ord. After that we were looking forward to a week-long break as we went cross country to Fort Dix in New Jersey, from there to England and then to the front. In the meantime, the four musketeers were working on a farewell surprise for the sergeant.

We'd dreamt up many schemes, but most required more skill or expertise than we could muster between us. One such scheme was to disassemble his personal car and put it back together in his office. Since it would take too long and none of us were mechanics, we had to scrap that idea.

We'd thought of getting him drunk and then taking some compromising photos. This might have worked, but since he knew we hated him the last thing he would do was accept a drink from any of us. Since one or all of us were forced to work in the kitchen for some minor infraction of the rules, we thought we could give the sergeant a nice case of the trots. That one also was shot down because we might have to make half of the camp sick just to get to the sarge.

It was one evening while I was peeling my thousandth potato that I had an idea. I had to wait 'til breakfast to explain it to the other guys. They listened intently and then began to pick it apart just like they had for all of the other ideas. This plan was bulletproof; for every problem they would bring up I had an answer. When you are doing mindless work like peeling potatoes you have plenty of time to think things through. It was settled; on our last day before we headed east to New Jersey we would pull off "Operation Spud."

The great thing about pulling this prank on our last day was there could be no repercussions. We would have graduated our basic training and would no longer be taking orders from the sergeant. The down side was we would be gone when he discovered the surprise and wouldn't be able to see his face. Well, "you have to take the bad with the good," as my mother used to say.

The evening before we were to leave I went to the back door to the kitchen. As I had suspected there was some poor private sitting there peeling potatoes. I walked in and told him that I'd been sent to relieve him and that he was dismissed to go back to his barracks. He didn't ask any questions and disappeared out the back door in a flash.

I signaled the other guys and they came in. They each hefted a fifty-pound sack of potatoes and headed out. I sat there and dutifully peeled the spuds in case someone came around to check. After about fifteen minutes they returned to get a second load. It was about twenty minutes before they returned this time.

"How many more do we need?" I asked.

Tiny said, "I think four more bags should do it, but we need to hurry. The guard on the motor pool changes in thirty minutes."

We each grabbed a sack of potatoes and headed toward the motor pool. On the way there we heard the sergeant coming out of the officer's club so we ducked into the shadows.

Turning toward the door he said to somebody, "I'm going to check on the private I left peeling potatoes and then I'm going to turn in."

I dropped my sack and managed to get back to the kitchen before the sergeant. I hunkered down over a pile of potatoes and was peeling for all I was worth. I heard him stop outside of the screen door to the kitchen, then I heard him strike a match and smelled cigarette smoke. I heard his footsteps grow fainter on the gravel path as he made his way back to his quarters.

Just when I thought I was out of the woods, I heard a deep voice say, "Private, get out here and explain this."

I knew the jig was up, but as I approached the door there stood Tiny nearly doubled over with laughter. Doc had been working on his impression of the sergeant and had gotten me good.

The next day we're on the troop train and headed for New Jersey. The guys were telling me how the sergeant's car looked full of potatoes. They said, "you couldn't see them till you were right up on it, but it was a solid layer of spuds from the window to the floor. If he doesn't see them before he opens the door, he'll be knees deep in potatoes."

We were laughing and carrying on when a lieutenant walks in and we snap to attention. He looks down at us and at a telegram in his hand.

"Parker, Gordon, Muldoon, and Plotnick, you are needed in the rear of the train."

We all looked at each other, shrugged, and headed to the back of the train. The car before the end car was the kitchen for the troop train. The very last car was food storage. We looked around and saw sacks and sacks of potatoes.

The lieutenant said, "This telegram is from your former sergeant. It says that you have a fondness for potatoes and I should keep you busy until we get to New Jersey."

He pointed at some vegetable peelers and said, "Get started!"

And that's how I became "Spuds" Plotnick.

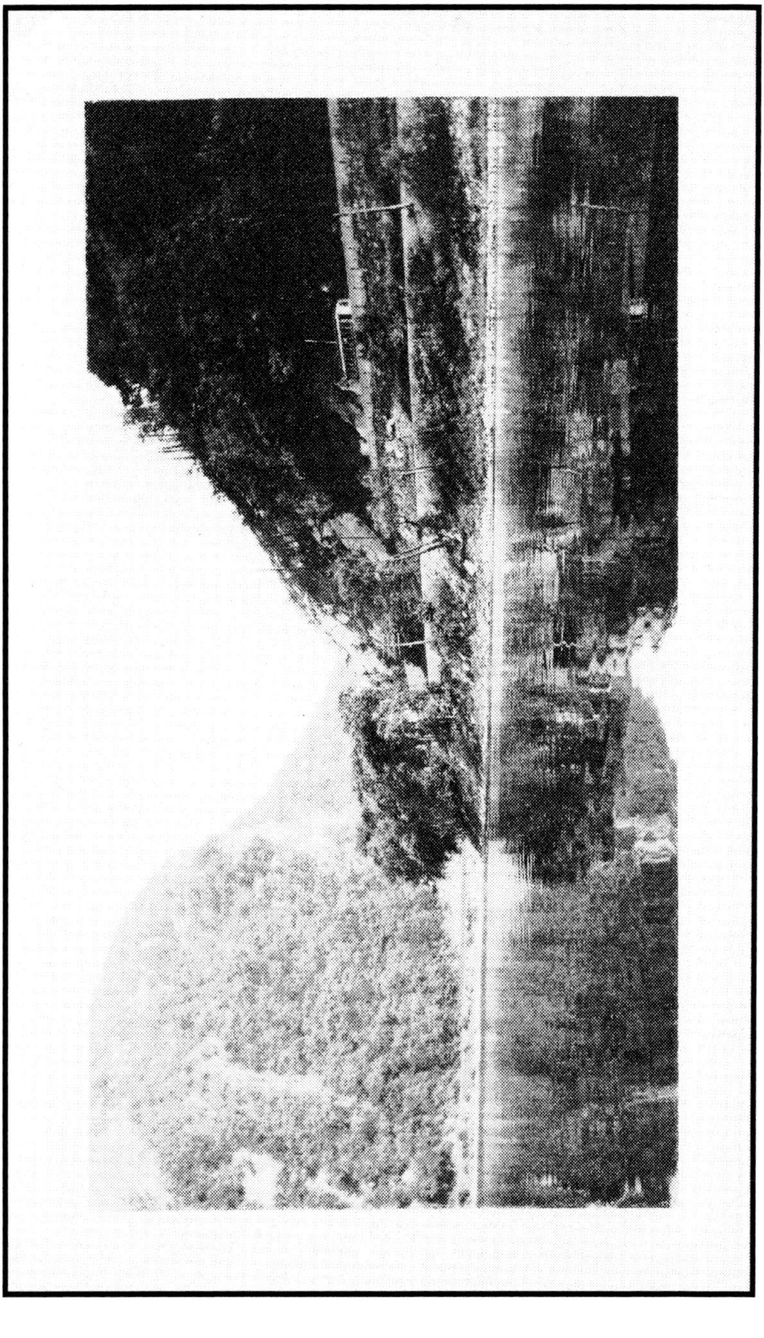

Loch Ness of the West

We'd rented a cabin up in the mountains thinking we'd get in some fishing and canoeing. The other three guys with me were Oscar, Sam, and Vince. We all worked on the loading dock and every year the company shut down for two weeks in the summer. The union had managed to get us paid for those two weeks so we were pretty well stocked on supplies.

The weather didn't cooperate with us. For the first two days we were stuck indoors while the rain pelted the roof. There was a leak in the roof and after a bit of searching, we found a bucket to catch it. We'd see lightning crack the sky and light up the lake and then moments later there would be the thunder echoing through the mountains.

The cabin had a good supply of paperbacks, mostly mysteries. We had a couple of decks of regular cards and one deck of pinochle. There was a checker board and a set of dominoes. We'd brought the Sunday paper from the city. There was also a counter top radio; it could only pull in a couple of stations. We weren't exactly bored but we were getting restless. We could have stayed home and played cards.

The second night I was tired of cards, dominoes, reading, and quite frankly the other three guys. I went out on the porch that overlooked the lake and sat in one of the rocking chairs and waited for the light show. I didn't have to wait long — a great fork of lightning lit the sky. I was staring out across the lake at the time. I was certain I'd seen something on the lake, something big and moving fast. Then I thought, "What idiot would be out on the lake in a boat in a thunderstorm with no running lights?"

I kept a lookout for that same spot on the lake, waiting for the next flash of lightning. When it came I had to rub my eyes because my brain couldn't process what I'd just seen. The boat was no boat. It looked like a snake but it was huge. Size was hard to judge without any point of reference but it stood out in the lake. It undulated across the surface and then disappeared.

I yelled to the guys to come out and see this.

"What is it?" Oscar asked.

"You just have to see it for yourself," I said.

So they all came out and took seats and waited for the next flash of lightning. When it came I said, "Look over there."

I was pointing franticly, but by the time they had looked where I was pointing it was too late and the light was gone.

"Keep looking in that area."

They did and when next the lake was lit up they saw nothing and neither did I. We tried a couple more times, to no avail.

Vince asked, "So what did you see?"

"I don't know. It looked like a huge snake to me. I saw it moving fast once. It's hard to judge size though."

Sam asked, "What do you mean, huge? Ten or twelve feet?"

"I think more like seventy-five or one-hundred feet. Don't look at me like I'm crazy. That's what I saw... I think."

"I think your eyes were playing tricks on you. I bet it was a submerged log just bobbing to the surface."

It was Vince who said this, but I think he was trying to reassure himself as much as anything.

We all finally got to sleep that night and awoke to a clear rain-washed day. The sky was a cloudless blue and the lake barely had a ripple on it. Our spirits had lifted with the passing of the storm and I think everyone but me had forgotten the events of the previous evening.

We fished and canoed for the rest of our stay and hardly saw another soul. We had the only cabin on that end of the lake and it was in a secluded cove. I guess the fish liked it too, because we had fresh fish for dinner every evening.

On our final day there we loaded the camera up with a fresh roll of film and went out in the canoe. We wanted some scenery shots and a shot of the cabin from the lake. We were about to call it a day when the canoe hit something that was submerged, so we back-paddled to see what it was. We saw nothing. Then the rear of the canoe struck something and we all looked at each other, the same thought running through our heads.

I told Sam to keep the camera ready while Vince and I paddled for shore. We hadn't gone ten feet when something hit the canoe and sent it rocking. Then we saw something I'll never forget. A head, more like a dinosaur than a snake, slowly emerged from the water. It was between us and the shore. The head swiveled on a long thin neck and then caught sight of us and dove in our direction.

All I remember other than the panic that was welling up inside of me was the constant click of the shutter and Sam advancing the film for another shot. We began to paddle like our lives depended on it and moments later the head emerged again, but this time behind us. The creature must have misjudged our speed. It dove a second time in our direction, but this time we weren't so lucky. It surfaced right under our canoe and nearly flipped us over. Sam was on the verge of falling over and flaying his arms. I grabbed him by the shirtfront just as the camera strap snapped. It flew about ten feet and landed with a large splash. This may have been our saving grace. The creature may have thought it was a big fish and went to investigate. This gave us enough time with all four of us at the paddles to make it back to shore.

The creature was gone, the camera was gone, and any evidence was also gone. If we told anyone they'd think us raving lunatics.

We decided to pack up our stuff and head out immediately, never to speak about the creature... and never to come back here for vacation.

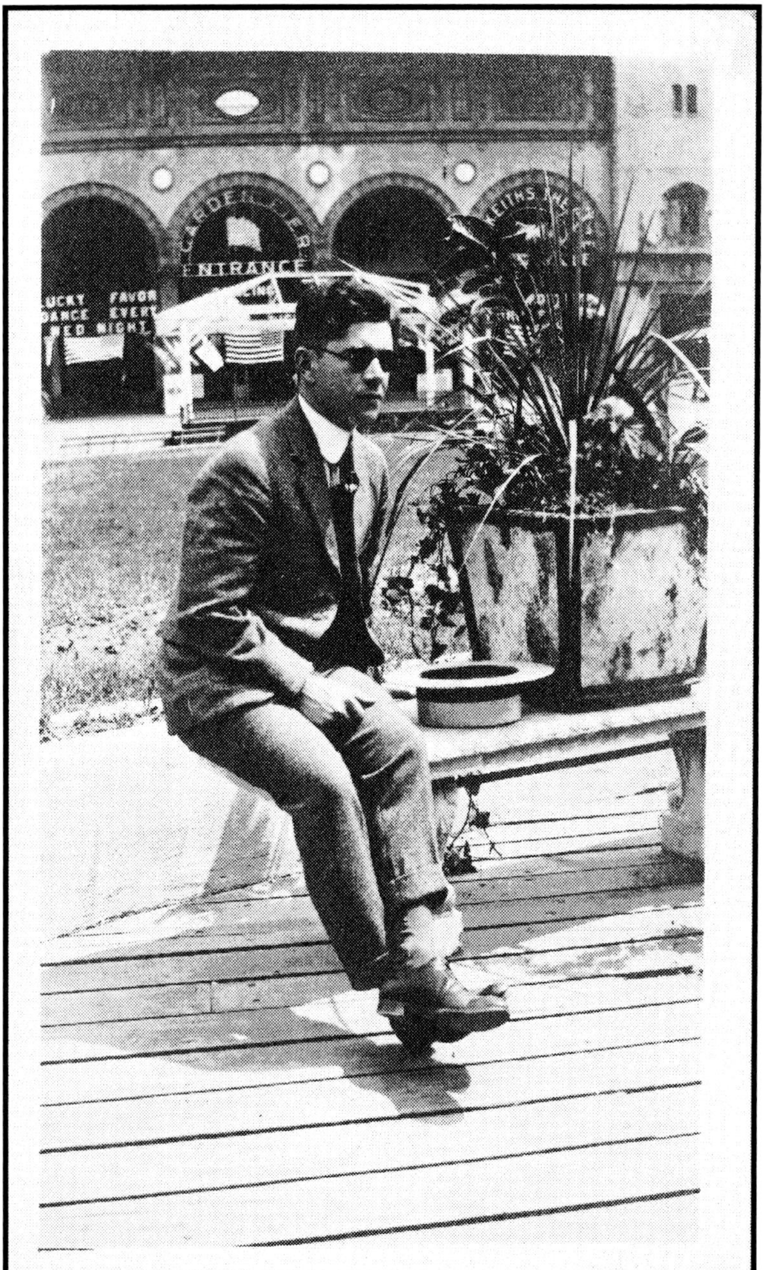
ENTRANCE
LUCKY FAVOR
DANCE EVERY
WED NIGHT

Missing Houdini

Oliver Fisher sat patiently waiting for his lady friend to show up. They had met at the ballroom here at the Garden Pier. While dancing, she had mentioned that the great Houdini would be performing at Keith's theatre the coming week. So here Oliver sat with two front row tickets in his coat pocket, waiting.

As he waited, his mind drifted. He imagined himself up on stage with Houdini as one of the committee that would examine the Chinese water torture cell. He wasn't sure what he would look for, but he would do his due diligence.

He had seen this performance once before in New York. Several members of the audience would be chosen as the committee to examine the water torture cell and to deem it inescapable. The torture cell was about six feet tall and maybe three feet square with a glass front. Houdini would issue a challenge before he exited the stage to change into a swimming suit.

Houdini would say, "Ladies and Gentlemen, introducing my original invention, the water torture cell. Although there is nothing supernatural about it, I am willing to forfeit the sum of one-thousand dollars to anyone who can prove that it is possible to obtain air inside of the torture cell when I'm locked up in it in the regulation manner after it has been filled with water."

The scrutiny became heightened after this challenge, but nobody could find anything out of the ordinary.

While Houdini was off stage changing, his assistants would fill the torture cell with water from high pressure hoses and caldrons of hot water. He would then return and lie on his back and have the stocks closed around his ankles. A block and tackle would then raise him over the tank and then lower him head first while his assistants secured the locks and positioned the curtain around the cell. One assistant stood by with a fire axe in case the glass had to be smashed to save Houdini's life.

The orchestra would begin to play "Asleep in the Deep," very apropos about sailors drowning at sea. Then the longest two minutes in the world would begin. At the performance Oliver had attended, a lady in the audience screamed to let him out after about a minute and a half. She was frantic, but just after the two-minute mark, Houdini threw aside the curtain dripping wet and took his bow.

Oliver pulled out his watch. It was two o'clock and the matinee had just begun. There was still no sign of Gwendolyn. He stood up and began to pace. He hated to be late and saw it as a character flaw in others. His first thought was that she had gotten stuck in traffic, but then remembered she was staying in a hotel close by and was walking to the pier.

Now he'd begun an inner dialog about how much longer he should wait. Should he go on in without her and leave the other ticket at the booth and let the usher know who to look for? As he paced he became more agitated. He pulled out his watch again; it was now ten after two.

At this point Oliver noticed an attractive young lady sitting by herself. He went over to where she was sitting.

"Excuse me miss, my name is Oliver Fisher and I know we haven't been formally introduced but would you care to see Houdini at Keith's this afternoon?"

She looked up in surprise and said, "Sir, I'm not in the habit of carrying on conversations with strangers."

Oliver thought he might as well go on in because by his watch it was quarter past the hour. The problem was he wasn't in the mood anymore and wasn't sure he would be even if Gwendolyn did show up.

He noticed the attractive young lady again talking to another man. Then he noticed that she was pointing at him. The other man straightened up and headed straight towards Oliver. Oliver didn't want a confrontation here in public, but he saw that look in the other man's eyes and realized that this wouldn't end without somebody being punched in the nose. Oliver had been on the boxing team at Yale and really didn't want to take this young man to task, but would if he had to.

"Hey, have you been bothering my girl over there?"

Oliver replied, "I didn't know she was with any one when I went up to speak to her."

"She says she doesn't know you from Adam and you were asking her to go see Houdini with you."

"Both of those statements are true but—"

"Don't give me any of your buts, I ought to give you a thrashing so you think twice before you try to steal a guy's best girl."

"I can assure you, my good man, that I had no intentions of stealing—"

Oliver had to duck at this point because the newcomer had taken a swing at him but only succeeded in knocking off his hat. By instinct Oliver countered with a punch to the solarplexus knocking the wind out of him.

Oliver grabbed the man by the arm and helped him sit down. His girlfriend came over and began to pummel Oliver until Oliver having had enough of this just yelled, "Stop."

She did and sat down beside the other man.

She said, "Andrew, are you all right?"

Andrew nodded, and then said, "I guess I was disappointed that the matinee was sold out and then when you told me about this guy I figured I could take out my frustration on him.

Oliver had at this point picked up his hat and overheard the conversation. He pulled out his watch, it was now twenty minutes after two. Gwendolyn wasn't coming.

He reached into his coat pocket and handed the two front row tickets to Andrew.

"If you hurry you can still catch most of the show, and probably Houdini too."

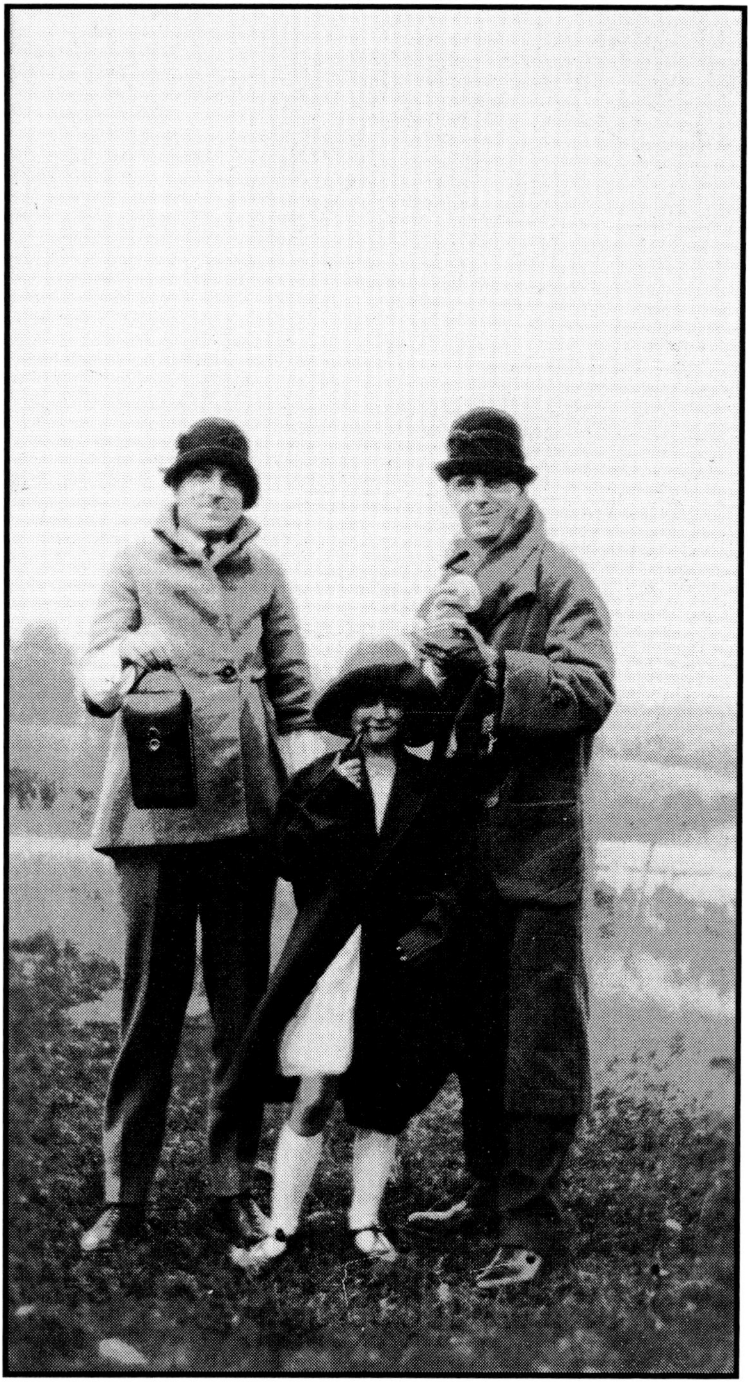

WANNA BET?

While on vacation our wives, Iris and Emily, had gotten it into their respective heads that George and I gambled too much. It was true that we would bet on nearly anything. We'd be betting on whether the next person coming into the room would be a man or a woman, tall or short, old or young. Since they were friendly bets just between us two, we saw no harm in it. One week George would be a couple of dollars ahead and the next I would be. It was all good clean fun, but apparently it had begun to annoy our wives.

I guess they had hatched up this scheme together. One day we were out having lunch and sitting in a booth next to the window, the ladies on one side and us on the other. There was a café curtain, so we couldn't see the street without moving it, but the exposed glass above the curtain allowed plenty of light in. It also allowed our wives to see the street in the mirror that was over our heads, but we didn't know that at the time.

Iris glanced up and said, "I'll bet you a dollar the next car coming down the street is blue."

George and I looked at each other and shrugged.

Then we said in unison, "You've got a bet."

About thirty seconds later we heard a car, and peeking out of the windows, saw it was indeed a blue car. We grudgingly paid Iris. She smiled and tucked the money away.

Next it was Emily's turn.

She had seen a gentleman come in the front door of the café in the same mirror.

She hurriedly said, "I'll bet you a dollar that the next person to be seated will be a man."

We accepted her bet and then kept an eye on the vestibule that led into the café. Sure enough, the waitress was leading a gentleman to a table. Once again we paid up. George and I were both out two dollars and wondering why all of a sudden the wives had decided to start betting us.

I looked at George and said, "I'll bet you a dollar he just orders a sandwich."

George said, "I bet he orders a full meal."

"You're on."

At this point the ladies excused themselves to go to the powder room.

We didn't know that while our wives went off to powder their noses, they were also interrogating the waitress about the current customer's order.

When they got back, we were still staring over toward the patron waiting for his order. Iris and Emily sat back down.

Iris said, "Emily and I will each bet you two dollars that the gentleman waiting for his food only gets a bowl of soup. It's a chance for you to win your money back."

Well, George and I looked at each other and I knew we were both thinking the same thing. They have been lucky twice in a row, it won't happen a third time.

"You're on," we both said.

Now we were all interested in the lone man at the table waiting for his food to arrive. After about five minutes the waitress comes out of the back with a club sandwich and heads in his direction. I was beginning to smile when she went right past him and took it to another table. About a minute later she reappeared with a steaming bowl of soup. This she proceeded to place in front of the waiting customer.

We overheard her say, "Will there be anything else?"

The Gentleman just shook his head. Well the girls were three for three and we were out four bucks each.

Emily said, "Don't you see how silly all this betting is?"

Iris chimed in, "We'd like you both to stop because we have begun to get tired of it."

George and I looked at each other.

George said, "I'll stop if Harry stops."

I said, "Wait a minute, I'm not making you bet. I'll stop because Emily wants me to."

Emily and Iris looked at each other and shook their heads.

Iris said, "We don't believe you can quit. In fact, we are willing to bet you that you can't quit for one full day."

George and I accepted the bet.

"Wait." said Iris. "You don't even know what the conditions of the bet are."

I said, "Whatever they are we accept."

Then Iris and Emily began to lay out the terms and conditions of the bet. And after they did and we had agreed, it was to begin immediately.

There were several times over the course of lunch that either I or George nearly blew it. We made it through lunch, through a shopping trip and dinner. By the time we'd all woken up and assembled for breakfast there were only a few hours left before we won the bet or so I thought.

George was sitting across from me at breakfast.

He looked at me and said, "I'll be—"

That was as far as he got before I kicked him in the shin.

He gave me a dirty look, and reached down and rubbed his shin.

"All I was going to say was, I'll be a son of a gun if that's not the same man we saw in the café yesterday."

I knew that wasn't what he was going to say; in fact the man he was gesturing toward looked nothing like the man in the café. I just gave him a hard look.

As we opened our menus to order I said, "I bet they don't have—"

That was the kiss of death. I had uttered those words. Had we won, life as we know it would have continued as usual and our wives would not mention the betting again. Ah, but if we lost... Our wives wanted us to dress up in their clothes so they could take a blackmail picture. If we ever were caught betting again they would send the picture to our lodge buddies and that would be a fate worse than death. When they finally took the photo, we had talked them into just coats, hats and hand bags. Our niece, who was staying with us at the time thought it was a hoot that Uncle Harry was going to dress up like Aunt Emily and wanted to get in on the fun, so we let her put on my coat and hat and pretend to smoke my pipe. Needless to say, my lodge buddies never saw it.

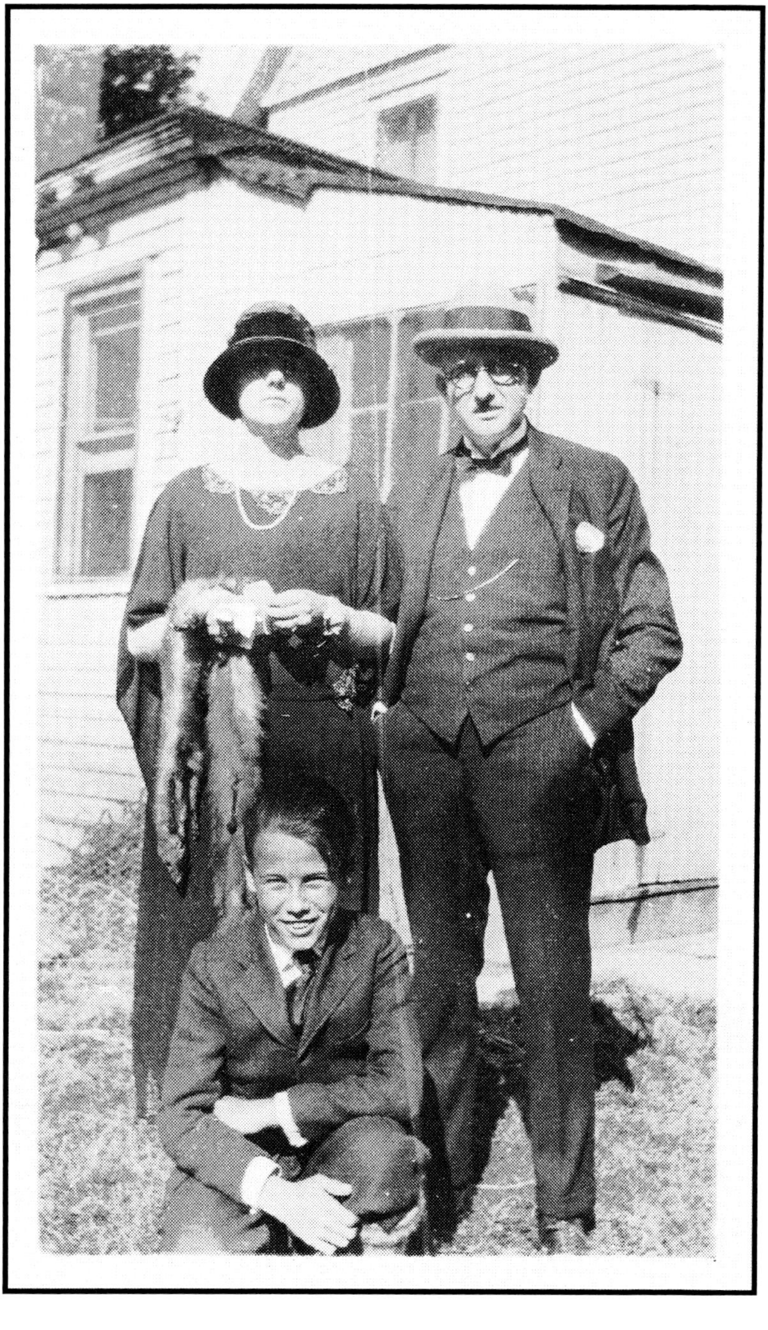

Love Conquers All

Mr. and Mrs. Eugene Featherstone had debated long and hard about what to do with young Harold. He wasn't a bad boy, but he could be mischievous. Some of the things he came up with were quite humorous, or so Mrs. Featherstone thought, like the time he crawled under the dining room table and tied every man's shoelaces together. As all the men got up to go smoke cigars, they all ended up in the floor. It was very hard for all of the women to stifle their laughter. Mr. Featherstone, on the other hand, got to hear about it on a regular basis at the office.

"What's that boy up to now-a-days?"

"Has that boy of yours learned to tie any new knots?"

Mr. Featherstone took it all with a light-hearted smile, but inwardly he was seething that he had to put up with the ridicule. Harold had done more antics than that, but it seemed like the most current one became the butt of all the jokes.

In his mother's eyes, he could do no wrong. After all, what mother wouldn't dote on her only child? Yes, he had gotten into some hijinks with the neighborhood boys. There was that matter with the neighbor's shed catching on fire, but Harold had sworn he had nothing to do with that. The occasional pie would go missing from a windowsill. To Mrs. Featherstone it seemed like the blame was always put on poor Harold. She knew he wasn't entirely innocent, but you couldn't blame an entire crime wave on one small boy.

Mr. Featherstone was always ready to blame Harold. If there was two cents missing from his trouser pocket, Harold must have taken it. If the neighbor's flower pot was broken, it must be Harold. So Mr. and Mrs. Featherstone had been at odds on this subject for nearly three years. There had even been talk of sending him to military school.

Harold had just turned thirteen and Mr. Featherstone was trying to find him an apprenticeship in town. Harold's history for shenanigans had not helped the endeavor. Nearly everyone Mr. Featherstone spoke to would just shake their head and walk away. The summer break was coming soon and Harold needed to be occupied at some kind of physical labor so that by the end of the day he'd have no energy left for mischief. With this end in mind, Mr. Featherstone went about a mile out of town and visited an acquaintance, Gus Peterson. Gus had a bustling farm and usually took on extra hands in the summer.

Mr. Featherstone pitched the idea to Gus.

"I don't know, I've heard some wild stories about Harold."

"Come on Gus, you can't believe everything you hear. Besides if he'd done everything that people say he'd be locked up in reform school."

"Well... I can't pay hardly anything. We're just scraping by as it is."

Gus thought this might get him off the hook.

"He'll work for free. I'll pay him out of my own pocket. You just make sure that you work him hard."

"Oh, I can do that. You send him on over as soon as school ends next week and I'll put him to work."

At that evening's dinner, Mr. Featherstone made the announcement that young Harold had a job for the summer working for Mr. Peterson on his farm.

"Harold doing manual labor!" exclaimed Mrs. Featherstone.

"How much does it pay?" asked Harold.

"The pay is ten cents a day and meals."

Harold thought it over. "OK, I'll do it."

He made this pronouncement as if he actually had a say in the matter.

The summer went by blissfully for Mr. Featherstone. Harold was occupied from sun-up until sundown, six days a week. After he got home from the farm he was too tired to do anything but eat and flop into bed. He was getting a healthy tan and developing a good set of muscles.

His mother, on the other hand, was continually worried about him getting hurt. She imagined all sorts of scenarios. He might stab himself in the foot with a pitch fork. He might get kicked in the head by a mule. He might fall out of the hay loft and break his neck. Of course, none of these things ever happened. In fact, he seemed content doing manual labor even though he would be exhausted at the end of the day.

July fourth came and both of his parents expected the worst. An almost fourteen-year-old boy with money in his pocket and the availability of fireworks made a recipe for disaster, but he didn't even purchase a sparkler.

We went down to the lake where they were having a small fireworks display.

Harold said, "I'm going to go get a snow cone. I'll be back in a little bit."

Harold had been gone for some considerable time so his parents went off to look for him. They looked near the snow cone vendor and all around and couldn't find him. They then ran into Gus Peterson and asked if he'd seen Harold. Gus motioned up the hill with his thumb. Mr. and Mrs. Featherstone turned to go up the hill when a huge burst of fireworks illumined the area. There was Harold with his snow cone, sharing it with Sarah Peterson. They were laughing and carrying on and pointing at the night sky. Just then they saw Sarah lean over and give Harold a peck on the cheek. It was suddenly clear that the miraculous change that had come over Harold wasn't due to Gus Peterson, but his daughter.

Mr. and Mrs. Featherstone headed back down the hill before they were seen.

250

Auras and Gris Gris

Uncle Wilber was a wonderful man. He and his wife Edith raised four daughters. Each of them married and gave them grandchildren. He was also a handsome man, but you would never know it from this photo or any others of him.

For some reason that nobody could explain, Uncle Wilber couldn't be photographed. Well that's not entirely true. You could take a snapshot of Uncle Wilber but there would always be some inexplicable reason that his face wouldn't show up.

This wasn't always the case. There are a couple of pictures of Uncle Wilber as a little boy. In those pictures, there is a bright-faced apple-cheeked boy. It was some time after he became a teenager that the strange shadows or blurring or anything else that might obscure his face began.

As a young man, when one of the family wanted to take his picture he would tell them that he'd just break their camera. If they insisted, he would go along and they would snap his picture. Later after having the film developed they would report back to Uncle Wilber that for some reason that picture didn't turn out. This went on for years.

Uncle Wilber traveled a lot for business and was periodically in New Orleans. During one of these trips he decided to find Marie Laveau the voodoo queen. He wasn't overly religious or superstitious but thought if someone could shine a light on his problem, it might be her. He came to find out after asking around that he was about fifty years too late to talk to Marie Laveau. However, he was able to find her great grandniece who still practiced the religion.

There was a five-dollar consultation fee and the price gave

him pause. Would he be throwing away good money on worthless information? Or could she maybe shed some light on why he couldn't be photographed? In the end, he figured it a small price to pay to possibly get an answer.

He waited in the outer chamber as a swath of humanity came and went. They were young and old, white and black, poor and well to do. They all went in seeming burdened with some problem and came out buoyed by some inner hope.

The outer chamber had all the trappings of a voodoo priestess. The air hung heavily with incense and candles flickered everywhere casting eerie shadows on the wall. On a shelf behind the "receptionist" were fetishes made of bones and feathers, bunches of herbs tied together with ribbon and small leather pouches whose contents were known only to the initiated.

As the last person left, the receptionist looked up from the appointment book and waved Uncle Wilber in. He didn't know what to expect, but the inner chamber was an amplified version of the outer one. He walked in and saw Marie Crocker looking down and fumbling with some beads that looked like a rosary. She looked up as he entered the room and stiffened as if she'd seen something that disturbed her, but then she settled down and asked Wilber to have a seat.

"You have come to see me because people have a hard time seeing who you really are."

She said this in a matter-of-fact tone as if it had been discussed at length, although Wilber hadn't uttered a word.

Wilber said, "That's pretty close to the truth."

He pulled out a couple of snap shots and showed them to her.

"This, or something like it, happens every time I have a photograph taken. Is there anything you can do to help me?"

Marie Crocker looked over the photos and then she stared at Wilber. She seemed to be looking just past Wilber and not at him directly.

"You have an aura. It is black as ink and I have never seen one like it before. It's as if somebody has cast an evil spell on you."

Wilber just laughed at this, but the look he got in return suggested that was not the best thing to do.

He cleared his throat, "I don't know anyone who would put a spell on me, and this has been going on for years. The last clear photo was taken when I was thirteen."

"You have had no bad luck in your life? No broken marriages, no children dying, no fortunes lost?"

"Oh no, none of that, I have a good business and wonderful wife and three wonderful girls and a baby on the way."

Marie shook her head, "I can only see this darkness foretelling a disaster. The fact that it has not manifested itself yet means nothing. Fate works in its own time."

"So, you think something bad is going to happen?"

"No, I know it will — it is only a matter of time."

Although not superstitious, Wilber was beginning to get worried. He wasn't concerned about himself, but didn't want anything bad to happen to his wife and children.

He asked, "What can I do to get rid of this?"

Marie shook her head again, "I don't think you will ever be rid of it, but I can make you up a gris-gris that should protect you and your family from the ill effects."

Here it comes thought Wilber, wondering how much this "gris-gris" was going to cost him.

Marie spoke again, "It will require a sacrifice."

She laid a white handkerchief on her table and asked to see

my left hand. I gave her my left hand and a quick as a snake she had sliced one of my fingers so that the blood dripped onto the handkerchief. I pulled my hand back and wrapped my finger in my own handkerchief.

"Why did you do that?"

"I told you the gris-gris required a sacrifice. Your blood is the sacrifice. I'll use the square of linen to wrap up the gris-gris and bind it to you before it goes into its leather pouch. You must have the gris-gris on you at all times. I suggest you even be buried with it. It will be ready tomorrow at about this time. You can pick it up then."

She pulled out a scrap of paper and wrote something on it.

"Please give this to the receptionist on your way out and you can pay her then."

Having been dismissed Wilber went out and handed the receptionist the paper.

She said, "That will be twenty dollars."

Wilber grudgingly handed over a twenty-dollar gold piece.

He picked up the gris-gris the next day and wore it faithfully.

The shadows in the photos never went away, but Wilber had a remarkably lucky life, until the day he died.

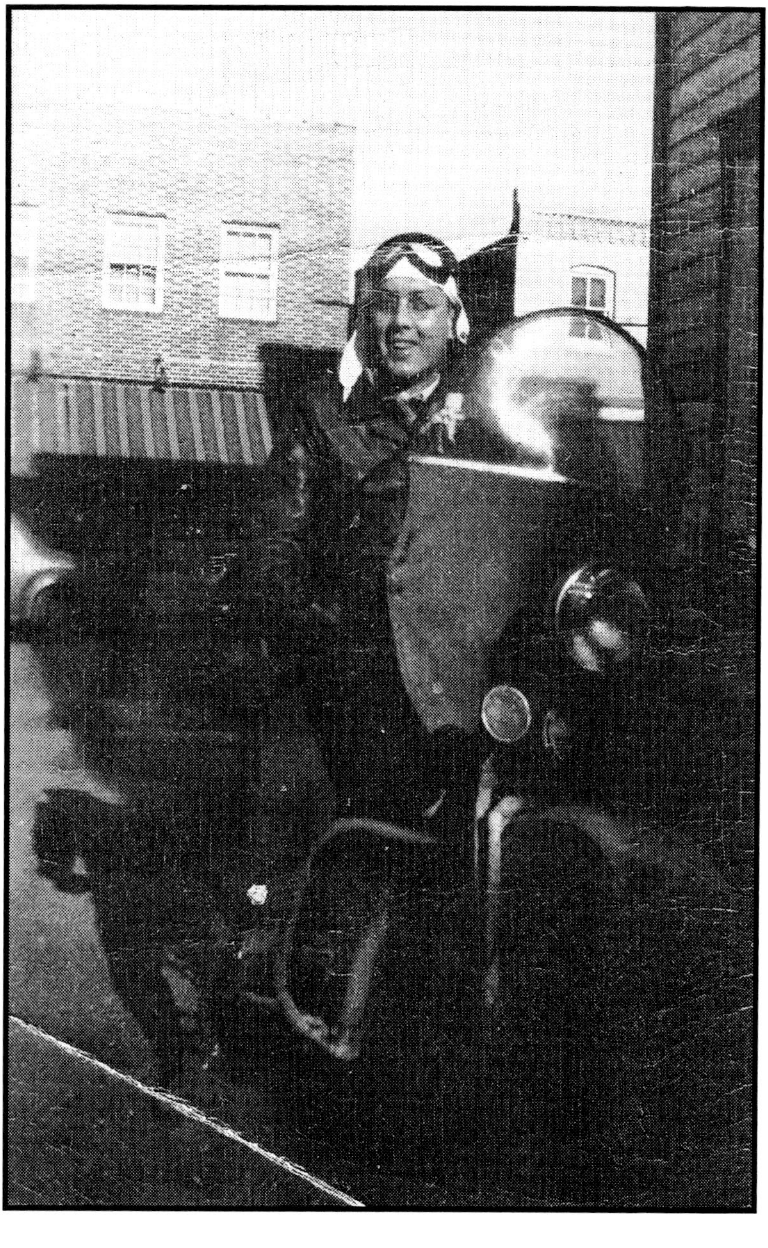

Two Wheels Move the Soul

There were only two women in the motorcycle club and Jane was one of them. She had read somewhere – "Four wheels move the body but two wheels move the soul." She firmly believed it. She was thirteen when her brother, after much nagging on her part, had let her ride his Indian Scout. Even though her toes barely touched the ground and it almost fell on her once, she was smitten. From that time on, her goal was to own a motorcycle — not just any motorcycle, but an Indian just like her brother's.

It took Jane five years of relentless scrimping and saving to come up with the money to buy a fifteen-year-old Indian Scout. The bike had seen better days, but she had been hanging around the fringes of the motorcycle world for five years and had picked up a lot of information along the way.

Her brother Elliot was a mechanic and had his own garage so she had access to all the tools she would need. He also had an unused bay that he used to store tires, oil and what not. She talked him into letting her use the bay to work on her Indian. Little did he know when he gave her permission that she was going to nearly live there for six months. Somehow she had acquired a maintenance manual for her bike and planned to tear it down all the way and rebuild it.

Jane was not for doing something halfway. Once she had it fully disassembled, she took the frame, fenders and gas tank to the local bicycle shop. She had worked for Mr. Small during the war, painting and pinstriping bicycles. Since all steel was being sent to the war at that time, new bicycles didn't exist. Mr. Small's shop would tear down an old bicycle, then re-chrome the handle bars, strip the frame and fenders and then lacquer them.

The final touch was to add the pin stripes on the fenders. It looked like a new bicycle when they finished with it.

Mr. Small took on the project and didn't charge Jane anything. He had some fire engine red lacquer ready to go. All Jane had to do was strip off the old paint and get it down to the bare metal. After everything was dry she used her pinstriping talent to do some fancy flourishes on the fenders.

There was still the matter of rebuilding the engine and re-assembling everything. Jane got a little help from her brother, but most of it she did in her free time when not working as a switchboard operator for the telephone company. She could have gotten her Indian back in shape sooner by paying to have the work done, but she wanted the satisfaction of having done it herself. She'd bought it in October and figured if she had it on the road by spring she would be happy.

Word had spread about this cute girl working on a motorcycle over at Hancock's garage. Her brother didn't encourage a bunch of motorcyclists hanging around, but he really couldn't chase them off either. They bought gas, oil and tires, so it was good for business. Besides, pretty soon it would be too cold and the guys would have packed away their cycles until spring. By then Jane should have her bike back together and be out of the storage bay.

Well, April rolled around and Jane unveiled the Scout. It was gorgeous. She had polished all the chrome and waxed all other surfaces. It nearly sparkled in the early April sunshine. Then she kick started it – it fired off on the first kick. It had a low throaty purr. She put on her helmet and took it for its maiden cruise.

Elliot was envious of her "new" motorcycle. Even though his was newer, her bike looked like it had just rolled off the assembly line. She rolled back in and asked Elliot if he'd like to take it for a spin. Elliot didn't want to look too eager but thought it might be a good idea to make sure nothing was wrong with it.

Elliot took it out and opened it up on the straight-away going out of town. He hit eighty miles per hour before he slowed down. It was perfect, no vibration, no hesitation. He had to admit it, she'd done a damned good job.

For the next month or so she took it out to every speed trial she could find. Every time she won, beating all other bikes in her class. Of course, she had tweaked it just a bit. She'd polished the cylinder walls, adjusted the fuel to air ratio to be optimal and a couple of other things that she was keeping to herself.

Word began to get around and many of the guys that had pooh-poohed a woman motorcyclist were eating their words. They were even coming to her for mechanical advice.

Jane realized she was spending too much time on other people's bikes and not having any time for her own. Something had to give.

Jane went and had a talk with Elliot and they came to an agreement. He would let her use half of the storage bay and his tools, free for six months. After that if she thought there was enough business he would start charging her rent, otherwise she would close up shop. They shook on it and the next day she turned in her resignation at the telephone company.

After the first month, she had a waiting list of customers for her service. After six months, she was paying Elliott rent and was happier than she had ever been. The business grew until she had to move to her own garage. At this point she was able to hire some up-and-coming mechanics, including one woman. Her reputation grew and she could be seen from time to time at the Bonneville Salt Flats in Utah consulting with one team or another. She was there in 1967 when Burt Munro broke the land speed record with his modified Indian. They were to become good friends and corresponded regularly until his death in 1978.

Jane never broke any speed records, but may have had a hand in some of them. Although she could now afford any motorcycle that she wanted, she continued to ride the Scout that she rebuilt. As parts wore out it was getting harder and harder to find them, but she always managed. She was seventy-three when she had a stroke. The doctors said if she hadn't been on that motorcycle at the time she may have lived.

She had made prior arrangements so that her headstone was engraved with a picture of her beloved Indian Motorcycle and the words "Two wheels move the soul."

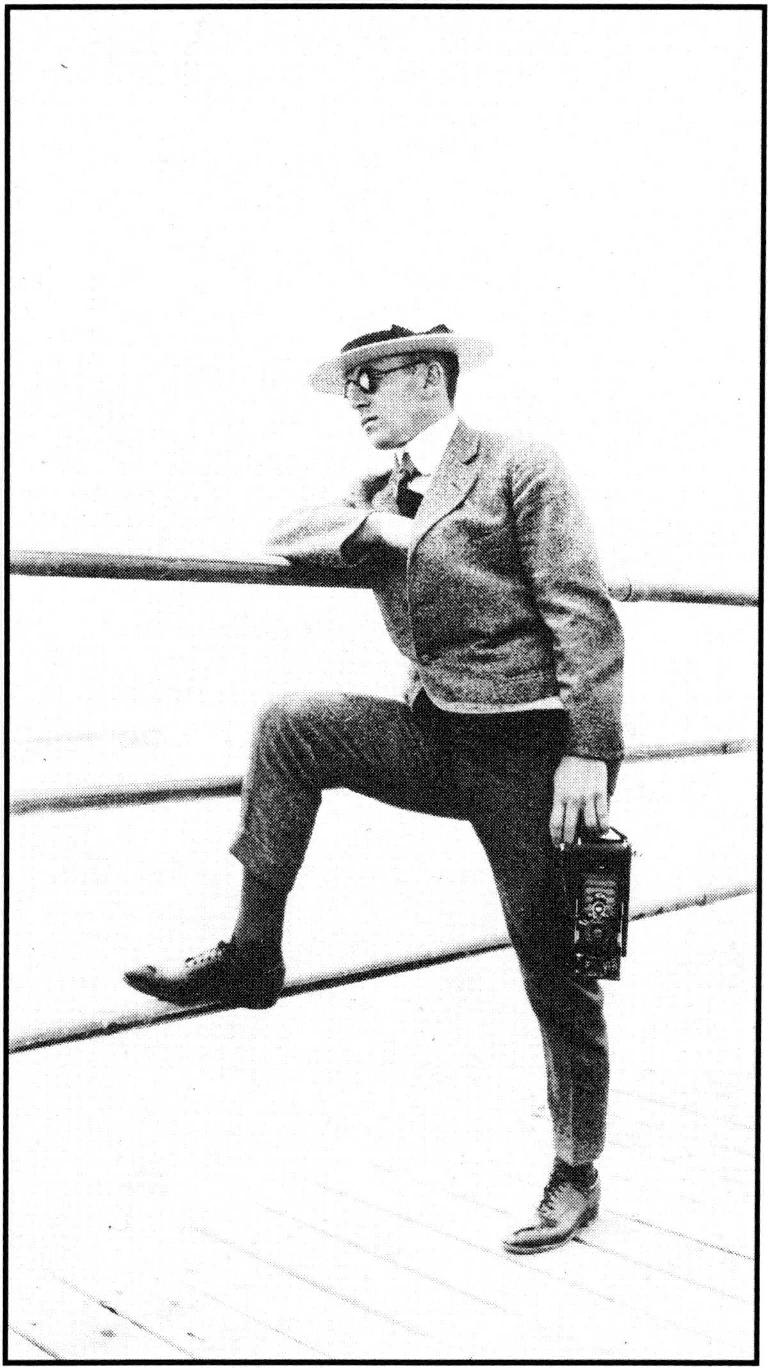

Private Eye

I was watching the entrance to the Schlitz Hotel because that was where my client said her husband had been seen coming and going with as she put it, "some floosy." Today was the third day and I'd seen no sign of him. I wasn't complaining, mind you, not at twenty-five dollars a day plus expenses.

My name is Jake Harper and I'm a private investigator. Most of my cases are a lot like this, either following a wife that is supposedly having an affair or vice versa. Unlike the pulp fiction that they churn out, I seldom have some long-legged blonde show up in my office promising me the moon and stars if I find her missing brother, or dog, or whatever, then placing a stack of cash on my desk for a retainer and a kiss on my lips just to keep me interested.

Of course, it's never the brother or the dog; it's usually the whatever that she never actually defines that she will want you to risk life, limb and your P.I. license for.

The closest I'd ever come to that kind of a case was about a year ago, when a woman was in the waiting room of my office. Her story was she'd had some of her jewels stolen and she thought it was someone in the house that had done it. She said that was why she didn't want to involve the police. I told her my usual fee and she plopped two-hundred dollars down on my desk and told me to let her know when I needed more. I wrote her a receipt for the cash and wrote down her address and told her I could be by this afternoon to look over "the scene of the crime." She batted her eyelashes at me as she left saying, "See you this afternoon Mr. Harper."

I felt my car and I were out of place as I pulled up into a

ritzy neighborhood. My tires crunched up a white stone drive surrounded by a lawn that rivaled most golf courses. I parked the car and ignored the doorbell and used the huge door knocker that was in the shape of a lion's head. The echo of the first wrap had barely faded when the door swung open silently on well-oiled hinges. A butler stood there and said, "Mr. Harper, you are expected. May I take your hat? Please wait in the library."

With that last utterance, he ushered me into a room off from the foyer that was lined floor to ceiling with books. The lady of the house entered moments later.

"What jewels were taken?" I asked as I pulled a notebook and pencil out.

"An emerald necklace and matching earrings and a diamond brooch."

"Can I see where you keep your jewelry?"

She led me upstairs to the first bedroom on the right of a long hall that must have opened onto half a dozen other bedrooms.

I asked, "How many servants are there and who else lives here?"

"There is the butler, the cook and the maid. It's just my husband and myself."

"Do you throw parties here?"

"Occasionally."

"Did you have any parties before you noticed the jewelry missing?"

"No, we had about a hundred guests here a month ago, but the jewelry was here two weeks ago."

"How do you know?"

I asked this because her jewelry box was stuffed to overflowing and I had no idea how she knew what she had.

"Because I keep them in their own cases."

She showed me the cases and I could see they were indeed empty.

"Nothing else was taken?"

"No, just those."

"Any insurance?"

"No, no insurance."

At least I could rule out an insurance scam.

"May I speak to your staff?"

"I guess so, but I'm sure it wasn't any of them."

"I'm not accusing anyone of anything yet."

Well, the long and the short of it was the husband had done it. Apparently, he had some heavy gambling debts. It took me a week and a lot of shoe leather to track down the pawn shop he had taken the stuff to. I was able to tell her where she could retrieve her jewelry and give her a full accounting of my time. I owed her five dollars but she just told me to keep it.

Back to the matter at hand. I saw a couple leaving the Schlitz hotel and raised my camera. I snapped several shots before I lowered the camera. It was a fiery redhead but she was with a tall lanky fellow in uniform. It was not the couple I was being paid to look for, but my girlfriend and some soldier boy.

I began to make a bee line toward them. They were headed away from me and she hadn't seen me. When I caught up to them I said, "Hello Judy."

She and her companion turned around and I saw Judy's face light up with surprise.

"Jake, what are you doing here?"

"I might ask you the same thing."

She turned to her companion and said, "Rob, this is my boyfriend Jake."

Rob looked at her and said, "You didn't tell me you had a boyfriend."

Uniform or no uniform I was about to punch this guy in the face when he suddenly stuck his hand out and said, "Rob Jones, glad to meet you Jake. It seems like my little sister here has some secrets even from me."

Flabbergasted, I took his hand and shook it.

"I'm so sorry. I thought you two..."

They just looked at each other and then at my red face and began to laugh.

"Rob has a couple of days leave from Fort Dix and so he came to Atlantic City. Come join us for lunch."

"No I can't, I'm currently on a case." As I said this I looked back at the hotel entrance and saw who I'd been waiting for these past three days. I turned and raised my camera and snapped several shots. Then I caught back up to Judy and her brother.

"So where are we going for lunch?"

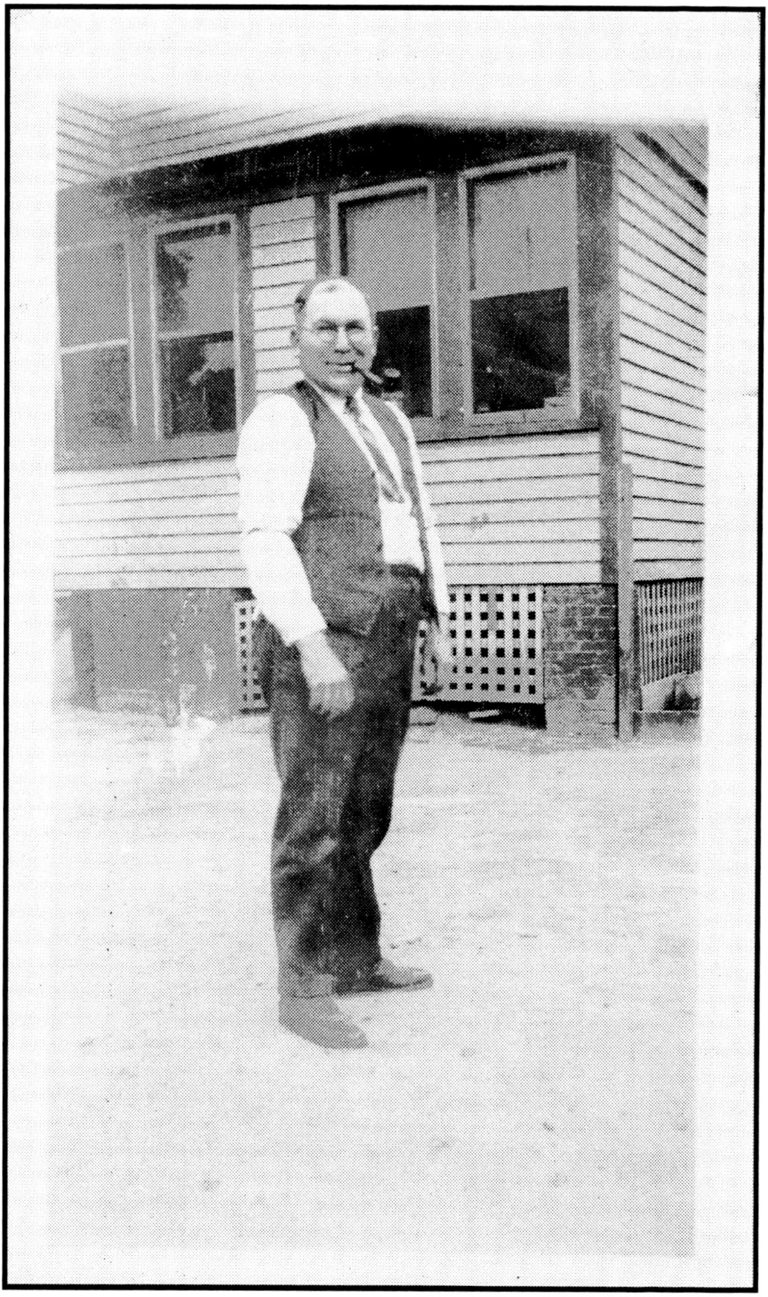

The Secret Life of Mr. Pomeroy

Mr. Pomeroy lived alone for as long as any of us kids could remember. Sometimes we'd hear the grown-ups talk about Mr. Pomeroy's wife and how nice she was and what a shame she died so young. We couldn't imagine him ever being married, or ever being young for that matter.

He had a garden out behind his house. We'd see him out plowing the field with his mule and know that before he got it planted, we could get out there and have dirt clod fights. Once he had planted his garden it was strictly off limits for us kids. He grew normal stuff like corn, green beans, potatoes, tomatoes and watermelons. Up closer to the house he had a small patch that he grew other stuff in. Mamma said she thought it was herbs to cook with but she wasn't sure.

During those hot summer days as the garden grew, when he wasn't hoeing weeds, Mr. Pomeroy would be sitting on a rocker in the shade of his porch. Sometimes it would just be him, his pipe, and a glass of sweet iced tea. Other times he'd have a couple other old men up there and they would have heated discussions about this and that.

He didn't have any kids of his own, but seemed to tolerate us neighborhood kids. His yard had some of the best climbing trees around and he always let us climb them. One day as I was coming down I slipped but caught myself on one of the bottom branches just long enough to break my fall. I ended up flat on my back winded. Mr. Pomeroy had seen the whole thing and for some reason it had struck him funny. He was laughing so hard that he could hardly get his breath. When he finally collected himself, he asked me to do that again because he'd missed it the first time and then began to laugh again. I left his yard never to return. Of course, I'd forgotten all about it by the next day.

As the summer wore on, we'd be out playing until way after dark, catching fireflies in a jar, playing hide-and-seek and anything else we could dream up to play in the dark. On most of those nights we'd notice Mr. Pomeroy's house was dark and we thought he went to bed awfully early, but then we noticed the lights were on in the basement. We wondered what he was doing down there. This went on for about a week while we came up with all sorts of stories. They ran the gamut from him being a spy to burying bodies in his basement.

Well, our curiosity got the better of us. One night we crept up as quietly as we could to try and peek in the basement windows. The first window we peeked into only showed us a laundry room with a big sink and washing machine. Some of the windows were too crusted over to see in, but we finally saw some shadows behind one of them and peered in. There was Mr. Pomeroy in a white coat and there were rows of test tubes and little gas flames under beakers. We'd seen some of this stuff at school in science class. So, what was Mr. Pomeroy up to?

Almost as soon as we got a glimpse, Mr. Pomeroy took off his coat and hung it on a peg and turned off the lights. All that illuminated the room now was the gas flame. We had a mystery to solve now.

I asked my mother what Mr. Pomeroy did for a living. She told me he was retired and didn't have to work anymore.

Then I asked her, "What did he do before he retired?"

"He taught science at the high school. Why all of this sudden interest in Mr. Pomeroy?"

"I was just curious," I said and ran off before I was interrogated further.

I talked to some of the other kids and they'd gotten the same information. This would explain the lab coat and scientific equipment, but what was he doing down there? We thought of breaking in and doing some snooping, but our parents would kill us if they found out.

Our small group discussed at length what he could be doing and we finally settled on moonshine. He grew the corn to make the mash and then turned it into moonshine. That must be it.

I was thirteen and the oldest of the bunch of guys that hung out and thought myself more grown up than the rest of them. They say, "curiosity killed the cat, but satisfaction brought him back." I was definitely that cat. My curiosity got the better of me and I couldn't stand it any longer.

One day all on my own I walked up the steps to Mr. Pomeroy's house. He was sitting there in his usual chair.

"Mr. Pomeroy, can I ask you a question?"

"You just did."

"What?"

"Never mind, what do you want to ask me?"

At this point my nerve failed me and I began to look at my bare feet and mumble.

"Your name is Orie isn't it?"

"Yes sir."

"Well Orie, ask me your question."

I blurted it out, "What do you do down there in your basement?"

He looked me over like he was sizing me up and he took a couple of puffs on his pipe. I was half expecting him to kick me out of his yard for good. To my surprise he asked me a question.

"Orie, do you like science?"

I thought for a minute and then said, "I guess so. I get pretty good grades in science class."

"If you want to know what I do, you have to promise not to tell anyone."

I promised and he led me through the house and down into the basement. It was cooler down there and he led me past all the test tubes and the gas burner into another room that we couldn't see from the window. In here were little glass dishes with some kind of plant sprouts in them.

"This is what I'm doing. I'm trying to develop a seedless watermelon. I've been working on it for the past five years and I'm getting close, but no cigar. Not yet anyway."

It was a bit of a let down, after all the crazy things we'd dreamed up. There was no need in worrying about me breaking my promise to secrecy because nobody would have believed me anyway. How would you plant a seedless watermelon? It was just plain crazy. Besides, half the fun in eating watermelon was seeing who could spit the seeds the farthest.

Hitchens
Salisbury, Md.

You Should Be In The Movies

She was born Bernice Wrightson but thought it wasn't flashy enough for the vaudeville stage to which she aspired. She called herself Angel Rockefeller, trying to get some mileage from a famous last name. She had the looks, but she wanted to be a singer like Lillian Russell. Her voice would never match her looks though, and she was lucky to get a spot on any of the vaudeville circuits.

She hired a voice trainer and worked for more than a year until she had mastered most of the foibles of her soprano voice. Her shortfall was the high notes; sometimes she could hit them and sometimes her voice would crack, and she never knew what it would do until it happened. She had tried all of the normal remedies such as gargling with warm salt water, resting her voice and taking throat lozenges. No matter what she did she could not guarantee the outcome.

Due to this fact, she might get a decent spot in the vaudeville circuit, but the first time her voice failed she would be bumped for the next up-and-coming soprano. It seemed that beautiful sopranos were a dime-a-dozen.

She decided to pack up her things and head to New York and try to break into the movies. Her voice couldn't betray her since the movies were silent. This was a good thing because her speaking voice was a bit on the high-pitched side. Her first stop was the Biograph studio in the Bronx. The Biograph had director D.W. Griffith and a range of stars including Mary Pickford and Lillian Gish, just to name a couple. Angel thought she could be the next Mary Pickford. She was given an audition with some no-name director and they told her that they would be in contact with her if something came up. Well, Angel knew that was as good as a "No."

Her next stop was Vitagraph Studios – not as prestigious as Biograph but it could be a foot in the door. She was interviewed by one of the underling directors who seemed to take a great interest in her and her career. It was during this interview that Angel learned the meaning of the word "casting couch." The first rung director promised her the moon and the stars, but first she needed to drop her knickers. Angel had run into this type while trying to break into vaudeville and flatly turned down the offer. She had a switch-blade in her purse if it came to that. She had only had to pull it on one old lecher while trying to get in on the Orpheum Circuit. This was strike two.

Her next stop was Jersey City, NJ where Pathé was filming "The Perils of Pauline" serials. It was here that she met a director who thought that she might just have what it took to make it as a film star, with no strings attached. He wrote her a letter of introduction and told her to take the letter to the Pathé Studios in Paris and this would get her an audition and the all-important screen test. This was wonderful for Angel, but steamer tickets to France weren't just laying around. She'd used most of her savings to come to New York.

She waited tables during the day and sang in beer halls at night to save up the money she would need. By scrimping and saving she was able to book a third-class passage to France. The voyage was hard on her. She was sea-sick most of the way there. When she arrived in France, she was a shadow of her former self. Physically she felt fine, but she looked a mess. Her hair needed work, she had dark circles under her eyes, and she'd lost about ten pounds. She couldn't turn up at Pathé Studios looking like this. She knew a smattering of French and was able to get a job as a waitress. This job allowed her to eat and find a place to live. She did this for a month and finally felt that she looked presentable. It had been nearly six months since she was given the letter of introduction and she hoped it was still good.

She arrived at the studio with her letter in hand. The guard at the gate looked it over and then pointed her to a building on the lot over to the far right and told her to ask for Mr. Charles Pathé.

She went in, presented her letter and was ushered into Mr. Pathé's office. He read over the letter and then said, "My brother seems to think you may have what it takes to become a star. We shall see."

Appointments were made for her audition and her screen test. Each went very well but they didn't have anything for her now. They put her on the payroll and used her as a general girl Friday. She ran errands, helped with makeup, and anything else that they could think of.

Her big break came when the studio made a couple of short films with her as the lead. These were filler before the major film ran, but she was in the movies.

Sadly, those were the only two movies she ever made. They say that timing is everything, and her timing couldn't have been worse. The silent films were on their way out and the "talkies" were taking their place. Her voice was once again her undoing.

This time she gave up and got out of the movie business, but this was all for the good because Pathé Studios had a rule in place to keep employees from fraternizing and Angel had fallen desperately in love with one of the cameramen, and he with her. They were married and she was able to travel all over the world because her husband became one of the best newsreel photographers of the day.

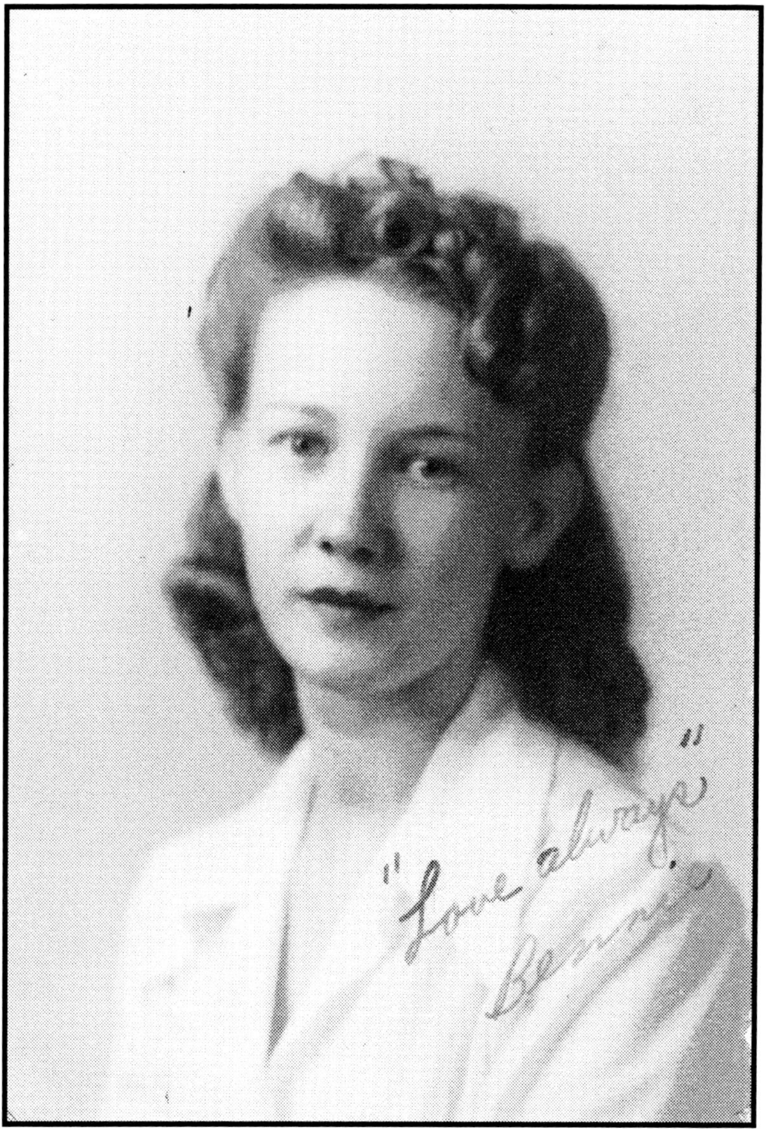

LOVE AND WAR

Her name was Bernadette, but everyone called her Bennie. This was her graduation photo but she hadn't changed much by the time we were married.

I enlisted in the Army on December, 8 1941. The line at the enlistment building stretched around the block. All the talk on the line was what we'd do to the Japs when we got overseas. They didn't know who they were messing with. How they were cowards. We had no thoughts of sweethearts except the idea of protecting them from the Communists, Nazis, and Fascists. When we finally made it through the enlistment process, we were each given a few days to tie up loose ends and say our goodbyes, along with a letter to report to Fort Dix that Friday.

Bennie and I had been talking about getting married, but hadn't felt the urgency that we did now. We both decided that it would be better if I got through basic training before we got married. That way I'd have nine weeks of a private's pay in the bank for Bennie to live on while I was overseas, at least until the Army started sending her the bulk of my checks.

Those nine weeks of basic training were the longest and the hardest I'd ever endured. Every hour away from Bennie seemed like a day, but I at least had her photo to comfort me. The drill sergeant was a piece of work. If you didn't fall in for calisthenics or snap to attention fast enough there was hell to pay. Out on the field, we learned to shoot, and crawl on our bellies under barbed wire. His motto was "if one trips you all fall." This did keep us on our toes because if you screwed up, your entire squad would be punished and they would take it out on you later. At the time, I thought that the man was crazy, a maniac. I can see in retrospect that he was just trying his best to get a bunch of green recruits ready to go to war. It was his training that probably kept most of us alive for the first couple of months. When I was going through basic training, I would have gladly punched him in the face many times over. If I ran into him today, I'd shake his hand and thank him.

After we all graduated from basic at Fort Dix, we were give a seven-day pass before we had to ship out. I hopped the first train home and went to find Bennie. She had made all the arrangements and we were married the next day. The honeymoon was in a one bedroom apartment that Bennie had rented for us. We called that apartment home for the next week before I had to leave.

I shipped out on February 15, the day after Valentine's day. There were tears and hugs and kisses goodbye. After landing in England we were deployed to the far-flung reaches of the British Empire and beyond. At first they had us defending the border with France and England and then there was talk of sending us to the Pacific theatre. We were just privates and corporals so we just took orders and kept out mouths shut. We were beginning to think that the generals didn't have a clue, but we only got a small sliver of the overall picture.

There was always a lot of waiting, and in those times you'd begin to think about home. It was then you'd see most of the guys writing letters back home, to parents, sweethearts or wives. I was no exception. I must have sent off a letter a day, even if I had nothing to say. I knew that I would get a response to most of them. And so it went – long periods of waiting, followed by short periods of intense fighting to gain or lose a hundred feet of ground. I knew deep down in my being that what we were doing was right, but there were days that I questioned the wisdom of it. I saw friends die in front of me and not be able to do anything about it other than get mad and fight harder. It was times like this I thought of Bennie and I knew that this war must be contained and won here and not be allowed to migrate west.

The highlight of our day was mail call. We would share our good fortunes and our bad because we had become more like brothers than just a bunch of guys that had been thrown together. It was mid June and another mail call. We had been in one of those waiting periods for a couple of days and the mail always relieved the tension. One of the guys, Joe Haskell from Detroit, got his mail and was tearing into it. As he read I saw his eyes begin to fill with tears and I thought the worst. A parent had died or his wife. Something bad had happened.

"What's wrong Joe?"

He could barely speak because of the lump in his throat. He finally just handed me his letter with a photo paperclipped to it. It read:

Dear Joe,

We love you and miss you. I had the neighbor take a snapshot of me and Timmy. He just turned three and wants to know when daddy is coming home. I don't know what to tell him. I thought I'd send the picture along since it should be close to Father's Day when you get this. Keep well and come home to us.

Love,
Betty

I handed back the letter and said, "I'm glad it wasn't something bad." I was thinking, what a sap to get all teary eyed over that.

Just then I was handed a letter. It was from Bennie of course. I began to read mine and suddenly my eyes were brimming with tears and I was the one with a lump in my throat. Joe gave me the same reaction I gave him, and likewise I just handed off the letter.

Dear Hank,

I hope you are sitting down because you are going to be a father. I'm five months pregnant and the base doctor says I'm doing just fine. I am happier than I've ever been. If you were here it would make things perfect. Take care of yourself and remember you are fighting for two of us back home.

Love always,
Bennie

Look who's the sap now.

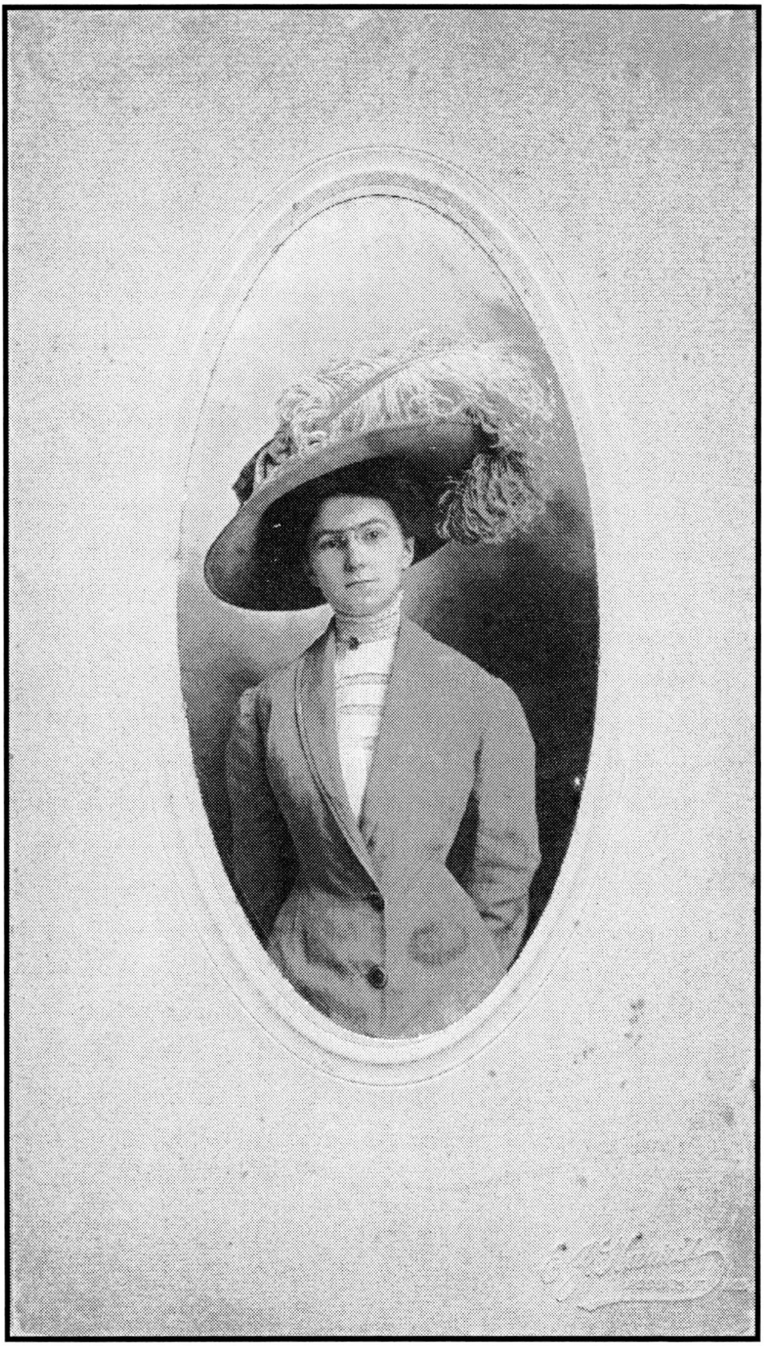

Women Get the Vote!

To say Emily Stockdale's family was well off would have been an understatement. Her family lived on an estate that covered nearly eighty acres. The house was huge, with eleven bedrooms and six bathrooms as well as the ball room, billiard room, the library, and many more too numerous to mention. This didn't count the servants' quarters.

Each evening there was a gourmet meal and everyone dressed for dinner. Emily was the youngest of three children. Her two brothers, who were ten and twelve years older than her, were hardly ever around. This didn't seem to bother Emily; she was treated more as an only child than one of three. She wanted for nothing her entire life. She had the best nannies and then private tutors. When she was old enough, her parents sent her to the relatively new Wellesley College. It had only been open for twenty-five years but was gaining a very good reputation. She graduated with honors and returned home. Her parents thought that now would be a good time for her to marry and began to extend invitations to all the eligible gentleman that would be in her social standing.

Emily was to have none of it, but for the sake of appearances she went through the formalities of meeting these young gentleman and politely explaining to them she wasn't interested in marriage at this time.

She had a small trust fund that would allow her to live as a woman of independent means and that was what she intended to do. On the other hand, there was no rush to leave her parents' house until absolutely necessary.

Emily began a series of social causes, but none of them held her interest for very long. Not until she heard a speech by Julia Ward Howe about the Suffrage movement did she find a cause she could get behind wholeheartedly.

Mrs. Howe was spearheading the suffrage movement and there was a rally a short distance from where they lived. Emily was in attendance and at once became enthralled. Her father decided this was not in keeping with what a young lady should be doing and ordered her to stop. Emily knew that now was the time she would have to leave her parents' home. She had expected this day to come and had been putting by some of her monthly stipend, so she had a tidy sum to bankroll her departure. She found lodging in town – not as grandiose as she was used to, but it would have to do.

Although her accommodations weren't exactly like she wanted, she could still dine out and get the food she had grown accustomed to. After about a month of this she realized she could not afford to live as she used to and began to tighten her purse strings. Luckily the new circles she traveled in didn't require new frocks in the latest fashion. She had several plain black or gray dresses that were more than serviceable for her day-to-day activities. She had become so immersed in her new life that she hardly thought of the old one.

Emily would write to her mother on a regular basis, but because of her father's stubbornness she was no longer on speaking terms with him. If only he could see women as independent human beings and not as underlings to men. Maybe that was too much for his generation to conceive of.

The years went by and the rallies went on. Between 1910 and 1914 ten states granted women the right to vote but the battles were hard-won. In 1917 she was arrested and jailed with about five hundred others who were protesting in Washington. She was released in 1918.

She knew that universal suffrage was just around the corner and she worked that much harder. Emily was noticing that she was fatigued much easier than she had been but she chalked it up to the inactivity in the prison and told herself that she would be right as rain in a couple of weeks. After a month she had gotten no better. Her mother had told her in her last letter to come home and they could take care of her. It wasn't until she collapsed that she condescended to be taken to her parents' house.

Her parents feared the worst; they thought she had the influenza. The doctor was called and Emily was inspected from head to toe. The doctor determined that she did not have influenza but that she was just physically exhausted and needed to recuperate and build up her strength. If she were to go back out and continue as she was, she would be in a weakened state and more susceptible to the flu.

Her brothers showed up to visit her; they had both become officers in the Great War. They would sit with her in the conservatory and tell her stories – none so gruesome as to offend a young lady. One day the younger of the two brothers came by with another junior officer. He walked with a cane so Emily assumed he was wounded in the war. Emily took a fancy to this young man, but had little experience flirting. She and he just sat and talked until her brother came to collect the officer and leave.

The young officer's name was Andrew and he was a few years younger than Emily but they were close enough in age to have things in common to talk about. He returned the next day and Emily seemed to be perkier when he was around. This went on for some time, and when Emily was no longer confined to her chair, they would take long walks in the gardens.

Emily had told him of her trials and tribulations with the suffragette movement. He was one of the few men she knew that believed that women should have the vote.

It was Wednesday August 18, 1920 that Andrew showed up with a newspaper under his arm. He handed it to Emily and showed her the headline, "WOMEN GET THE VOTE."

Andrew looked at her and asked, "So what are you going to do now?"

"I don't know," she said.

"I have an idea" he said as he went down on one knee and pulled out a ring box. "Marry me."

Emily paused, thinking over all the possibilities. Then she shook her head and Andrew's shoulders drooped. She saw this and realized how it looked.

"That head shake wasn't for you. It was me dismissing all the other possibilities. Yes, I will marry you."